# DIRTY DEALERS

*By Tia Louise*

This book is a work of fiction. Names, characters, places, and incidents are products of the author's imagination or are used fictitiously. Any resemblance to actual events or locales or persons, living or dead, is entirely coincidental.

*Dirty Dealers*
Copyright © Tia Louise, 2017
www.AuthorTiaLouise.com
Printed in the United States of America.

Cover design by Hang Le.
Photography by Sara Eirew, Photographer.

All rights reserved. No part of this publication can be reproduced, stored in a retrieval system, or transmitted in any form or by any means—electronic, photocopying, mechanical, or otherwise—without prior permission of the publisher and author.

*For those who like a little darkness
with their light.*

BOOKS BY TIA LOUISE

## THE DIRTY PLAYERS DUET
*The Prince & The Player* (Book 1), 2016
*A Player for a Princess* (Book 2), 2016

*Dirty Dealers*, 2017
*Dirty Thief*, 2017

\* \* \*

## THE ONE TO HOLD SERIES
*One to Hold, One to Protect, One to Save* (Derek & Melissa)
*One to Keep* (Patrick & Elaine)
*One to Love* (Kenny & Slayde)
*One to Leave, One to Take* (Stuart & Mariska)
*One to Chase* (Marcus & Amy)

\* \* \*

## PARANORMAL ROMANCES
*One Immortal* (Derek & Melissa)
*One Insatiable* (Koa "Stitch" & Mercy)

## Contents

Chapter 1: An Assignment     7
Chapter 2: Resignation     15
Chapter 3: Reasons     31
Chapter 4: Learning     41
Chapter 5: Floodgates     51
Chapter 6: Closer     63
Chapter 7: The Truth     71
Chapter 8: Reality     85
Chapter 9: Reminder     97
Chapter 10: Debts     105
Chapter 11: Failure     121
Chapter 12: The Whole Truth     133
Chapter 13: Confrontation     145
Chapter 14: Struggles     157
Chapter 15: Dirty Hands     165
Chapter 16: Bait     173
Chapter 17: Leaving     179
Chapter 18: Watching     191
Chapter 19: Explanations     199

| | |
|---|---|
| CHAPTER 20: THE FIRST MOVE | 215 |
| CHAPTER 21: A PLAN | 221 |
| CHAPTER 22: HEARTBREAK | 231 |
| CHAPTER 23: DISCOVERY | 239 |
| CHAPTER 24: STRENGTH | 251 |
| CHAPTER 25: SEARCHING | 257 |
| CHAPTER 26: EXECUTION | 261 |
| CHAPTER 27: RECOVERY | 271 |
| CHAPTER 28: NOTHING BUT THE TRUTH | 279 |
| EPILOGUE: AFTER | 291 |
| ACKNOWLEDGMENTS | 307 |
| EXCLUSIVE SNEAK PEEK: *THE PRINCE & THE PLAYER* | 309 |
| ABOUT THE AUTHOR | 317 |

## Chapter 1: An Assignment

*Kass*

*The sound of rain.*
*Metal scraping.*
*Fast breathing; accelerated heartbeat...*

"It's empty." Blix's voice is cold, and my nerves fly to red-alert.

We're in a warehouse where dim lighting casts black-and-blue shadows, and the smell of rain grows stronger.

*Petrichor, the scent of rain on dry earth.*

Lunging forward, I reach inside, frantically feeling around, raking my fingers through layers of what feels like crimped strips of paper. "I don't understand." My voice is a cracked whisper. My life is on the line.

"You don't understand," he mocks.

"No..."

My shoulders try to shudder, but I take deep breaths, doing everything in my power to stay calm. Fear is a sign of weakness, and weakness is like fine wine to my cruel boss. If I beg, he'll shut down, and then I'll be lost.

"Another job compromised. Even more of my money gone."

*Control.*

"Last year I made you a million—"

"And you lost it all in one night."

*Calm.*

"He betrayed us both."

"You fell in love with him."

My stomach roils as I reject that accusation. I've only been in love one time in my life, and it wasn't with some lowlife Miami drug dealer.

"He was a dirty dealer," I counter. "He made us believe we could trust him. We let him get too close, and he betrayed our trust."

"*You* let him get too close." He hits the *you* hard. "Now *you* owe me even more. And you will pay. Make no mistake. Everybody who owes me pays."

Ice filters through my stomach. He takes a slow step away, turning his back to me. I hold my breath, listening to his heels click on the damp concrete. Raindrops begin a staccato thrumming on the roof. The rhythm grows faster, and the metallic smell of damp asphalt floods my nose. The pungent sting of tobacco cuts it as he lights a cigarette.

A cloud of blue smoke surrounds me. "What am I going to do with you, Kass?"

An ironic smile is in his words, and my throat closes. I've never been in the room when it happened, but I've heard what Blix does to people who disappoint him. I've cowered away from the noise of grown men screaming like girls, and I've smelled the noxious mix of vomit and urine as their bodies fight his torture. Certain sounds stay with you forever. The dull snap of Blix's wire cutters as he removes his victim's fingertips is one of them.

My response is fast, breathless. "I know where he's staying. I can take you to him."

"And how are you going to do that?" Another cold smile. "In your car?"

*Vile, evil, villain*. The words appear in my mind like flashes on a touch screen. None of them are strong enough. A bead of sweat rolls down the center of my back, and it takes everything in my power to hold still as he steps closer, so close, I feel his warm breath on the tiny hairs at my temple.

I fix my gaze straight ahead, mentally seeing his pale blonde hair, his flat white-blue eyes as I answer. "Call Taz. Tell him to go to Port Everglades. There's a motel across the street, a Crown Inn."

He raises his hand, and I wince, bracing for the blow. Instead, I hear the grinding of his thumb over the metal wheel, and a burst of orange fire shoots from his lighter, straight up in front of my eye.

"No!" I jerk back, whimpering.

It only makes him laugh. "He'd better be there."

I pray he is, although I know what it will mean when they find him.

"Taz will bring him here, and we'll have a short lesson on stealing from the boss." He's still beside me, exhaling cigarette smoke around my hunched shoulders, evaluating me.

I have to turn this around. Clenching my jaw, I force the knot in my throat to relax. I force my shoulders down. "I don't need that lesson," I say in a low, steady voice. "You left me in charge because I've never let you down."

A sharp pinch on my upper arm makes me cry out in pain. "*Never* is a long time. Running this unit is a man's job. They steal from you because you're weak."

Swallowing, I control my voice. "I am not weak."

"He's been slipping an empty box into every shipment for the past six months. I've got suppliers all over the Caribbean demanding blood. I'm about to give it to them."

I still focus straight ahead. I won't let him see the fear in my eyes. "So you'll kill Davis. Then what? Send them my head as a peace offering?"

"Not your head…" The tip of a knife blade bites the top of my cheekbone. "But perhaps your blue eyes."

My will slips, and I shriek. "NO!" My hands fly up, cupping around my face.

He only laughs again. The click of his heels echoes in the large warehouse as he walks away from me. The noise of the rain has quieted. "Apparently, I have to use my own eyes," he mutters.

"Or eyes you own," I say still holding my face in my hands.

"They're worthless, but at least the color is nice."

I can't stop shaking. Constant shudders rack my body. I hate being alone with him. I hate when he treats me this way. I hate the power he has over me—the power I gave him when I made that first deal so many years ago, all those years ago when I was desperate and had no other choice. That day I was so low, I hoped this job would kill me. I have so many regrets.

Blix's buzzing phone distracts him from his game of torture. "Blix." The voice on the line is unintelligible, but I know it's Taz, his sergeant at arms, his capo. "Yes… At the warehouse… Bring him here… I have everything I need."

He finishes the cigarette. Stomping it out, he moves quickly to the back of the warehouse, and I know he's lost interest in me. I know the way his features are changing, and the dead focus entering his eyes as he prepares to deal with a traitor. He's detaching from whatever human feeling is left in his black heart.

Drawers and cabinet doors open and close, and he lifts out tools, dropping them each with a sharp *Bang!*

on the metal countertop. I'm not going to die, at least night tonight, but dread still twists my stomach. I know what's coming when Taz arrives with Davis.

"So you're back." My voice is demure, not challenging. "Why?"

When Blix left six months ago, I'd heard he was running from some government job gone wrong, and all I could hope was never to see him again. I was wrong. The worst ones never die.

He doesn't even look up. When he answers, he's under the cabinet moving heavy objects. "I came for you."

His voice emerges just before the sharp *Zee!* of a power drill slices through the air. I flinch sharply both from his answer and the noise.

"Me?" My eyebrows pull in a frown.

I've been in Miami five years overseeing this arm of his drug smuggling operation. I tell myself I'm not as bad. I'm not a dealer, and I never even touch the merchandise. We're not supposed to touch it. We receive shipments of poppy and opium from cargo ships out of Turkey. Then we ensure they get onto cargo ships headed to South America and the Caribbean. That's it. No further involvement.

Davis got greedy. He saw the rise in prescription drug addicts and thought he'd line his own pockets by stealing just a little here and there.

Davis is a fool.

I'm a bigger fool.

When these guys go down, I'm going right along with them.

"Since your eyes have failed me, I'm going to see if your body is still worth anything."

My stomach turns at the suggestion. "I don't do that. I've never done that..."

"Now you do." He pushes past me, but I follow right behind.

"You promised—"

All at once he's in my face again, seething with fury. "I promised not to take the boy. You promised to guard my lines. Which check are we going to cash?"

My chest is tight with fear. My little brother Cameron isn't as little as he was when I started working for Blix. Back then he was only sixteen, but now, at twenty-two, he's old enough to be one of Blix's foot soldiers. Men who are always one screw up away from a cruel and horrifying death. I won't let that happen to him.

"What do I have to do?" I'm quiet, resigned.

He touches my cheek with the tip of his finger, tracing a line to my ear and into my hair. "So easy to control." He twists a lock of my pale blonde hair around his finger. "So beautiful. Your assets are wasted here."

"It's where I want to be." *Far from my past.*

"Too bad." That flicker of gentleness is gone and I hear a car pulling up outside. "We'll discuss your new assignment tomorrow."

Ice is back in my stomach. I don't want to be here when the torture starts. I don't want to hear it, but I don't have a way to leave. Doors open and slam

shut, and I hear Davis's fast-talking pleading. Soon they'll turn into high-pitched screams for mercy.

He won't find it.

"I will say," Blix pauses, giving me one last bit of his time. "It's a job you might enjoy."

*I will not.* I don't say the words out loud. I barely have time to think them before Davis's voice enters the back room. He laughs nervously, trying to buy time.

"Blix, it's me! Your right hand. Your pal! I wouldn't—AHH!" His voice breaks, and I know Taz has jerked his arms back, looping them behind his back and tying them with yellow, nylon rope, as per usual. "Blix! Wait!"

He's still pleading when the deafening *Zee!* of the power drill cuts through the night.

Blix's voice is loud, flat. "Thirteen suppliers across the Caribbean have been shorted in the last six months. They will each receive a piece of you as retribution, and to show I have zero tolerance for theft."

"It wasn't theft!" Davis's voice is hoarse as he tries to shout over the power drill. "I got you a better price here in town. In South Beach!"

"I'm going to start by removing the kneecaps."

The noise of the drill goes louder. Taz's meaty chuckle is cut off by Davis's raving screams. I run for the back door, pushing through to the outside and sliding down the wall until my ass hits damp grass. My knees are bent, my face slick with tears, and I wrap both my arms over my head, trying to block out the screams.

It's not enough. It's never enough to kill that sound. I can only pray one day the person screaming isn't me.

## Chapter 2: Resignation

*Logan*

The waters of Occitan are emerald blue and clear as crystal. I stand at the broad French doors on the balcony of the royal estate and look down on the small family I've been trusted to guard, mother and child.

I've been with them for almost a year now, ever since Zelda Wilder ran away from Monagasco, leaving her younger sister Ava behind with the crown prince. A lot has changed since that day last spring when I was sent after her, to find her, to protect her and ultimately to bring her back.

For starters, the crown prince is now the king, Ava is now his wife, making her the queen regent, and I'm in his office waiting to request a release from this assignment. My time is done, the threat is neutralized, and I need a change.

I watch as Ava lifts her baby niece into the air, laughing and gently rocking her side to side. As queen regent, Ava is always refined and elegant, but when her sister visits, she becomes a completely different person—she becomes more like Zee.

Formal gowns and designer dresses are discarded in favor of bikinis and cut-offs, and the two spend every day here beside the ocean, running around the grounds barefooted.

I confess, I like them better this way. It tugs at old memories I thought I'd put behind me long ago.

The little girl squeals with delight, and Ava lowers her so their noses touch. Belle's chubby hands grasp her aunt's pretty face. She's a sweet baby with a halo of pale blonde curls around her small face. She's Zelda and Cal's child, and she's part of the reason I can no longer guard their family.

I got too close. I let my feelings get involved, and now I can't be around them without wanting things I can never have. It's inappropriate and unprofessional, and it goes against everything I vowed to uphold when I entered the service.

"It's a beautiful day, Logan," Rowan's voice cuts through my thoughts. "Why such an angry expression?"

My brow immediately relaxes, and I turn away from the door, bowing to the king. "Your majesty," I say.

"I think we can be a little less formal, considering all we've been through." He reaches out to give my hand a firm shake, patting my shoulder at the same time.

The king and I are equally matched in height. We both have the dark hair and blue eyes of our country's heritage. Our only noticeable difference is my muscle mass, which serves two purposes—it gives me a more intimidating appearance to potential attackers, and it relieves the tension of suppressing these feelings. The burn of pumping hundreds of pounds of steel takes the edge off the constant longing and regret.

*God, I need a break.*

"What's on your mind?" Rowan's voice is controlled, and he moves with the calm dignity of his position as leader of our tiny nation-state by the sea. He's so different from his brother.

"With all due respect, sir, I'm here to ask you to release me from service."

He's visibly taken aback. "You want to retire? But why?"

"I'd like to go to Italy... Perhaps join the foreign legion." My answer is mostly true.

"And start all over again? In the desert?"

I understand his disbelief. Six years ago, when I entered our country's military, I'd had nothing—no money, no clear goal. I thought being a part of the guard, defending our way of life, was a noble endeavor. Monagasco is small, but we have a long history holding the border between France and Italy. For eight hundred years we've been one of the richest countries in western Europe.

It was a smart choice. Apparently my temperament is exactly right for the service. I'm focused, controlled, and it's only taken me a few short years to rise to the top of the food chain. I serve directly under the king, I earn more money than I have time to spend, and I travel everywhere the royal family goes...

Now, all I want is to get out.

Rowan laughs, momentarily breaking the tension. "So you've had a taste of adventure. Now your work here is too boring for you. Is that it?"

"Not at all." It's true the events of the past year have been dramatically more exciting than my usual role, lurking in the background, shadowing the royal family, but I don't care for such high stakes.

I don't like finding mutilated bodies in seedy motel rooms. I don't like knowing that one wrong choice could mean finding the queen's sister in a body bag. We'd been lucky in our last job.

"What is it, then?"

Hands in my pockets, I step away from the patio doors. "The job is over. Matters here are under control, and I'd like to travel... while I still can."

For a moment, he only regards me, steel eyes slightly narrowed. Then he shakes his head, and my insides tighten. "I'm sorry, Logan. I won't accept your resignation."

"You must." My tone is sharp, and my gaze instantly drops. "Forgive me, your highness, but you must."

Rowan is quiet as he walks to the door where I'm standing. He looks out at the scene before us. My eyes slide closed as I wait, knowing what he sees, knowing he's working out the truth behind why I'm asking to be let go. How I've been compromised.

For several moments, he doesn't speak. I never served directly under the king, but his reputation is one of studied thoughtfulness. He was never like his father or even Cal, both of whom were more impulsive. The second hand on the clock ticks loudly as I wait.

"You're controlled, Logan, a born protector. It's what makes you our best guard." His voice is thoughtful, measured. "When Zelda was kidnapped, you worked around the clock, digging into her background, learning her story, and following where it led."

My jaw is tight as I answer. "I wasn't alone in that task."

"No, but you were the most dedicated."

"It was my job to find her and bring her back to safety."

He turns to face me, and I bring my eyes from the floor to meet his. His dark brow is lowered.

"Freddie would sleep. Hell, even I would sleep, but you—"

"Did what I've been entrusted to do, sir. She is the Queen Regent's sister, the mother of the princess, the Duchess of Dumaldi."

"Not yet."

I can't answer him. That clock ticks louder as I wait. Finally, he exhales and crosses the room to the large mahogany desk positioned in front of the empty fireplace.

"My answer is firm. I will not accept your resignation." My stomach drops, but I hold my posture straight. I watch as he opens the top drawer and removes a beige envelope. "I respect your feelings. I respect you... However, it's possible matters aren't as locked down as you think."

"What are you saying?"

"I'll transfer you back here, to Monagasco, immediately. A more serious threat has emerged, one that requires your level of commitment."

His words intrigue me more than the frustration twisting my insides. Returning home, getting away from Tortola, could be enough to ease the tension in my chest. Something serious could help me regain my focus. "What is it?"

"I received this letter a few weeks ago." He removes a folded sheet of paper from the envelope and holds it out. "I want you to read it and tell me what you think."

Stepping forward, I take it. A quick glance, and I see it's a ransom note. It's an unsettling, old-school style note, with letters cut from assorted magazines.

*Wade Paxton owed me twenty million pounds sterling. I want my money. Instructions for delivery are pending. Don't make me move on your family again.* -B.

The words change the tightness in my chest to anger. "What the fuck?"

There's only one *B.* who would send such a message. Blix Ratcliffe is the sick bastard who eluded us when we shut down the operation in Uranu, the tiny island now appearing on all maps of the waters surrounding Aruba. We brought every man associated with that hidden brothel to justice and placed the women in homes and rehabilitation.

Blix Ratcliffe is the sick bastard who hurt Zelda. He's the monster who killed her partner and shot Ava, and I've been waiting for the chance to deal with him.

"What makes you think he's coming here?" I ask.

"I don't know what he'll do." Rowan takes the letter back and puts it in the envelope. "I only know I want my best man guarding my wife."

My jaw tightens, and my eyes flicker to the doors. "What about—"

"I'll increase security around the princess." He goes to the door and pauses before exiting. "We'll be in Tortola several days. I give you leave to stay here and take some personal time. Use it to relax, reset... Get laid."

My eyes cut to his, and I'm not sure he's joking. "Is that a royal command?"

He almost smiles. "It's a friendly suggestion. When we return, you are solely responsible for the safety of the queen."

I don't have to ask if that's a command, and I'm ready to accept it.

"You have my word. She will not be hurt."

\* \* \*

Night Three of self-imposed "personal time," and here I am, at the Royal Casino bar again. A short tumbler of whiskey is in front of me, and I tilt the cool glass side to side, watching the amber liquid slide over the perfectly square ice cubes. I couldn't be more alone in this opulent space filled with aristocratic gamblers.

I asked for this. Hell, I'd wanted it permanently. If Rowan had accepted my resignation, I'd figured I'd travel to Italy or France—perhaps even Turkey—get away and start over. As it is, I'm stuck in Monagasco, waiting to resume my position in the elite guard. I have nothing else, and I'll start another term guarding a life that isn't mine.

I entered this line of work hoping for adventure. I wanted to travel, be a part of something powerful and important. I got my wish, and now I might as well be a knight. I've dedicated my life to this cause, and the reward for good work is more work. The penalty for my dedication is solitude.

An older woman wearing a sparkling gold evening gown passes in a cloud of perfume. I watch as she takes the arm of a fellow around her age, and he kisses her cheek. She gives him a familiar smile, and it's clear they've been together a long time.

*Consenescere: to grow old and grey together.* Her voice drifts through my mind like a phantom, an unwelcome memory.

"Why did I come here?" I say through an exhale, pinching the bridge of my nose.

I know the answer. In a world where I'm always on guard, my friends are security. In a world where my job is to follow the royal family wherever they go, I haunt their favorite places like a ghost. Bartenders recognize me. They fill my glass without question. It's familiar, easy.

As if to make my point for me, Brian nods at me from across the bar. "Ready for another?"

"I'm good," I say, studying the half-inch left in my tumbler.

I wonder if I have time to take a trip. Maybe visit the desert, see if I really would prefer the foreign legion. It feels strangely quiet in the casino, and I realize what's missing. No mob of paparazzi lurks around every corner ready to chase whichever royal I'm shadowing. I can take my time, take in my surroundings. It's depressing.

With a slow sip, I finish my drink. For two nights I've sat in this fucking chair looking at this fucking bar. Turning away, my eyes go instinctively to the gleaming brass roulette wheel turning, flashing red and black. I can still see her sitting there... No. I push back on that memory. I have to move forward.

Rowan told me to reset. *Get laid*. Yeah, fuck that, I've never been a playboy. The thought almost provokes a bitter laugh. Almost.

I'm so far removed from any sort of personal life. A fleeting memory is all I have left of the one person... the one girl...

"Scotch and soda, please," a soft voice says, and I almost drop my glass. The voice is firm, filled with authority, and it's so, so familiar. It's as if I conjured the memory simply by allowing her to flicker through my brain.

*Is it possible I imagined it? Why would she be here?*

Brian places the short tumbler on the glossy wood and starts to pour, and she speaks again. "Thank you."

My insides clench. *It's her. But... How?*

The warmth of her small body is at my side, and I push out of my chair. Turning, I step back to face her. A leather barstool is between us, and my eyes travel quickly up her slim arm to the silky black fabric of her dress. The sleeves have long slits starting at the shoulders, revealing her pale ivory skin. Her platinum blonde hair is swept up, leaving her slim neck on display. A few soft pieces float around her cheeks, and the only new thing is a pair of tinted glasses perched on her small nose.

"Cassandra?" My voice is quiet, filled with disbelief.

Her body stiffens, and she doesn't answer. She doesn't even look my way. A few bills are quickly dropped on the glossy wood, and she takes her drink, quickly exiting the bar area.

I'm right behind her, but she doesn't stop. In fact, she seems to pick up the pace. She's through the enormous French side doors, her black heels clicking on the travertine, before I'm able to catch her.

"Cassandra, wait!" Reaching out, I grasp her arm, positioning myself in front of her, blocking her progress. I can't let her disappear without a word. It's been so long.

Her voice is flustered, and she still won't meet my eyes. "Leave me alone or I'll call security!"

That almost makes me laugh, considering who I am. I release her, but I won't let her pass. "Don't you remember me?" Studying her face, I see her blinking quickly. *Is she trying not to cry? Is she afraid?*

"It's me," I say as gently as possible. "Logan."

"I can't believe you recognized me," she says not looking up.

My stomach tightens with a sensation I haven't felt in years at the soft sound of her voice.

"How could I not?" I say. "You haven't changed a bit."

"Not a bit?"

*Is she teasing me?* "Well, you're not wearing a bikini," I go for warmth.

She's elegant and sophisticated as hell in her little black dress, but I still recognize the feisty, skinny girl with long pale hair, running through the surf in shorts and a tank top and bare feet. We'd spent every waking minute together, before I was sent away for training. Ten months in the desert, and I came back to find her gone.

Her eyes flutter and her chin drops. I want to catch it and lift it, pull her into my arms and hold her like I used to all those years ago, every single day that summer. My last summer…

"What are you doing here?" she says. She's still not smiling, and I'm not sure how I feel about that. "I thought you were gone—"

"I was in the Caribbean most of last year," I say. "But… when did you come back? I looked for you when I got back from Morocco. Cam said you'd moved to America."

"I took a job there." She's so tense standing here as if she's under arrest. It's making me crazy. "I just flew back a few days ago."

Softening my voice, I dip my head to try and catch her eyes. "I'm so glad to see you, Sass."

With those words, her entire posture changes. Her shoulders drop, and the stern line of her jaw melts into a smile. She covers her face with her hand, and I hear the smallest laugh. "Did you just call me Sass?"

Blue eyes cut up through her fingers to mine, and warmth floods my chest. *There she is.* "Perhaps I was out of line?"

"I suppose your familiarity could be considered inappropriate." Her tone is taunting, like it always was, daring me.

"I hope not... Sassy Cassie," I say, doing my best not to laugh when her blue eyes narrow behind those glasses.

We're standing so close. She places a hand on my chest, and I mentally note she's not wearing a ring.

"It's Kass now. With a *K*." A gentle push, and she glances over her shoulder behind us. "It's been a long time since those days."

As much as I hate it, I move back, giving her space. "Are you here with someone?"

Her head snaps to me. "Why would you say that?"

"I just noticed... You were looking around."

I don't want her to say yes. I don't want her to leave. My insides are a tangle of anticipation and curiosity and all the feelings I gave up years ago. On the tip of my memory is the ease we had with each other. I crave it.

We were barely adults when we knew each other six years ago. She was nineteen and I was twenty-four, and we'd been pretty hot together. I'd lost count of all the places we'd had sex around the coast—under the pier, behind the cabana, in the ocean... so many times in the ocean. I'd perfected the art of holding her in front of me, slipping in from behind. I can still feel her skin against my chest, her clenching around my dick.

Heat floods my pelvis, but her voice interrupts my steamy reverie. "I came with friends, but they left early. I was just planning to leave myself."

"You haven't finished your drink."

She tilts the short glass to the side. "It's almost gone."

"We could walk down to the fountain and talk. Catch up?"

I can't get a read on her. She isn't giving anything away. She has changed, and seeing her here now, this smart, beautiful woman, I can't help wanting her. I want to know how much has changed and how much is still the same.

Her lips press together, and she exhales softly, almost as if she's conceding something. "I guess I have a few minutes."

It's not the level of enthusiasm I'd hoped to get from her, but it's not a no. We start to walk, side by side, not touching. My hands are in the pockets of my dark slacks, and we make our way down the beige stone steps.

Motorcycles are parked in a shining row, and across the enormous lawn the laughter of men and women dining outdoors at the Paris Hotel drifts to us on the sea breeze.

Glancing up over the tops of the buildings, the mountains surrounding the city are pale blue in the growing twilight. We're entering the gardens at the back of the casino, where the choreographed fountains rise high overhead amidst dancing, colorful lights.

For the moment, they're still, and the peaceful trickle of the smaller fountains hidden in the walls creates an ambient noise.

"It's so lovely here," she says, looking out across the darkening gardens.

"I remember sneaking onto these grounds with you." A grin is in my voice. I remember doing more than that on these opulent grounds.

"We would hide in the shadows up on that hill and watch the men and women in their fancy clothes coming in and out." A wistful tone is in her voice.

"They were always surrounded by cameras flashing and dozens of people."

"They still are."

She pauses in her walking and turns to me. "You're one of them now, aren't you?"

"No." We're facing each other, the moon highlighting the planes of her cheeks, the silky bend of her hair. "I'm the shield between them and the rest of the world."

"Yes, keeping them safe from urchins like me, dreaming of things I'm not allowed to touch."

Quiet surrounds us as we walk. The only sound is our shoes crunching softly on the gravel path.

"You'd like these new royals. They're very much like you and I were in those days." In that moment, I understand the pull Zelda Wilder had on me.

I'm looking at the ghost from my past Zelda conjured just by being herself, and I feel like a fool that I didn't see it sooner. I didn't understand my obsession with saving her until now, walking in the moonlight with Cassandra. Kass... The girl I lost so long ago. I was so blind.

"The Americans," she nods. "I've heard about them. Cam says the queen is like a Cinderella, and her sister is some sort of criminal?"

"She reminds me of you."

Another little wince moves through her, and I notice her pale brows draw together. "Why do you say that?"

Pulling up short, I reach out to stop her again. "She's lively and strong. She's a survivor like you always were."

Again, I seem to have found the correct combination of words. Her shoulders relax, but she shakes her head, not smiling. "It sounds like she got lucky falling in love with a prince."

"Maybe, but she didn't get off easy." I don't want to elaborate on the grizzly details of what Zelda went through before we found her. I don't want to spoil the moment. Instead I redirect. "How long are you in town? Are you back to stay?"

"I'm only here a little while. I wanted to check on Cam, and I... I have a job to do." That sadness is in her voice again, and all I want is to take it away. I have time. I have several days left in this personal leave.

My insides are tight, and I feel like I've been walking on eggshells since the moment I touched her. Still, I have to try. "Would you have dinner with me?"

She's quiet, and I'm actually holding my breath. At last she does a little nod, but still no smile. "Okay," she says, barely above a whisper. Her expression is resigned.

I don't understand, but I'll take it. Reaching into my breast pocket, I pull out the slim phone hidden there. "Tell me your number."

Another momentary hesitation, and she's reciting the digits. I punch them in quickly and hit send, waiting as her clutch starts to make music and buzz softly with the vibration of her ringtone.

"Hey," I say, ending the call and catching her shoulder, causing her to look up at me. "I can't believe I ran into you tonight..." I hesitate, but after all this time, goddammit, I'm not holding back.

Moonlight glistens in her eyes, and she blinks it away quickly. "Me either."

Her voice wavers, and that's when I see the smile lifting the corners of her mouth. It's like winning a fucking marathon. I mentally do a fist pump.

Stepping closer, I catch her chin, just touching it with my thumb and forefinger so lightly. "Cassandra," I say, leaning closer.

Our breath swirls together, mixing with the air between us. I can still taste her kisses, cherry lip gloss, cinnamon gum, and salt water. Entranced, I lean closer, still holding her chin. She doesn't pull away. Her eyes are fixed on my mouth, and her breath skates over my cheek as I draw closer. She smells like clean jasmine and fresh air. She's the dream I had as a young man, when I was careless and naive, when I believed I could go away for all that time, and she'd still be here waiting for me when I returned. She's a splinter of moonlight, beautiful against the darkness of my skin. Our lips touch, the softest velvet against my mouth, and it's all back.

All of it.

Her chin lifts out of my fingers, and her lips part. She's kissing me in return, and a little noise aches from her throat. It's electric, but only for a heartbeat. Just as fast she pulls away.

"I'm sorry," she exhales. "Goodnight, Logan."

She turns and takes off across the grass practically running. This time I don't chase after her. I stand and watch her as my insides begin to relax, my breathing returns to normal. Fate just threw me a lifeline, and there's no way in hell I'll lose it this time.

*You're running away, Sass, but I felt what you want. I'll have you in my bed, and no matter what it takes, I won't lose you again*

## Chapter 3: Reasons

*Kass*

My insides won't stop trembling. I knew seeing Logan for the first time in so long would be hard, but I had no idea how overwhelming it would be. It's like being hit by a thirty-foot tsunami. No survivors.

The moment I heard his voice, I chickened out. I ran away, hoping he didn't recognize me, but of course he did. Of course he chased after me. Our past is too strong, too fierce and demanding for him not to.

I couldn't breathe. I could barely speak. I was defenseless against the onslaught of feelings simply being near him provoked. So many memories assaulted my mind. I'm surprised I kept my footing.

Returning to my tiny, second-floor walkup, and I can't shake the memory of his mouth covering mine. The firm brace of his lips and the soft scruff of his beard…

He's so much bigger than he used to be. He's always been tall, but back then he was lanky, playful, and teasing. *Sassy Cassie. Oh my god!* I can still hear him saying it with that cocky grin. I can still remember going wild with fury, jumping on his back and beating my palms against his skin, demanding he take it back.

He'd only laugh and run us into the ocean, drag me out to sea as he covered my mouth with his, slipping his long fingers into my bikini bottoms, stroking me until I would moan with need. All the anger would disappear when he slipped inside me, rocking me to a swift orgasm as I kissed him like he was the most delicious thing I'd ever tasted.

*He was...*

Now he's a mountain of a man, tall and dark. He has a beard that bristles against my skin when he kisses me. He's so different, yet so familiar. I'm a little afraid of what will happen if he takes me. *If...* As if there's even a question after that kiss.

Our reunion in every sense of the word is a foregone conclusion, and I'm simultaneously thrilled, nervous, devastated, and heartbroken. I know I'll never recover from this.

We're both in vastly different places than we were that summer six years ago. I was taking care of my little brother and struggling to hold down three jobs. Logan was old enough to join the military, and he saw it as his ticket out of the working class. He was the most gorgeous thing I'd ever seen with that dark, silky hair and those hazel-blue eyes. Yes, he was playful, but he was also focused, even then. He hid a seriousness that only I saw.

Now he's one of the king's elite guards, and I've forfeited the right to even dream about him.

Only I do dream about him. I never stopped.

The click of nails on hardwood fills the air, and I hear soft yipping around my feet. Dropping to sit on the top step, I greet my neighbor's little dog.

"What are you doing out, Henri?" My voice is soft, cooing, and he licks my chin, going for my mouth. I only laugh, catching his soft muzzle and moving it down. "You're so French," I tease, and he nods his head, attempting to free his face so he can lick me again.

"Stop now," I say gently, placing my hand on the top of his head and sliding it down his back. He calms at once, dropping his nose. I continue stroking but the action of petting him does little to ease my raging insides.

"Oh, Henri, I'm in trouble now," I whisper. The small dog scoots further into my lap. "I thought I'd packed all those emotions up tight, but now I see how wrong I was."

A little further down the hall, a door scrapes open, and the dog's head pops up. "Henri!" I hear Luc, my neighbor's crackled call.

A gentle pat, and the little dog jumps up to scamper home. *"Ah! Vous êtes là."*

*There you are*, I hear Luc saying to his dog, and I long for a simple life of walking the dog, staying up late, getting up early.

"*Bonne nuit, Henri. Bonne nuit, Luc*," I say softly. *Good night.*

His door pushes closed, and I assume they didn't hear me. I enter my lonely apartment, thoughts of Logan still spinning in my head.

Sliding the zipper down my side, I push the silky black dress off my shoulders, letting it fall to the floor. I step out and cross the small, studio apartment to the queen sized bed that takes up most of the space. Unfastening my bra, I let it drop as I climb onto the soft duvet, pulling a pillow against my chest and curling around it.

*Limerence: The euphoric feeling of desire and wanting to have it reciprocated.* Curling my tongue over the *L*, I rub my hands over my upper arms, remembering how Logan's rough palms felt against my skin.

I'd been so close to tears as I walked with him through the garden. He's still so beautiful, perfect and strong, and I'm so broken and dirty. God, I don't know if I can do this. I don't know how I can go through with it…

He said I was the strong one, a survivor, but he has no idea all I've had to do to survive since I saw him last. I can't tell him how the hits had kept coming, harder and harder, like the storm surge in a hurricane, walls of water knocking me down to my knees, to my face. The only thing that kept me going was Cameron. I had to do what I could to keep him safe until he was old enough to stand on his own.

My phone lights up, and my heart plummets. I don't want to look at it. I don't want to see the text. I wait, lying on the bed, feeling my heart pounding in my chest as my mind trips over this evening at the Royal Casino. Seconds slip past, and it buzzes again. If I don't respond, he'll come and check on me. I can't have that.

With trembling fingers I reach for the phone, and just as fast, my insides release when I see it's a number not yet saved in my contacts…

*Just wanted to say goodnight again. It was hard to let you go, Sass. I'll pick you up tomorrow at six. Bring a swimsuit, and text me your address.*

Tears flood my eyes, and all the dread is pushed aside by the warmth of Logan's words. Holding the phone against my chest, I breathe…
*Inhale…*
*Exhale…*
*Calm my galloping heart.*
*Oh, Logan, what am I going to do? If only you could help me.*

I text him my address and fight every urge in my body to say more, to ask him to come here, hold me through this misery. It's so wrong of me to want him this much, but there's no way in hell I could ever tell him no.

My phone buzzes again, and joy sizzles in my veins. I want all his words, precious words, and I lift the phone quickly to see what he's said. It all comes crashing down, when I see it's what I originally dreaded. It's Blix.

*Good work tonight.*

It's all he says. I don't even respond. I reach out and put my phone back on the nightstand and curl around the pillow again. For a little while I'd been able to let Logan take me away from my reality. Now I can only hold the pillow closer against the empty hole that used to be my heart.

\* \* \*

*Two clicks.* "A bench," I say. My little brother pulls my arm, and I stop short. "Lamp post."

"Impossible!" he cries, and I start to laugh.

"I told you, it works!"

A skinny arm flops around my neck, and I loop my arms around his waist. Cameron is sixteen, but he'll still let me hug him.

"Why do you have to go back to Miami?" he complains. "Stay here with me this time."

"And do what?" I cry. "You have to go to school, and I have to earn the money to pay for it."

"I don't have to go to such an expensive school."

It's not an argument I intend to have with him again. "It's a place for you to live..." He tries to interrupt, but I push on. "And they have classes you *need. I won't have you stuck in a cheap school living in public housing."*

*"But if I didn't go to such an expensive school, you wouldn't have to work so hard, and I could live with you."*

*The tone in his voice makes my heart ache. He's lost so much family, and I know family is as important to him as it is to me. Still, I could never make the money here I make in Miami... And he has no idea why I have to go back, the debts I owe. I keep that part far from him.*

*"Then you'd get sick of me," I tease, scrubbing my fingers through his light brown hair.*

*"I'd never do that." His voice is quiet, and I pull him into a real hug...*

Not much has changed in six years.

"Come on, Kass! Tell me why you can't go!" Cameron holds my arm, and I smile at his persistence. That sixteen year old peeks out less and less these days.

"I have other plans tonight." I reach out and tug a handful of his long, thick hair. "And you need a haircut."

"Fuck that!" he teasingly slaps my hand away. "Chicks love my hair."

"How are you ever going to get a real job like this? You look like a pot head."

"How would you know?"

"Trust me," I say bitterly. "I know."

It's been six months since I've seen my little brother, and he's gotten even taller. He's as free-spirited as any other young man his age, and his hair hangs past his jawline.

My phone buzzes, and I lift it, turning away so I can cup my hand around the face as I read the text.

36

His voice is suddenly serious. "You don't have to do that, you know."

My insides tense, and I lift my head. "What are you talking about?"

"You don't have to hide it from me."

Lowering my oversized phone, I reach for his shoulder. "Habit."

A sad smile curls my lips. Any sign of weakness is deadly in my world.

Cameron closes the space between us, wrapping his arms over my shoulders. I don't resist his hug.

"You're so tall now," I say, burying my face in his shirt. It smells like laundry detergent and something new... something manly.

"And my hair is too long," he adds. "It's darker, but I still have our blue eyes. We still look alike."

We're quiet several moments. I listen to his heartbeat, his breath swirling in and out, and I think about the sacrifices I've made to keep him safe. I'd do it all again. No questions asked.

"You don't have to worry. You're going to be fine," I say, wrapping my arms around his narrow waist and giving him a squeeze. "You're not going to be like me."

"If I were like you, I'd be smart and clever, able to face down whatever life handed me. How is that a bad thing?" He rests his chin on top of my head.

I don't want to argue with him, so I change the subject.

"What are you planning to do with this hair? Be a model?"

I'm only part-teasing. I'm desperate for him to find a job where people count on him and expect him to show up every day. It's another layer of protection, in addition to me, against the evil creeping around his door, watching him to see what kind of foot soldier he'll make.

"I'm waiting tables for now," he says, releasing me and moving to the other side of the room where he rustles around in some boxes. He turns to me again with a dramatic flourish and the sudden *Thrum!* of guitar chords fills the air. "I'm going to be a musician!"

My eyes go wide, and the protest is out before I can stop it. "Cameron, no!"

He starts to laugh, and just as fast, he plays another chord, quickly followed by a waterfall of notes as his fingers travel the neck of the guitar, hammering out a melody. It's clear he has talent, but I just can't even. It's the exact type of thing that will lead him straight into harm's way.

"We're not rich people, Cameron," I say, trying to temper my knee-jerk response.

"Which is why I'm waiting tables." He's on his feet and crossing the space between us. "It's okay, sis. I'm friends with the managers of two really popular restaurants. I've even met the commodore of the yacht club."

That draws me up short. "The yacht club? The *Monagasco* Yacht Club?"

"One and the same." Pride is thick in his voice, and I shake my head with a little laugh.

"If you get in with those rich old snobs, my work here is done." Picking up my hat, I take my phone and drop it in my pocket.

He follows me to the door. "I'm little more than a court jester as far as they're concerned."

"Still," Reaching out, his hand meets mine, and I run my fingers over the calluses on his fingertips. "You've been doing this a while. You're very good, and these calluses are thick."

My hand moves from his fingers to his square jaw. Lightly touching his face, I can't deny he's a handsome man. "You'll meet some princess, and she'll fall madly in love with you. Then you'll be set for life."

"Only if I love her back," he calls as I make my way down the stairs of his building. "When will I see you again?"

Stopping at the door, I lift my face in his direction. "It's probably best if I don't spend too much time here. You have my number. Text me if you need anything. I'll keep in touch."

"I love you, sis."

His words squeeze my heart, and I can't stop the memories of him as a little boy, all blue eyes and towheaded. He was so adorably cute and so trusting of me. I'll never forget the way he'd clung to me when our aunt died, the way he cried. She was the only mother he'd ever known. The job fell to me after that, and I swore I'd never let him down. I've done my best to be there for him. Now it's time for me to step out of his way. Funny how fast that time comes.

"I love you, Cam."

I'm out the door just as the noise of my Uber greets me from the curb. Jumping inside, I close the door and look back out of habit. My little brother isn't little anymore. I'll do what I must to get him to safety, then I'll let him go.

## Chapter 4: Learning

*Logan*

I'm on fire after spending less than an hour in her presence. Pushing through the door of my apartment, I hardly notice the bare walls, the absence of photographs, and only the most basic furniture. All I can see is her—her beautiful hair, her soft lips, her gorgeous body—all of which my memory is able to conjure perfectly. Every curve, every slope, every sweep is clear as a bell in my mind. How did this happen? It's the most amazing stroke of luck I found her.

I pace the enormous space, desire humming in my veins. This luxurious loft-studio is basically a crash pad for me between shifts at the palace. A maid service keeps it clean, otherwise it's still white walls, dark wood floors. A king-sized bed made up in navy sheets is against the wall in the far right corner, the dark wooden headboard a stark contrast to the sparse surroundings. A full-length mirror is beside it, but I don't even pause.

I head straight for the bathroom, ripping off my blazer and throwing it on the chair. I pull the shirt over my head and unfasten my jeans, shoving them to the floor as I step into the glass-encased shower. Spinning the dials, I let the warm spray cover me, rubbing my hands over my face, trying to get a handle on this.

Expensive body wash waits on the rack. It smells of rain forests and some such shit, but the suds are rich and lubricating. I lean my head against my forearm and work out the frustration of needing her right here in my fucking expensive-assed shower.

With my eyes closed, I'm immediately back, her beautiful body wrapped around mine, the cool salt water swirling around us as I hold her against my chest and sink into her warm depths. Soft lips touch my ear and her little moans send electricity straight to my cock.

"Kass..." I groan, massaging as the sparks of electricity snake up my legs.

I remember the feel of our kiss tonight, the noise that ached from her throat when I claimed her. I could still see the dark, hardened peaks of her nipples, feel them between my lips, until I finish with a low groan of longing, of needing to have her with me.

Fuck, it's like the least-fulfilling appetizer in the most expensive restaurant along the Avenue Princesse Grace.

One restless night and one endless day later I'm on a motorcycle headed into the La Condamine as fast as the city traffic will allow.

Her flat is in a series of converted warehouse buildings in the port district. My chest is tight, and *fuck*, I can't wait to see her again. I park the bike outside the industrial-styled structure, prop my helmet on the seat, and exhale as I let my eyes travel up the colorful doors of the warehouse building. Out here in the alley, the hanging lights over the cafés are growing brighter as the sun starts to set.

I have no idea how she feels. Hell, she could be seeing someone. That kiss last night was amazing. Our chemistry is something we never could deny, but it's not a guarantee of anything. Six years is a long time.

Glancing at my watch, I'm a few minutes early. I debate walking around the colorful block as I leave my bike beside the wooden tree-box. Just then, the door to her apartment starts to open. I jog forward to catch it, my eyes straining for her beautiful face, when I draw back quickly.

"*Tasses-toi de mon chemin!*" A stocky little man in a grey driver's cap pushes past me. His head is at my ribcage and he's holding the leash for a grey terrier dressed in a plaid jacket.

"*Excusez-moi,*" I say, catching the door over his head.

I almost laugh at myself. This grumpy old man is *not* the vision of loveliness I was straining to see. Still, I'm here, holding the front door to her walkup apartment. A narrow flight of stairs leads to a landing above, and I step inside, letting the metal door close behind me with a slam. My humor is gone when I realize this is not safe at all. I could be anyone walking in off the street without her knowledge.

The lighting is dim. I've only taken three steps up the narrow passage when another door opens at the top, and in a swirl of pale blonde and bright red, Kass jogs down the stairs toward me. I'm frozen, watching her slim hands fumble with the strap of her bag. She's wearing a pair of dark sunglasses, and her pace doesn't slow as she gets closer. She's beautiful.

"Hey," I say, catching her arm, and she jumps, letting out a little yelp. I pull her closer, and her hands clutch my biceps before quickly moving up my shoulders and to my cheeks.

"Logan!" she exhales, and I feel her body relax.

"I'm sorry for scaring you." My voice is low compared to hers. "It's way too easy to get into this building. It isn't safe."

"I'm always safe with you." Her pink lips part, and she's panting.

Her scent of fresh linen and jasmine surrounds us, and the need I've been wrestling with heats my skin. I turn her so her back is against the wall. Her fingers move from my cheeks into the hair at the back of my neck.

Every touch is electric. My eyes close, and I lean forward, claiming her mouth, pushing those lips apart and sliding my tongue inside to taste her fresh mint.

Hesitation disappears as her fingers tighten in my hair. With a whimper, she kisses me back, molding her body to mine as she pulls us closer. Our mouths chase each other's, lips grasping, tongues tasting, and my hands slide down her sides to her rounded ass. Shit, I want to lift her against the wall and fuck her right here in this stairwell. She cuts us short, releasing my hair and pulling back.

"Aren't we going out?" she says, still breathless.

We're both breathing faster, and I want to see her beautiful eyes hidden behind those enormous sunglasses.

I touch them lightly. "What's this? Jackie O?"

"You said to bring a bathing suit. I thought we were going to the beach." She glances down the stairwell, and I lean forward into her hair, grazing my lips over the top of her ear.

I'm rewarded with a shiver, and I smile. That little erogenous zone is still intact. My mind travels to the other ones—all the ones I found that summer we were inseparable.

"We'll go to our beach." I'm not hiding my desire, and she melts further into my arms. "Only, I changed my mind. Who needs a bathing suit?"

Her sexy laugh is a sound I've missed more than I realized until this moment. Again, she steps out of my arms and starts down the stairs. "So where are we going?"

Catching up, I reach down and pull her slim hand into the crook of my arm. "Do you have a helmet?"

"No..." Her pretty brows clutch together.

We stop outside beside my bike, and I smooth the line in her forehead with my finger. "It's okay." Reaching to the side, I take my helmet off the seat and gently slide it on her head.

"Oh!" She ducks at first before reaching up to hold the sides, positioning it behind her ears. The sunglasses are replaced by the tinted visor over her eyes, and her chin and mouth are exposed. She gives me a cute grin. "But what will you wear?"

"If those were aviators, I'd wear them." I point to the sunglasses now tucked in her shirt. "As it is, I'll be okay for the short drive."

Her hands immediately fly to the shiny helmet. "You should wear this! I'll be behind you."

"You forget," I say with a smile. "Protection is my job."

I can tell she wants to argue, but I climb on the bike before she has a chance, kicking it to life with a loud roar.

"Get on!" I shout, and she reaches out hesitantly for my arm. "Trust me."

Her fingers tighten on my sleeve and she carefully gathers her dress up her long, silky legs. I don't even try to hide that I'm watching the hem of her skirt rise, but she doesn't seem to notice. In a swift move her leg is across the seat and her body is pressed against my back. The heat between us is undeniable.

"I wish you'd warned me." Her lips just graze the skin of my neck as she speaks, and tightness crosses my fly. I want her. "I would've worn something more appropriate."

"You look amazing," I say, twisting back to steal a kiss, another hit of my favorite drug. "Now hold on."

Slim arms hug my waist so tightly, and I'm pretty sure this is the greatest feeling in the world. Easing into the speed of the chopper, we head off into the late afternoon climbing the mountains, following the winding, narrow roads of the countryside.

The salt air is at my face, and the sun is going down in a blaze of pinks and oranges and burning yellows. Kass's head is on my shoulder; her arms hold my waist. Her body is pressed to mine, and I wonder how long it would take to get to Paris. Too long.

Instead, I turn in at the Robie House restaurant, a Frank Lloyd Wright-style establishment on the cliffs overlooking the ocean. Naturally, we sit outside, and the way it's built, the patio juts out from the mountain. It's like we're on the edge of a cliff, and a light breeze surrounds us.

"And here I thought you wanted to *apricate*," she says with a little smile.

Taking my seat across from her, I grin at her old hobby. "Still collecting unusual words? What would I be doing if I were to *apricate*?"

She leans toward the table and wrinkles her nose. "You'd be basking in the sun."

"Good one," I take the roll of silverware off the table and place the utensils beside my charger, the napkin in my lap. "I'd like to see you apricating in one of those string bikinis you used to wear. How about tomorrow?"

"You're very sure of yourself."

"I'd say I'm optimistic."

That earns me a laugh. She places her own napkin in her lap, sliding her fingers back and forth on the fabric. "These linens are very soft. What expensive taste you've acquired, Mr. Hunt."

"Only the best," I say with a wink. One benefit of working nonstop and keeping a studio apartment is my bank account is ridiculously full. I want to empty it on her.

We're quiet a moment, and I don't want us to be awkward. I want to see her beautiful blue eyes. Those dark glasses are back in place on her nose, and I'm just about to say something when the waitress appears to take our drink orders. I ask for a bottle of champagne and the young woman disappears. Kass slides her fingers over the menu.

"Are we celebrating?" she asks.

"I'm feeling lucky this evening."

That gets me another laugh from behind her menu. She lifts her chin in my direction. "Tell me what to order."

"You want me to order for you?"

"Sure," she wrinkles her nose and puts the heavy folder aside. "You know what I like. Save me the guesswork."

I love this playful side of her. "Do you still hate salads?"

"Ugh!" She pretends to cough. "Lettuce is what my food eats."

"Still like clams?"

"Les fruits de mer!" she exclaims, and I decide.

The waitress returns, and I order us both the linguini aux vongoles. Kass's eyebrows rise behind those dark shades, and a smart little grin curves her lips.

"We always wanted to go to Campania," she says once the woman has gone. "Spaghetti alle vongole is one of the most popular dishes there."

"Did you ever go?"

A little head shake. "We only talked about going there together. Remember?"

I want to say I remember everything we dreamed of doing together, but I don't. Instead, I say what's been on my mind since the stairwell. "Do you have to wear those sunglasses?"

"Oh..." Her lips part, and she hesitates before continuing. "I-um... They're prescription."

My eyebrows rise. "Something new." Thinking back, I remember last night at the casino and the slim glasses perched on her nose.

Shifting in her seat, now she does a little shrug. "Apparently, I always needed them. I never knew."

"So you're Monet?"

I watch as her fingers slide over the tablecloth until they collide with the stem of her champagne flute. She spreads them over the base before lifting the glass to her lips.

"Something like that." Her smile is sad again. "If only my world were as beautiful as his."

"I thought it was his myopia that created the beauty."

"Myopia..." Her white teeth press together in a smile. "That's an unusual word."

Sitting forward in my chair, I slide my hand across the table to cover her slim one. She flinches slightly before relaxing, threading her fingers through mine. I love the sight of her slim, pale hand captured by my larger, darker one. It's like she glows.

"Myopia isn't so unusual," I say gently, watching her pink lips press together. I wonder if she's thinking of our kiss in the stairwell like I am. I wonder if she'll let me have her tonight.

A young man with a large tray of our food appears at the table, breaking our moment. Small plates are set in front of each of us containing the flat noodles with opened clams, red sauce, and slivers of zucchini garnish. I assure him we need nothing more, and he disappears.

Kass leans forward, a conspiratorial smile on her face. "It smells delicious. I might eat every bite!"

I don't stop my laugh. It's been a while since I've felt happy. "I hope you do. God knows you can afford it." She's as thin as she always was.

Her soft laugh surrounds me, and I watch as she slides her fingers over the silverware before lifting her knife and fork and digging in. I don't waste time following suit. The sooner we eat, the sooner I can decide whether I want to take her to the ocean or back to my apartment.

## Chapter 5: Floodgates

*Kass*

My mind is still on Cam when I grab my dark shades and slide them over my eyes. I instantly regret my decision when I dash out into the stairwell. I might as well have shut off the lights altogether. Stifling a swear, I make my way fast down the stairs, knowing the sun will still be blasting full force once I get outside.

Blix's text from last night is on my mind. He didn't say much, but I know he's watching. He's always watching. I'm lost in thought when a pair of massive arms closes around me, stopping my heart.

"Where are you going so fast?" The deep voice is right in my ear, and I almost faint from relief.

"Logan!" I gasp. My body instantly responds to him. Heat floods my panties as his scent surrounds me. It's warm cedar and fires burning. Even in this darkness, I can see his lips curling in that grin I love. "You startled me."

His warm breath skates over my cheek, and I want him to kiss me again. I trace my fingers up his massive biceps to his broad shoulders. *Shit*, I can only imagine him naked. He's so familiar, but at the same time, he's different, bigger.

Threading my fingers in his soft hair, my wish is granted when he leans in and covers my mouth with his. Our tongues collide, and it's hot and luscious. The soft brush of his beard moves against my cheek, and my fingers tighten, pulling him closer as my body melts into his.

Nothing has changed between us. He could fuck me right here in this stairwell, and I wouldn't stop him. Only, I have to stop him. I'm not going there with him, especially not now, not with all I've done and what's hanging over my head.

Reluctantly, and with a final pull on his warm lips, I step back, putting a little space between us, trying to regain control.

He makes a comment about my building not being safe before leading me the rest of the way down to his waiting motorcycle. I almost laugh at the irony. A helmet is on my head, and he's roaring the engine before I can even protest. I'm on the back, holding his firm body against mine.

The helmet only covers the top and back of my head, and my nose is at his collar. I smell his rich, masculine scent. The heat of our torsos is electric, and I rest my cheek on his shoulder blade. It's the most amazing feeling of speed and power and freedom and Logan's body against mine. I allow myself to dream we could keep going forever, run away from everything, never look back. It's only a dream, but it's so seductive.

Once we've slowed down enough to talk, I can't help teasing him. "You're a bad boy now."

I feel his body vibrate with laughter, and a thrill moves through me. I love that I can make him laugh. "I'm actually pretty good at some things."

A sigh, and I remember how good he is at those things. The memories rush back on the strength of the sea breeze surrounding us as he takes off again.

He'd been my first. I'd wanted it to be him the moment I laid eyes on him under that boardwalk where I sat reading my silly book. It was so unlike me.

I'd always been focused on books and music, and honestly, I was a little nervous around guys—especially big, masculine guys like Logan.

Still, he walked by, and all I could think was *Quatopygia: The enticing movement of a man's rear end...*

"What's that you're reading?" he'd said, dropping to sit beside me on the sand.

The sea air pushed his glossy, dark hair around his face, around his straight nose and dark brow. His easy manner relaxed me, and I didn't care he was a bit older than me. I'd been a year out of high school, nineteen and unsure whether to work or try to continue with college. He turned those gorgeous blue eyes on me, that perfectly square jaw, and I would have given him anything. Then he smiled, and my last shred of resistance disappeared.

After our first time, we were insatiable. He explored my body with all the enthusiasm of a modern-day pioneer—anywhere and everywhere—and it was thrilling and sexy and so incredible. I've never been the way I was with him that summer. I was wild and free. It was the best summer of my life, a dream. I had no idea everything would come crashing down shortly after he left.

Still, those memories are a blissful imprint on my brain. The bike starts to slow as we arrive at our destination, and I regret the loss of his heat when he gets off the bike. I take his hand, allowing him to lead me inside to a table covered with thick, fine linens and the most delicious smells of tomato and cheese and basil.

He orders champagne, and I can't resist a tease. "Are we celebrating?"

My dark glasses still cover my face like a mask. I can't help wondering if I take them off, if I show him everything, if he'll see all the awful things I've done since he left me. He went away to become an honored member of the elite guard, and I stayed behind to slowly devolve into this thing I hate, my debts far outweighing my ability to pay.

"I feel lucky," his low voice moves thorough my insides in a sizzling vibration that makes me laugh.

He'd ordered for me, and I'd been thrilled that he remembered Campania—the pastel-hued district in the shadows of Mt. Vesuvius. Naples is there, the ruins of Pompeii... We'd always dreamed of visiting its dreamy coastline, lost in time and so romantic.

We'd finished, and as if in a trance, I'd taken his hand, followed him through the busy restaurant to the bike.

Now, walking on our beach, all I can think of are the hours we spent here telling each other everything, sharing everything. Holding my arms tight around his waist, I rest my cheek again on his shoulder. I remember how he'd wanted to travel, too. It had been why he'd entered the military.

"Italy, Morocco, the desert..." I can still see him lying on the sand, long and bronze in the sun, telling me his hopes and ambitions. I'd wanted to stretch my body along the length of his and soak up his warmth like a cat.

"Go to exotic locations, meet the natives, and kill them?" I teased, quoting something I'd read and not really meaning it. I didn't expect his defensive response.

"It's not like that, Sass. I'd be protecting our leaders. Guarding our country's existence."

"I'm sorry," I'd said quietly, wishing I could die. "I didn't mean it."

He'd touched my face and smiled, catching the wild strands of my hair blowing in the ocean breeze. "I know."

Sitting beside him, I'd leaned my head on his shoulder. "You could be killed. Doesn't that bother you?"

His answer was thoughtful, serious. "It's who I am. Protection, keeping people safe, these things just seem to come out of me. It's what I feel when I look at you."

My bottom lip is caught between my teeth. I'd always been so fiercely independent, yet sitting there with him, hearing his sincerity, I would willingly cede my power to his. I never wanted to lose him. I'd wait for him to come back, and I'd let him protect me. I'd vowed this to myself.

Only that isn't what happened.

Now he's here. He's the best of the best, like I always knew he would be, and I'm facing a debt I've only one way to repay.

My stomach is churning with the reality of what's to come, but Logan's voice pulls me from my thoughts.

"How is your aunt?"

A little start. I hadn't expected us to go there. "She died shortly after you left," I say, blinking down.

Logan's body stiffens at my side, and his warm hand covers my upper arm. "I'm so sorry."

I listen to the shushing of the waves moving across the sand, the tiny bubbles sizzling in their wake. I think about that day, and what I thought was the most devastating moment of my life. I had no idea it was only the outer bands of the storm moving in to destroy me.

"What happened?" he says gently.

Pushing a strand of hair behind my ear, I see her

face in my mind's eye. Her light brown hair streaked with grey, her kind brown eyes in a lined face. She'd raised my brother and me after our mother died of cancer. We never knew our father.

"She was riding her bike." I can't believe how easily the words flow from my mouth. For so long, I couldn't even think them. "A man driving a truck ran a stop sign and hit her."

My eyes heat, and before I can resist, I'm in his arms. Strong arms surround me, and my cheek is against his chest. His hand strokes the back of my hair, my neck. He kisses the top of my head, and I melt into him. It's so incredibly soothing.

"You were alone. You must've been devastated."

My insides cling to him. *How does he know what to say? How has he always known?* Swallowing the thickness in my throat, I lift my chin, closing my eyes as I inhale.

"I didn't have time. I found a job... We could stay in her apartment, but I had to prove I could take care of Cam."

Then the unthinkable happened.

"I wish I'd known." His arms loosen, and I step back, turning my face into the wind.

"You were training," I say quietly, remembering those nights when I cried for him. "You couldn't have come back."

"Still... I could have done something."

My eyebrows pull together as I think about this. "What could you have done?"

We start to walk again, and he doesn't answer right away. He'd been as broke as me back then. We were like gypsies, sneaking and borrowing everything we'd done. Laughing and living on the razor's edge of being caught at every turn.

"You're right," he finally says. "I had nothing and I couldn't leave. Still... I could have comforted you."

It's a sweet sentiment, but as much as my noble warrior would have wanted to help me, he would have been as powerless as I was in the face of that year.

The waves echo in the shelter of the boardwalk, and Logan stops. "Here we are." A smile is in his voice, but I'm confused. "Don't you recognize it?"

I'm on the spot, and I'm racking my brain for the right answer. "We spent a lot of time all over this place."

He catches both my hands. "I saw you for the first time right here. You had your back against that post, and you were reading... something."

Reaching out, I slide my hand down the weathered wood. "The sun was so bright that day."

"I was jogging, and there you were."

"You went right past me then turned around and came back. Why did you do that?"

"Hm..." He takes a few steps away, toward the water. "You were so beautiful. You were so absorbed in that damn book. I'm pretty sure your nose was touching the pages."

"I was trying to hide," I say, remembering. *Quatopygia*... Embarrassment heats my cheeks. "I was checking out your butt when you suddenly turned around and caught me."

Happiness and sadness fight it out in my stomach. I'd been so innocent back then.

Logan steps closer, his large hands covering my waist. That sexy grin is in his voice, and I can't deny the hum it sets off under my skin. "You were checking me out?

The heat from our bodies is intoxicating. My fingers move from his wrists up his muscled arms, and

I can't seem to breathe normally. "It was a new experience for me."

"I remember your level of experience." He leans forward, and my lips are heavy. I remember my first time, our first time. He'd been so gentle, so amazing.

"Don't tell me it wasn't a new experience for you." I try to tease him. "I'm sure you'd never been attracted to a bookworm before."

"Every guy has a sexy librarian fantasy."

"Even massively handsome jocks?"

"Those in particular."

*Jesus*, that grin in his voice has me right back to all the ways he'd made me feel — light and free and so sexy. I'd never felt sexy a day in my life before him.

"Logan—" His name escapes on a sigh just before he takes my mouth.

As always, his kiss is consuming, and I'm right there with him, holding the sides of his face and opening my mouth. Our tongues collide, and heat floods my pelvis. I'd decided earlier it would be best not to sleep with him, but when he lifts me and slowly eases us to a sitting position, me straddling his lap, I know I won't be doing what's best.

His hands are on my waist, and my knees dig into the soft, cool sand as I push up on them, holding his face in my hands. I kiss him like I'm tasting fine wine, so delicious. Large hands grip my legs, sliding under my skirt, moving higher to the tops of my thighs. My mouth breaks from his, and I exhale a moan. The desire is excruciating.

In my kneeling position, his face is right at my breasts. I feel the scruff of his beard against my skin, and I quickly pull the string of my bikini top. It falls loose, and I rake my fingers desperately along the V-neck of my dress, spilling out my breast and allowing him to pull a tight nipple into his mouth.

"Oh, god, yes," I gasp, clutching his cheeks and tracing my fingernails through his soft beard.

He makes a groaning sound as his hands find the seam of my bikini bottoms, teasing me. My thighs shake with desire. My forehead is hot. I can barely take it anymore when a thick digit goes inside me, and I lose control.

"Logan..." My nails dig into the skin of his shoulders.

"Shit, Kass," he hisses as his fingers invade, deep and curling. His voice is low. "You're so wet... I want you so much right now."

"Please..." I slide my tongue across his top lip before pulling it into my mouth. "Please don't stop."

I barely have time to react. His hands move down my back, and he rolls us so that I'm lying on the hill of sand under the boardwalk. His head is at my waist, kissing a line along my hip bone, moving lower. "I want to taste you."

My hips jump when his beard teases the crease of my thighs, and I gasp as he pulls the material aside and circles his tongue around my clit.

"Logan!" My back arches, and he begins his slow assault, massaging and sucking, the groan of his hunger vibrating through my body.

Pleasure fizzes through my pelvis, snaking down my thighs. His hands cup my ass, holding me to his mouth as he continues circling, teasing, sucking, until my body erupts in a shuddering orgasm. I'm moaning and whimpering, and he takes one last sweep of his tongue.

Nothing has changed. He's up, leaning forward to pull my lips with his mouth. Only a moment he breaks away, rising above me like a dark, sexy mountain. I hear the rip of foil, and I'm breathing so hard. I remember this so well.

Reaching out, my fingers fumble over his thick cock, sliding down his shaft as he rolls the condom over it. *So big...*

He leans down to kiss me again, long and slow. Everything about Logan is big. I slide my hands over his cheeks, down the length of his neck, inside his shirt that's now unbuttoned. I trace my fingers through the coarse hair on his chest—another new thing. With a shiver, I think *he's a man now*. I touch a beaded nipple, and he groans and kisses me deeper. I trace the lines of his torso, and he rocks his hips, moving closer to my core.

My knees are bent at his waist ready for him, but as always, he's taking his time, kissing my face, my neck, my eyebrows as the orgasm cooling inside me rages to life again. My hands are at his narrow waist, and my thumbs move forward, tracing the V along his pelvis. I feel his erection touching my thigh, and I'm aching, dying for him to fill me.

"Please, Logan," I whisper, and he kisses me again, rocking closer to the center. "Oh, god, please."

Then he pushes into me in one swift move. My back arches again, and I cry out from the incredible fullness, the intense pleasure mixed with a touch of pain.

"Oh, fuck, Kass," he groans, kissing my cheek and rocking a little faster. "You're still so tight."

I don't tell him it's been quite a dry spell since I last had him. I don't say I've been dreaming of him ever since. I only moan as he rocks into me faster, kissing me again, his warm lips full, pulling mine with his. I lift my hips and he bucks into me harder.

"It's been so long," he gasps, leaning down to kiss my neck, pulling the skin between his teeth and sending an explosion of pleasure through my core. He kisses my ear, and my thighs shudder.

With another groan, he rises up, holding my thighs and pushing into me. "Kass..." He pinches my nipples, pulling and teasing them, sending surges of electricity clenching my insides.

He kisses the arch of my foot before moving my leg around so he can lay behind me on the sand. He pulls my body into his as he pumps me so deep.

My orgasm is sparking, racing to the top, and he kisses the back of my neck, causing me to break into tremors.

"Oh, god!" I sigh, falling forward before arching back to hold his cheek, bucking my ass against his pelvis.

Small hairs tickle my back. Large hands cover my breasts, squeezing and massaging. Warmth rushes up my spine — my senses are overwhelmed.

The orgasm extends, jerking my body, clenching the muscles inside me holding his massive cock. His mouth open at the back of my neck, and his teeth graze my skin as he finds his release with a loud noise.

He grips my hipbones so hard, I know he'll leave a mark, moving me against him, and I feel him pulsing, filling the condom. I feel his stomach shudder, and my eyes squeeze closed. It's the most erotic sensation, and I remember it so well.

His hands move to my stomach, holding me against him. Warm lips touch my neck, and chills skate down my arms. I thread my fingers into his soft hair as we come down together. Turning my head, I find his lips again, and salt touches my tongue.

Our bodies are slick with sweat, and all I can think is *Oh, god, Logan*. I want to cry and I want to laugh and I want to hold him. I've missed him with my whole being, and I'm so amazingly satisfied. Another kiss and he reaches down to hold the condom as he slides out. I roll onto my back and reach out to touch his chest, to slide my fingertips over his skin. He's everything I ever wanted. He's more.

I still love him so much, and I am so fucking screwed.

## Chapter 6: Closer

*Logan*

Sunlight streams through the blinds, and I'm lying on my bed. All I can think about is Kass. From the moment I held her in the stairwell through our ride on the motorcycle, throughout dinner when we laughed and caught up I wanted her. I wanted to feel her coming apart on my cock like she did so many times before.

I'd wanted it, but I'd prepared myself for it not to happen. I didn't want to be a presumptive asshole, thinking someone as beautiful as her didn't have anyone. I never asked that question. I couldn't bring myself to do it.

If she had told me no, if she had pushed me away, it would have been over. She didn't. We made love with all the passion and intensity of those early days. Our reunion was spectacular, and I had wanted to bring her here, spend the night reconnecting a few more times.

She'd wanted to go back to her place... I couldn't tell, but she seemed shaken. The thought makes me grin. I complied with her wishes, but not before making plans to spend all day today with her. I can't wait to have her in my arms again.

Maneuvering my bike through the winding streets to the warehouse district, I glance up at the colorful awnings. I'd started out dreading this personal leave, and now I never want it to end. Rowan was right about time away and resetting my thoughts, but neither of us could have predicted I'd find this precious thing I lost.

Kass always loved visiting bookstores—the smaller and more obscure the better. A new one opened in a shotgun shack by the public beach, and a small café and ice cream shop are nearby. I want her to know I remember everything. Our time together was the happiest of my life, and I want her back if she'll have me.

I don't know the details of how it would work with my job or if she would want to move here... But I'm confident we can work these things out if she feels the same.

I'm still on my bike trying to wrap my mind around my decision when she skips out the door of her apartment building to meet me. She's dressed in a beige tunic top and her long hair ripples in pale waves around her shoulders. The bow of her swimsuit peeks out at the back of her neck, and again, those silly sunglasses are over her eyes. Any doubt I might have had about my feelings for her disappears. She's amazing.

"We are going to the beach this time, yes?" Pink lips curl into a smile, and I can't resist. I reach out and catch her by the waist, pulling her to me for a kiss.

She melts into me, clutching my broad shoulders. I've only just tasted her when I feel her teeth against my lips. She's smiling, and happiness tightens my chest.

"Yes," I say. "We'll *apricate*, grab some lunch, and then I have a surprise for you."

"A surprise?" Her eyebrow arches. "Sounds interesting."

"If you keep looking at me that way, I'll have to rearrange our day again."

"How so?" Her breath skates across my neck as she leans into me, tossing a leg over the bike and taking her place at my back.

"I'll take you to my apartment and spend the day making love to you instead."

Her hands tighten on my stomach, and her chin is on the top of my shoulder. "I like that plan, too."

It's a warm purr at my ear, and heat rushes below my belt. *Fuck me*, I have to focus on how much she's going to love that tiny bookstore, or I will seriously do it. Hell, we have time for everything. If I can convince her to give us another chance, we'll have all the time in the world.

"Tomorrow," I say, turning my head to capture her lips once more. "You're staying with me tonight."

She drops her chin so that her cheek is against my back. "But I didn't pack anything. I don't have a toothbrush—"

"I'll buy you whatever you need." My tone is final.

Her hands tighten around my waist, and I love the feel of her body pressed against my back. I'll do everything in my power not to lose her again. A sharp roar, and we're off, headed for the ocean and our favorite place.

It isn't long before we're walking on the beach, holding hands. Our fingers are entwined, and our palms press together. I glance over at her and smile. She's swept her hair up in an adorable bun, and she's stepping lightly, keeping closer to the edge of the water, while I'm up on the softer sand, dodging shells and driftwood.

"So!" She's more animated today, and I swear she seems as happy as I am we've found each other. "Tell me your favorite thing about being a member of the king's elite guard."

"Good question," I say, smiling at the way she says my title, punctuating the words like they're very important syllables. I suppose they are.

"You do love it, don't you?" Her brow lines, and I can only imagine what her eyes are saying behind those Jackie O shades.

"I do," I nod. "But you asked my favorite part. That's more precise."

"You're as serious as you ever were," she grins, looking out at the ocean. "You're allowed to change your answer later."

Pulling her hand up, I kiss the back of it. "I only ever want to be completely honest with you."

Her smile dims slightly, and I wonder why. *Has someone lied to you, my Kass?* She's hinted at bad things happening in those years we were apart. I want to know what happened. I want to help her repair the damage.

In the meantime, I'll answer her question. "The strategy of tracking and finding the bad guys."

She lifts her chin, making a little impressed face. "Please elaborate, Mr. Hunt."

Stopping short, I pull her to me for a kiss. "You're adorable."

Straight white teeth appear as she smiles, and she places her palm on my cheek, touching my mouth with the pad of her thumb. "You're distracted." With a skip back, she pulls me to start walking again. "Tell me about your *strategy*!"

I think about my most recent job. "Last year, when we were tracking a kidnapper and trying to find where they were hiding, we searched manifests, satellite imagery, even security cameras piecing together the trail. We put together piece after piece until we found what we were looking for."

A little nod, and her expression is focused, listening closely. "It sounds interesting."

"It's definitely more interesting than standing around watching the royals and pushing back paparazzi."

Her cute nose wrinkles. "I don't think I could do that."

"It's an important part of the job."

She makes a little noise of disgust and shakes her head.

"Your turn," I say, pulling her arm gently. "What did you do in America?"

Her smile falters at my question, but she recovers quickly. I make another mental note.

"I worked in shipping," she says, looking up. "You know, logistics, importing and exporting... Pretty boring compared to what you do."

"How did you get mixed up in that line of work?"

"I speak French!" She holds her hands out and shrugs. "And Spanish."

"And very obscure English," I wink.

"I guess once you've mastered two languages, adding a third isn't so hard."

We walk a little ways, and I decide it's time. I don't want to wait anymore. "It's pretty amazing we found each other, don't you think?"

She's quiet, watching the water rush over her feet. I wonder if she heard me until at last she answers softly. "Yes."

My optimism is dampened slightly by the return of her sadness. "I think the odds of us crossing paths again would be slim."

Her brow lines. "I disagree! I mean, you live here, and Cam lives here. It was bound to happen some day."

"Yes, but I'd been in the Caribbean most of last year. I'm always working." She has no idea how lucky we are. "I don't remember you gambling. What brought you to the casino that night?"

She shrugs. "I told you, I was with friends."

"What friends? Who do you keep up with here?"

"What is this?" she laughs, pulling my hand. "The inquisition?"

I look forward, across the sea, thinking. "I've lost touch with everyone outside of my work."

"I have, too." Her voice is quiet. "Those people weren't really my friends."

Now I feel guilty. I remember the loneliness that consumed me in the days before we met, and I don't want to bring her down. We're approaching the bookstore, and I pull her to my chest. She's so small wrapped in the safety of my arms.

"Forget the past. We're here... By some amazing stroke of luck we found each other again." I lean down and kiss the side of her neck. Her shoulder rises as she laughs. "And this is your surprise."

Releasing her, I turn us to face the small, white house with the sandy steps leading from the beach up to the wooden porch. At the top is a sign reading Poseidon's New and Used Books.

She doesn't answer right away. Her slim brows pull together over her glasses, and it's like she's not spotting what I brought her here to see.

"It opened just a year ago, and I figured you wouldn't know about it. Since you've been gone..." My enthusiasm dims a bit. "Was I wrong?"

"No!" She's a little breathless, shaking her head. "I guess I was just so surprised, I didn't know what to say. It's amazing!"

Clasping her hand again, I pull her to the steps, jogging up them and holding the door. She touches my arm lightly before passing through into the bright little house. Natural light surrounds us, and the interior is all white. Painted, weathered boards give it an antique appearance, and a few of the windows have large cushions in them—I presume for sitting in the sunshine to read.

Kass stands at the front entrance a moment, then all at once she clasps her hands together over her mouth. Still, she can't hide her enormous smile, and relief hits my chest. I return to where she's standing and pull her into a hug.

"Logan!" It's a soft whisper. Her arms are trapped against my chest, and her head turns in all directions. "What is this place?"

"Well, you see, those are grapefruits." I tease, tilting my head toward a stack of books.

She laughs, and I can see her blinking rapidly behind those silly glasses.

"What's wrong, Sass?" I ask softly, kissing her cheek. "Don't you like it?"

Her fingertips touch my jaw. "I can't believe it. You remember everything."

"I tried to forget when you left, but after last night, I realized I hadn't done a very good job."

Her hands rise to my cheeks, and she pulls my face down to hers. Our lips meet, and her kiss is so full of emotion. I lift her off her feet, sliding my hands under her ass and boosting her higher. Her arms go around my neck, and I kiss her deeper, momentarily forgetting everything until the soft clearing of a throat brings us back to reality.

"Excuse me," the voice says, and I break away, looking down at an older woman with short grey hair.

A wry grin is on her lips. "The romance section is in the far left corner."

I quickly lower Kass, who covers her mouth as she laughs. "Sorry!"

Taking her hand, I lead her through the store. She bumps into a table, and squeaks a little "Whoops."

I reach back and help her straighten it. "The place is yours to explore."

Walking through the rows, she lightly traces her fingers along the spines of the shelved books. I watch her a moment before slipping down a parallel row and stepping into her path when she reaches the end. She walks right into me and laughs as she hugs my waist.

"Thank you," she whispers, and I kiss the top of her head owning the joy simmering in my chest, knowing I'll do whatever it takes to keep her this happy as long as I can.

## Chapter 7: The Truth

*Kass*

He got me.

Logan is huge and strong and fierce. He takes orders, and he gives them equally well. He'll take a bullet. He's trained to kill. He *has* killed men in the line of duty... And yet he goes through the trouble of finding this little bookstore, bringing me here because he knows it will make me happy.

Never in a million years would I have expected it to play out this way. I'm completely caught in the most incredibly heartbreaking way imaginable, and I can't bring myself to say the words.

I'm standing here, surrounded by the smell of old paper and the warmth of my favorite characters, and all I want to do is keep going as long as I possibly can, even if the clock is ticking down on how much longer I can hide. I can't bear the way he'll look at me once he knows. Everything will change, and it breaks my heart.

Taking a volume off the shelf, I hold it to my nose, my chest. *It's too soon. I'm not ready...*

"What's that?" Logan is with me, and a smile is in his voice. "*Monster: An Illustrated History of the Cockroach.* Unexpected..."

My cheeks heat, and I put it back. "I didn't read the title," I say softly. "I was... just thinking."

"Do you want to buy something?" My hand is engulfed in his larger one again, and he's leading me through the store. "We've been here a half hour, and you've only walked around touching and smelling things."

"We book people are a strange folk," I say, smiling up at him.

He pulls me close. It's an automatic gesture I've quickly grown to love. "You're not so strange." His voice is warm. "But I do think the shopkeeper is ready to close up."

"After our grand entrance?" I pretend to be offended.

"I think especially after that."

I can't keep the smile off my face. I have no idea how to respond, but I'll be damned if I kill this moment. "Pick something for me," I say. "What's your favorite book?"

"Well," he steps back still holding my hands. "How about this?"

He places a thick tome in my hand, and my nose wrinkles.

"Not a *Game of Thrones* fan?"

"Too depressing. Pick something else. Something for us."

He chuckles stepping away again, taking the heavy book. He's back just as fast and now I'm holding a skinny one.

"How's that?" he says.

My insides drop along with my chin, but I hold on a bit longer. "It's perfect," I say, forcing a smile.

He kisses my head. "We can read them and decide which one we like best."

I smile, and he takes it from me to the register.

"I should have known." The woman I assume is the shop owner greets him. "*Poems of Rumi*. This edition has illustrations."

A few moments, and he's with me again, lacing our fingers and leading me outside where the air has grown cooler.

"The café here is supposed to be good..." He stops, and my hand is in the bend of his arm. I press my body to his.

"But?" I smile.

"What if we head back to my place, read a little, and order in?"

"You want to read?" When I lift my chin, our faces are closer.

He leans down and covers my lips with his. It's a long, slow kiss, and when he pulls back, my entire body is humming. "No."

"Me either."

My thoughts swirl as we zip through the streets on his motorcycle. My front is to his back, and my eyes are closed as the wind pushes against my face. He's so warm, and I tighten my hold on his firm torso. We're at his place—I've never been here—and he parks along the curb. Grabbing the bag, he pulls my hand into his arm again, and I'm right beside him, waiting as he fumbles with his keys before opening a large door.

"Your place is huge," I say, walking beside him up the stairs. "Does anyone else live here?"

We reach the top and he leaves me, crossing the open floor plan to what must be the kitchen. I turn away from the stairs, sliding my fingers across the back of a slick, leather chair.

"It's just the one big room," he says, and I hear the pop of champagne. The sound of bubbles in glasses is next, and he's crossing the space to me.

"When you said you had a studio apartment, I expected something like mine."

"Yours isn't like this?"

A cool champagne flute is placed in my hand, and I take a sip. "No," I say, laughing. "I can barely turn around in my place. It might be two hundred square feet."

A large hand slides around me, over my lower back. "I'm barely ever here. I sleep and occasionally stay a few nights."

My hand is on his chest, and I trace it over the soft cotton tee he's wearing. "How are you having so much time here now?"

"The royal family is in the Caribbean," he leans down to kiss the side of my face. His beard scruffs the sensitive place behind my ears, and desire shimmers through my insides.

"Why aren't you with them?" My voice has grown thick as he continues kissing into my hair.

"The king thought I needed a break." Straightening, he takes my flute and sets it to the side along with his. I hear the clink of the crystal glasses against each other.

Just as fast, he's back with me, pulling my hips against his with both hands. He slides them back and down, softly over my ass, and heat floods my pelvis.

"Come." His voice is low, seductive, and he takes my hands, pulling me as he walks backwards, leaning down to nip my lips every few steps.

"Careful." My entire body alive and sensitive to his touch.

He pauses and drops to sitting in front of me. His head is at my chest, and large hands clasp my upper thighs. My hands are on his shoulders, and my eyes flutter shut as he slides his hands higher, his thumbs grazing my center, before he pulls my tunic off my body.

Cupping his cheeks, I lean down to kiss him. "I want you so much."

His hands move faster, pushing my bikini bottoms down and off before reaching back up to slide two fingers back and forth across my slit. My legs shudder at the sensation, and I gasp a little moan.

"You are so beautiful," he murmurs, reaching up to pull the strings of my bikini top. In two pulls, I'm bare before him. My stomach tightens as he leans back, his gaze burning over my skin.

Just as fast he's back up, pulling my breast into his mouth, licking and biting at my beaded nipple. I can't help gasping as his large hands trace down my back and down my ass from behind, dipping into my core.

"You're so wet," he murmurs, devouring my skin, pulling little bits between his teeth.

"Oh, god, Logan," I whisper, fumbling with his shirt. "Take this off," I gasp. "I want to feel your skin on mine."

In a sweep, his shirt is off. He stands and quickly pushes his trunks away. I'm in a haze of longing as he reaches around my waist again, lifting me and pulling me onto his lap as he slides us both back onto his bed.

I'm in a straddle, and I reach down to wrap my fingers around his thick shaft. He exhales a hiss, and I don't waste time, scooting down, I place both hands on the bed at his hips before dipping down to flick my tongue all around the hardened tip.

"Yes," he groans, his large hand gently stroking the side of my face as I take him in one hand to guide him into my mouth.

His hips jump when I tickle my fingers down his shaft to feel a large vein straining. He's huge, and I lean down, but I'm not halfway before he's touching the back of my throat. Lifting up, he's out with a pop, and I thread my fingers over and down him.

"Come here," he groans, grasping my hips again and pulling me to him.

My breasts flatten against his chest, and his arms are all around me, hugging me as his mouth plunders mine. His tongue is in my mouth, and he's kissing me again and again, moving me so I'm right above his rigid cock.

His fist is between us, right beneath me, and with a swift thrust, he's inside.

"Oh, god!" I gasp a moan. We were just here last night, but still it's an amazing sense of fullness.

"I'm clean," he murmurs, kissing my bare shoulders, pulling my body against his mouth as he nips and kisses my breasts. "I want to feel you on me."

"Yes," I hiss, rocking my hips and massaging my clit against him.

I'm on fire from his burning kisses and touches. My head is spinning, and I breathe his intoxicating scent. Leaning down, I kiss his broad shoulder, slipping out my tongue to taste him. Salt from the ocean is on his skin, and now it's in my mouth.

My thighs jump and shudder as he lightly traces his fingers down the curve of my ass, scooping me closer to his pelvis, rocking me as his thick shaft massages in and out, picking up speed. The assault on my clit sends fiery sparks to the arches of my feet.

"Oh, Logan," I gasp. "I'm going to come!"

He doesn't slow the pace. He moves faster, gripping my hips and moving me against him with more force, driving his hips up and into me.

With a wail, my body breaks into spasms, clenching and pulling all around him inside me.

"Oh, fuck," he coughs out, and I feel him pulsing, letting go just after my orgasm starts.

His groans and shudders mix with the orgasm racking my body, and I'm rocking my hips in time with the sensations, resting my forehead against him as my body continues to jerk.

"Oh, god, Logan," I whimper, holding onto him as the waves subside.

Massive arms surround me, holding me close as he kisses me back to this planet, this room, this bed. Coming back into focus, I feel he's still inside me. The evidence of what just happened is slick on both of us, but I don't care. I need to hold him right now.

Finding my voice, I manage to murmur, "That was..." In all my collecting, I'm not sure I've found the word for what we just shared.

"Incredible," he rumbles, kissing my ear, his beard sending another tiny after-shock through my insides.

All of it — tasting, smelling, feeling him... the sensory overload was... "Yes," I say with a little smile. "Simply incredible."

Shifting our position, he rolls us onto my back. His body hovers large over mine. My eyes are still closed, but I'm smiling so big as I reach up to trace my fingernails lightly through the beard on his cheeks.

"I like this," I say quietly. "It was different at first, but I like it now."

"I'll keep it for you," he says, leaning down to kiss my lips before straightening again. His large hand cups my chin, fingers spreading along my jaw. "Look at me," he says.

My smile falters. My heartbeat quickens, and I try to wriggle out of his hold.

"Kass?" He pleads as he rolls to the side releasing me. "Please. I miss your beautiful blue eyes."

Sitting up on the side of the bed, I let my hair fall in a curtain between us as I try to decide how much I'll tell him. Just as fast, he's up beside me, reaching for my waist to pull me over his legs again. I'm facing him in a straddle, and I know I'm trapped.

"What's wrong?" His voice is so tender and strong.

My eyes heat with tears. "I don't want to lose you," I whisper.

"The chances of you losing me are unbelievably small." A smile is in his voice, and I lift my face slowly.

I know where his eyes should be in relation to the sound of his voice, the dark outline of his soft, wavy hair. Holding my face straight, I do my best to meet his gaze.

For a moment he's quiet. I can't breathe, and dread twists a painful knot in my stomach. One hand leaves my waist, and the pad of his thumb lightly touches the top of my cheekbone.

He's trying to understand why my eyes won't connect with his. He's noticing the slight jump when I try to force them to focus.

He's seeing my truth.

"Kass?" Quiet confusion is in his voice, and I feel him blinking, trying to process.

I feel sick, but I manage to speak in a voice so small. "I'm looking at you…"

His body breaks, and he pulls me to him again. This time his hand holds the back of my neck through my hair. He's got me flush against him, skin on skin, the warmth of him moving into me, and I feel him breathing as fast I am.

He holds me, and my eyes squeeze shut. I hold him as well, never wanting to let him go, but even more than that—never wanting him to change how he thinks of me.

"What happened?" he finally says. He eases me back, but his hands are still on me, moving up to cup my cheeks. "Were you in an accident? I would have come to you."

Reaching out to cup his cheeks, I cast my eyes down. "It's genetic," I say quietly. "My aunt knew… she hoped it wouldn't show up in Cam or me…"

"Is Cam—?"

"No." I shake my head. "He's fine. He won't ever…" I can't say the words.

Logan pulls me to him again, moving us higher on the bed so we're lying face to face. My eyes are closed, and he lightly trails his fingers over my cheek.

"You would say the sun hurt your eyes," he says.

"That was the beginning stages." *Photosensitivity is an early indicator…* the doctor's words echo in my mind.

"I thought you were exaggerating," his voice is rough. "I was such an asshole."

"No!" My eyes widen, and I fumble for his lips, placing my fingers against them. "Don't say that! You were the greatest thing… You are…" I can't finish.

He's quiet, but my fingers remain on his lips. I trace the outline of them, noting their serious shape, until they move. "So all this time, you've been… *blind*?"

Pulling my lip between my teeth, I do the slightest nod.

"That's why today… In the bookstore." He rolls onto his back, and I scoot closer, placing my cheek against his chest. I hear his heart beating. It's only slightly elevated.

"I'm sorry I didn't know what you'd done for me at first."

He tenses. "Don't apologize to me. I should apologize to you. I was making you choose books and walk through the store like you'd been there before. I was a complete dick."

"You treated me like I could see," I say softly. "I want you to continue treating me like I can see."

Rolling toward me, we're facing each other again. I know he's studying me. I can feel the weight of his attempts to understand.

"But your eyes are still so beautiful." His voice is tentative. "They're not clouded or blank. Are you in darkness?"

"No… It's more like a dense fog." I'm speaking faster. He isn't afraid or freaked out or trying to find an excuse to leave, and the relief pulsing through me with every heartbeat makes me want to cry. "If things are very close, I can still see them."

At once he moves so close our noses touch. "Logan!" I squeal, pulling back. He catches me.

"I want you to see me." His voice squeezes my chest, and this time my eyes do mist.

"I see you," I whisper. "Your face is one of my most vivid memories." My fingers touch his beard. "This is new, but I see your tanned skin and straight white teeth. Sometimes I can hear your cocky grin when you tease me—"

"Cocky grin," he repeats, still not pulling away or pitying me. Instead he pulls me closer. "Oh, Kass. How can I ever let you out of my sight now?"

"What?" Of all the things he might say, that wasn't what I expected to hear.

"Shit, I'm going to be a fucking wreck whenever you're away from me. What if someone tries to hurt you? What if a car pulls out when you're crossing the street? *Jesus!*"

"Stop right there." I sit up fast, pulling the sheet around my naked body. "You're freaking yourself out, and I will not let you do this. I've managed my condition going on five years now—"

"Five?" He pushes up to sitting beside me.

"Five. Which means, I'm not made of glass." My lips press into a frown, and my brows pull together. "Don't treat me like I'm handicapped."

He blows out his breath and turns his back to the headboard. "I'll be honest. It's going to be hard."

I'm so offended, my voice is almost a shout. "Not to treat me like I'm handicapped?"

"No!" He catches me and pulls me to him. "Damn, you're still so feisty."

Pushing against him, I straighten. "I can take care of myself."

"Clearly you can..." His tone is thoughtful. "It's just... I had already noted all the ways your apartment building isn't safe, and I didn't even know about this."

My anger cools slightly. "What are you trying to say?"

"My job is protection, Sass." He touches my cheek. "I can't help what's in me. I will protect you, and now—"

"Now?" Yes, I'm still a bit defensive.

"Now I'm going to have to figure out a mantra of some kind. Extreme meditation. Anything to keep me sane. Unless you're content never to leave my side... Any chance you might consider that option?"

Two blinks and I'm at a loss for what to say. I actually consider the prospect of never leaving his side, and I start to laugh. "Oh, Logan," I say, shaking my head. Cocking my head, I look up at him through my lashes. It's a gesture of habit, since all I can see is a hazy dark mass where I know he's sitting. "Shut up and kiss me."

A low growl, and he pulls me onto his lap in a straddle. I catch his cheeks and dive for his mouth, pulling and kissing him. His hands are sliding all over my naked body, waking my insides again. I reach down between my legs and give his cock a few gentle tugs.

His face breaks away, and he looks up groaning. "Ah… that feels good."

"I know what else you like," I purr at the side of his jaw, pulling his skin between my teeth.

"You give great head for a blind girl."

I jump off his lap at that, pissed and ready to go. Just as fast, he breaks into a loud laugh, diving across the bed and grabbing me before I can dodge his hands.

"Let me go!" I struggle, but he lifts me easily, holding me under the ass against his chest.

"Stop struggling. I was only teasing." His voice is strong, his hold even stronger, and I relent. "I'm amazed by you," he continues, causing me to melt. "You blow my mind. You always have, but shit. Now you're like super girl." My fingers thread in his hair and he starts to walk. "Let's hit the shower. I'm nowhere near finished with you tonight."

I hold him as he carries me to the bathroom, resting my head on his shoulder. He's the one who amazes me. He's so far past anything I ever expected. I'm perfectly blissed, but that tinge of dread is never far away. As much as I love this, as much as it's everything I want to do… it's what I'm here to do. I'm following orders. I want to cry.

Logan thinks I'm special, but he hasn't heard my whole story. I don't know if he'll be as understanding once he knows everything. If he ever knows everything.

We're in the bathroom, and he stands me next to the cool shower stall while he adjusts the water. I reach out to trace my fingers along the lines of his shoulders. I let them travel down, learning every inch of his new physique. His younger one was my old memory, now this sexy man is burning new memories.

When he comes back, he carries me under the warm spray. Our mouths reunite and fresh water combines with the salt of our kisses. Long fingers slide down between my legs, teasing and making me moan. Round 2 is just getting started.

Internally, I make a decision. No matter the outcome, I will tell him everything. He might hate me, but he deserves the right to that decision. It's a good plan, just and noble, and first I want to enjoy him one more time.

## Chapter 8: Reality

*Logan*

*Kass is blind.*
 *Blind.*
I'm still reeling from the revelation.

Don't get me wrong. It changes *nothing* about how I feel about her. If anything, my feelings have intensified… But I don't know how to handle this knowledge. It's like a sucker-punch to my most vulnerable, basic instinct.

Protect, guard… these things are my life. Can I ever go back to the palace and leave her alone — especially knowing what's out there? Especially knowing the kinds of maniacs we deal with, and their expertise at finding our weaknesses. She'll be a sitting duck.

*Jesus!* I think about that shitty apartment building where she lives. I walked right in off the street, and she never even saw me coming. She almost ran right past me in the stairwell, but I caught her, backed her against the wall, and kissed her. I could've been any intruder grabbing her that way.

Her initial shock makes a hell of a lot more sense now. It's a wonder she didn't mace me.

I'm a fucking asshole.

She needs a can of mace.

Sunlight streams through the window, and she's right here, curled at my side, her pale blonde hair spread around us on the pillow. Dark lashes touch the tops of her cheeks. She's so damn beautiful. She's ethereal, and she looks so young with her face relaxed in sleep. I want to touch her, but I don't want to wake her.

She's the same girl I knew that summer, yet she's different. She's stronger, better. I try to remind myself she's survived this long without my help. At the same time, I know how fast she could be taken from me. I can't help wondering if she's already a target.

I'm breathing harder as my protective anger rises. Just let anyone try to lay a hand on her. I'll break their necks. At the same time, I'm going to have a fucking aneurysm whenever she's out of my sight. What the hell... I already tried to resign, but Rowan wouldn't accept it.

How can I protect Kass and Ava at the same time?

Maybe I can get her a dog. A badass dog, like a Rottweiler or a German Shepherd...

"What's wrong?" Kass's soft voice pulls me from my spiraling thoughts.

Her slim brow wrinkles as she rolls onto her back and holds out her hand. I take it and pull it to my lips. She immediately pushes into a sitting position and holds out the other one. "Can I touch your face?"

Her hair hangs in pretty, messy waves around her shoulders, and her eyes are downcast. I kiss her hand again with all the warmth I feel. "Of course you can."

Her brow relaxes, and a little smile curls her lips. She carefully places her fingers on my cheeks, sliding them up to my brow before moving them down to my jaw, where she rakes her fingernails through my beard.

"You're angry. Why?"

My hands circle her waist, and I pull her onto my lap in a straddle, burying my face in her neck. She squeals a little laugh and wraps her slim arms around my neck as I kiss her collarbone.

"Your beard tickles," she sighs, and I'm getting hard.

I speak between a kiss to the top of her shoulder. "I'm not angry."

"You were breathing fast, your body is tense, and I can feel you frowning. Don't lie to me, Logan Hunt." The gentle reproving tone in her voice makes me catch her cheeks, pulling her mouth to mine. Even after all the times we made love last night, I want her again.

"Oh!" She struggles to break free. "Don't kiss me. I've got morning breath!"

That makes me laugh, and I kiss her anyway, albeit a closed-mouth kiss, warm and tender against those soft pink lips. Her eyes flutter closed, and I feel her smile just before she scoots back.

"Tell me why you're angry."

"I'm trying to remember," I tease. "Were you always this stubborn?"

Her head tilts to the side as if she's thinking. "Probably not. I've changed since we've been apart."

That makes me frown again, and I smooth my finger along the line of her hair. "I know." My voice betrays my emotion, and I'm going to have to learn just how perceptive my girl is even without sight.

Her chin drops. "It's the blind thing, isn't it." Her voice is full of something like... embarrassment or shame?

"Hey," I catch that chin and place another soft kiss on her lips.

"Please don't. You don't have to do that." She starts to move away, but I've got her by the waist. She's not going anywhere.

"I don't know what you're thinking right now," I say, "but you've got it all wrong."

She shakes her head. "It's a lot to take in, a major bomb to drop. I can only imagine how you must feel."

*Dammit, I can't take one more second of this.*

"Listen to me." My voice is stern, but my hand on her cheek is gentle. "I'm still trying to believe my luck in finding you again." She starts to interrupt, but I keep going. "If I seem angry, it's because, well, dammit, Kass. I don't know how to deal with these urges running through me."

Her slim brows clutch. "What do you mean?"

"You know what I am, what I do for a living."

"You're... one of the king's guards." I can't believe she's still confused.

"You are the most precious thing in my life right now, and you're essentially the most vulnerable as well. I don't know what to do with that. How can I ever let you leave, walk around in the world, without me beside you?"

Pink floods her cheeks, and she looks down as a brilliant smile lights her face. "Logan," she says quietly, blinking fast again. "I've been getting around on my own for years now."

"I'm trying to tell myself that, but it isn't working. Especially now with the added danger of you being associated with me."

Her lips press together, and she's adorably bossy. "You'll just have to try harder. If you start thinking of me as a... a *disabled person*, you'll never be able to think of me as anything else."

For a moment I run my eyes over her tiny frame sitting in my bed. She's like a stubborn drop of sunshine in my navy sheets, and the only thing covering her body is one of my thin white tanks. The dark peaks of her breasts are visible through the fabric, and my semi is turning to full hard-on.

"You said that before. You think I won't find you attractive?" I'm grinning as I slide the back of my finger up and down the fabric, over her beaded nipple. She jumps and does a little gasp, sliding her hand over mine.

Her other hand rises to touch my lips. "That cocky grin."

The flush in her cheeks spreads down her neck, and I'm ready to remove all doubt from her mind about how attractive I find her.

"My attraction to you is something you never have to worry about." My thumb closes over that hard peak.

"Logan..." her voice is a soft warning, and I catch the hem of my shirt, pulling it quickly over her head. She lets out a little startled laugh, and I wrap my arms around her slim frame, pulling her to me.

"Come here," I growl, moving my lips over her soft skin, starting at her ribcage and working my way up to her breast. "I've dreamed of this body for years."

A beaded nipple is between my lips, and I give it a hard pull while I stroke and tease her other breast. She exhales a moan, and her fingers thread into my hair.

Turning our bodies, I lay her back on the pillows, rising on my knees a moment to study her slim frame, back arched and legs spread. Her hair fans around her, and her dark lashes just skim the tops of her cheeks. A pretty flush covers her breasts and upper body where my beard has left traces. I'm surprised by how much I like the signs that I've had her body... that her body is mine.

Leaning down, I hook my arms around her hips, pulling her to my mouth before giving her pussy a long and lingering French kiss. Her hands slap the mattress beside me as her back rises.

"Oh, god!" She cries as I slide my tongue across her clit faster and faster. "Ahh!"

Her hips rotate in time with my movements. I feel the shuddering breaking through her thighs, which are wrapped in my arms. Her hand moves frantically in my hair, and she starts to wail, shaking and coming apart on my mouth.

She's trembling a bit as I kiss the inside of her thigh, moving my mouth to the top of her hipbone. As much as my cock is aching for her wet heat, I pause to give her hip a little suck, a pull to mark her pale body. Her fingers thread in my hair, and every brush of my beard against her sensitive skin makes her jump.

"Come to me, Logan, please," she gasps, reaching for me.

I break away from her, planting a little kiss on the bright red hickey now tattooed on her hip.

"You want me, Sass?" Sliding my chest against hers, I rest on my forearms, holding the backs of her shoulders in my palms.

Her slim knees rise, positioning her entrance right at my tip. "Please," she whispers, and I don't make her ask twice.

With one swift thrust, I bury myself in her, balls deep. "Oh, god," we groan together. My forehead drops to her shoulder, and I pause a moment, doing my best to get control, to make it last a little longer.

Kass lets out a whine and shifts her hips back and forth against me, pulling me with her clenching insides. My eyes squeeze shut, and I can't hold back any longer. I grab her face and kiss her deeply, rocking my hips in a fast pace with my building orgasm.

"Oh, Kass," I break away with a ragged groan as pleasure explodes through my pelvis. My body shudders, and I wrap my arms around her, holding her to me as the aftershocks tumble through my insides.

Her legs wrap around my waist, and with her arms around my neck, we're as close as we could possibly be. I have her right where I want her—so close, so safe.

"Hmm," she lets out a contented little sigh right at my ear. I can hear her smile, and warmth floods my veins. "The most precious thing in your life?"

I hold her and turn us to the side so she's cradled in my arms. She moves forward to press her face against my jaw. "I've thought about you off and on, pretty much nonstop since you left. I thought I knew how it would be if I did see you again. I was wrong. It's so much more."

Her fingers trace the lines up and down my biceps as she listens. We're quiet a moment when I've finished speaking, and I close my eyes as I hold her, listening to her breath, feeling her warmth against me. Her body vibrates, and I hear the faintest words drift by on a whisper. It almost sounds like *I'm so sorry.*

"What?" I frown, leaning back to catch her eyes.

That shadow is in them, that sadness is back. I'm confused, but she quickly changes, returning to light, teasing. "I wonder…" she smiles. "Do you still make the greatest coffee I've ever tasted?"

I prop my head on my hand and look down at her shimmering blue eyes, lifting a strand of silky blonde hair away from her face, wondering what could be left for her to hold back. I opt for patience and answer her question.

"Maybe. I don't have the opportunity to do it as much anymore. And I don't know whose coffee you've been tasting while we've been apart."

Her lips curl in a bigger grin at the unexpected

innuendo. "I've actually had very few coffees since we've been apart. They might as well have been tea compared to yours."

Leaning down, I cover her mouth again in a slow, lingering kiss. When I pull up, I'm rewarded with another little contented sigh and a smile.

"Let me see what I've got," I say, rolling to the side and climbing out of bed. I walk to the kitchen naked, and I'm opening and closing cabinets when I notice Kass slip out of the bed and gingerly make her way around my apartment.

She's surprisingly accurate, considering her vision. She makes several cute little clicking sounds with her mouth and as a result, she manages to avoid the sofa, the lamp, and even my low coffee table. Without a word from me, she makes it to the bathroom and closes the door.

My eyebrows rise, and I shake my head as I start the Ninja. She's amazing, and she's right. She is not disabled. I still don't know what to do with this, but I won't make her feel weak or insult her ability.

It isn't long before she's back with me, cleaned up and wrapped in the thin robe I keep on the back of my bathroom door. It's black with white pinstripes, and it's enormous on her.

"Here." I hand her a mug of coffee.

She scoots onto the stool at her hip, and I watch as she cups the mug in both hands, taking a slow sniff before sipping it... just like she always did. Lowering the cup, she smiles and lets out a satisfied noise.

"That is the best coffee I've ever had."

I shake my head and take a sip from my own cup. It is pretty damn good, but I can't take all the credit. "It's the coffee maker. It's one of those 'perfect cup every time' models."

"No, it's you."

I reach out to cover her hand with mine. "So how do you do it?"

Her brows quirk. "Do what?"

"You made it all the way around my apartment like you grew up here. And what's with the little clicks."

"Mm," she takes another sip of coffee. "It's echolocation."

For a moment, I only study her expression. She's completely serious.

"You mean like what bats use?"

"And dolphins!" The offense in her tone almost makes me laugh.

"I'm sorry. I just… I didn't know humans did that."

"I didn't either." She holds out her mug, and I step to the pot to give her a refill. "Thanks. So I heard about this guy. A blind guy who can ride a bike."

"No way."

"I know, right?" Her blue eyes are wide and animated as if she can actually see me. I almost feel like she can. "I didn't believe it at first, but I took a few of his classes, and I practiced it myself. You'd never think about it because you can see, but when the world is hazy or dark, the different ways it echoes creates an image. It's amazing."

"I still wouldn't ride a bike if I were you." The thought of what happened to her aunt who was not blind makes my stomach churn.

"I won't." She holds the mug up to her lips. "It's not fool proof, though. I couldn't find my dress."

"Are you kidding? That robe has never looked better."

That gets me a grin, and I suddenly feel inspired. "Let's take the bike into the mountains today. We can pack a lunch and picnic on the grounds of one of those old estates."

"Okay..." Her smile grows, and I want to scoop her up in my arms and kiss her. "Then what?"

"Then what," I repeat as my eyes travel over her pretty face, her hair, her shining eyes and full pink lips. All I want is to have her body pressed against my back, her slim arms around my waist. "Then we can just drive, sight see."

Immediately I regret the last thing I said. "I don't mean sight see."

Kass doesn't skip a beat. She leans forward on her elbows. "Do I get to hold you close and rest my cheek on your shoulder while we do it?"

The sleeves of my enormous robe drop down exposing her slim forearms. I reach out and cover one with my hand.

"I hope—" My black phone beeping and vibrating on the counter across from us cuts me off. It's my secure line, which means the only texts or calls I get on it are from the royal family.

"You have two phones." Her tone is quiet.

"Don't move," I say, stepping over to pick it up.

It's Rowan, and my stomach sinks when I see his words.

*En route from the islands. At the palace by noon. Want to meet and discuss our steps going forward ASAP today.*

The device is quiet in my hand, and my arm drops by my side. All I can think of are my plans for today, Kass alone in the city, my god-awful hours working at the palace. I'm trying to formulate a reply when it goes off again.

*Hope you had a relaxing, lucky break.*

I shake my head, knowing the implied meaning there. It's unlike the king to be so informal, but I suppose after the year we've had, I'm more like family now.

*Safe travels. See you this afternoon.* I text back. Then I look up at Kass, who's sitting at the bar tracing her finger around the lip of her near-empty coffee cup.

I walk over to where she sits, and as if she has extra-sensory vision, she asks. "Is something wrong?"

Moving around behind her, I put both hands on her shoulders and lean down to kiss her head. "The royal family will be back at the palace by noon. That was the king. He wants us to meet and discuss our plans going forward."

Her body tenses briefly, and she moves her hands from the cup to her lap. Her chin drops, and when she speaks, her voice is quiet, tentative. "Is he sending you away again?"

"No," I say, turning her to the side so I can wrap my arm around her shoulder. "I'm working directly with the Queen Regent now. It's a new assignment. He probably just wants to go over the scope of my duties."

Kass's eyes close, and a brief wave of something like resignation passes across her face. "You're working directly with the queen."

It's not a question, and I'm concerned by this change in her. She seems to be pulling away somehow. I don't understand.

"It's a job," I try to reassure her. "Let's meet for dinner. I'll pick you up at your place, and we can see where the road takes us."

"Can you do that?" Her chin lifts, and genuine confusion is on her face. "I mean... are you able to set your own hours?"

*Is that what's bothering you, beautiful?* The truth is, my hours are bothering me a little now, too. "I'll talk to Rowan. If Ava's not going out, I should be able to get away for a few hours."

"In that case, I'd love to." She smiles, but it's a little less bright. Slipping off the stool, she walks toward my bed. "Do you happen to see where I left my clothes?"

"Are you asking me for help?"

"No…" her head tilts to the side. "I'll find them eventually, but I've never been here before. It's a bit like being in a country where you don't speak the language."

"Languages never gave you much trouble." I squeeze her hand as I walk over to my large sleeping area.

I reach down and retrieve the filmy tunic from halfway under the bed. Her bikini is beside it. Returning to her, I place them in her hand. "Right where I took them off of you."

She smiles, but I hold her a beat longer. "I'm going to talk to him about us. I'm going to see what I can do about getting more flexibility in my schedule. I meant it when I said I don't want to lose you again. We can make this work."

Her only reply is a wistful smile.

She might be doubtful, but I am determined to do what I can to hold onto this woman as long as she'll let me. Rowan will have to understand.

## Chapter 9: Reminder

*Kass*

With a kiss and a promise to meet this evening, Logan is gone. I'm standing at the door to my apartment building, and the sun is shining strong against my skin. My sunglasses are gone. I must have left them at Logan's. I've lost my mask. I have no way to hide.

For a moment, I lean my back against the building and lift my chin. I want the hot rays to burn against my skin. My body is sore from last night, but I feel so deeply satisfied.

Still, my debts, the job hanging over my head looms in front of me. The royal family is back. Blix expects me to complete my assignment. If I don't...

All at once, the sun feels too hot. I don't want to be outdoors. I'm tired and heavy with guilt, and my eyes sting with unshed tears. As Logan held me close, telling me how much it meant to him that we had found each other, I almost broke down. Burying my face in his chest, I could only allow my lips to say the words twisting my insides. *I'm so sorry...*

I can't summon the energy to find my key, so I press the buzzer in the little rhythm Luc and I use to let each other know we're home. The loud clang of the lock indicates the door is open, and I pull it hard, stepping into the dim hallway.

It's quiet, and the lack of proper lighting makes it impossible for me to make out anything with my limited vision. At least in the bright light, I can make out shapes. In this situation, I have to rely completely on my ears.

Right now, they're telling me the stairwell is empty. It's the same thing they told me when Logan was here, but at least that ended well. I can't help a tremor of fear at who could be lurking, watching me without my knowledge.

I'm about to call for Luc, when I hear his door open. I hear the click of doggy nails on wood, and Henri yips at me from the top of the stairs.

"Is it safe, Henri?" I whisper, facing where I presume he's standing.

He lets out a little bark, and I hear him start to come down to me.

"You're a good dog," I say taking the first two steps and doing my best to calm my rising nerves. "You are no *kyoodle*." He breathes loudly, and I can just see his little smiling terrier face in my mind's eye, tongue hanging out.

"Do you know what a *kyoodle* is?" I'm halfway there, and my stomach is so tight, it's hard to breathe.

*Two more steps.*

*Happy terrier breathing.*

*One more step.*

At last I'm at the top. I made it. No one is here except this little short, coarse-haired dog and me. My body is weak from the adrenaline, and I sit on the top step, exhaling a laugh and feeling silly.

Henri steps into my lap and as usual, he licks me right in the mouth. I do a fake spit, and my hand fumbles to his muzzle, blocking more mouth-licks.

"A *kyoodle* is a noisy, yapping dog," I say. "That is not you. You're a good doggy. Yes you are! You're a good doggy!"

My voice is a sing-song, and his entire body wags. I smile, his joy making me feel better.

Just then Luc's door opens, and he snaps, "*Henri, viens!*"

He's telling him to come, and the little dog happily takes off, back to his owner.

"Bonjour, Luc!" I call, but he doesn't answer. "Au revoir, Henri," I say quietly as their door closes.

Luc is not a bad neighbor, and the two of us have worked out a mutual coexistence in the building. Still, I'm lucky if I get a greeting from him. Only Henri is my cheerful friend when I come home. All eleven pounds of him.

I'm still sitting on the top step when my phone starts buzzing in my hand. Instinctively, all my tension from before races back, and with a shaky hand, I lift it close to my cheek, the screen bright in the dim hall. I'm bracing for Blix, hoping for Logan, and relieved when I see it's only Cam.

*What are you doing tonight?* He texts.

I tap out a reply. *Nothing definite. What's up?*

*I'm playing at the Café Steele. Come see me.*

Pulling my bottom lip between my teeth, I think about my little brother's request. Logan had said he might only have a few hours this evening. Stopping in to check out Cam's gig could be the perfect thing.

*Sure!* I text back. *What time?*

*Really?* I can almost see the playful gleam in his eyes. If he were here, he'd probably be hugging me.

*Really. I'm very curious to see how this hair is working for you.*

*Chick magnet. I told you.*

That makes my eyes roll, and I do laugh this time. *See you tonight.*

Pushing on my knees, I stand and turn toward my door. Luc can't help me with this one, so I dig in my bag for the keys. I haven't been here since I left to spend the day with Logan yesterday. I need to take my birth control. As much as I love feeling of Logan inside me, no barriers, a baby is a slip-up I can*not* make. Not with all the shit I have hanging over me. Maybe not ever…

The thought provokes a twist of sadness in my chest, but I shake it away. I can't pile sadness on top of sadness.

On a lighter note, I probably have a pile of mail to carry in. Funny how the junk mail always seems to find you.

My fingertips graze the metal pieces in my bag, and I drag out the large key ring. Bag on my shoulder, I place my left hand on the door, using my thumb to guide the key into the lock. I don't realize I'm pushing against the wood until it slides open with a *clatch*.

Pulling back, I suck in a sharp breath. Fear shoves out every emotion in my chest. I'm paralyzed, standing in the hall facing my open door.

*I know I locked it before I left yesterday. I remember distinctly…*

I don't move. I'm not sure if I should go forward or run away… or get Luc. I'm so good at getting around and feeling out the world despite the thick haze clouding my vision. Still, it's situations like this where I feel my disadvantage all the way to my bones. Logan's expressed desire to keep me by his side sounds pretty great right now.

"No," I whisper, squaring my shoulders. "This is my place. I won't be afraid."

My keys are in my hand, and I make a fist around them, positioning the key I had planned to use between my middle and index finger. It's sticking straight out like a small knife. If anyone tries to grab me, I'll jam it straight into his unsuspecting neck.

With a trembling step forward, I hear my breathing loud around me in the small room. My teeth are clenched, and I reach to the side with my unfisted hand to turn on both light switches. The small studio fills with light, and I begin to make out the hazy shapes I know. I intentionally left the walls stark white to help with this process.

*Bed in the corner... dresser against the wall... small table with chair...*

*Dark shape appears to be sitting in my chair...*

My heart slams against my chest. I freeze then take a step back. "Who are you? What do you want?" My tone is stern with only the slightest wobble — miraculous, considering how close I am to hyperventilating.

A shiver starts in my back, low in my waist, but I fight it. "Who are you?" I say louder. I inhale deeply, searching for a scent.

His scent greets me at the same time his humorless laugh ripples across the space between us, turning my blood to ice.

Blix is here.

"You never cease to amaze me, Kass." A shuffling noise, and he rises. "Just when I've decided you're useless to me, you turn out to be so... fucking... valuable." He's standing in front of me, and with his final words, he does a little tap on my nose.

The meaning of what he's saying isn't lost on me. I feel the nausea tightening my throat. I know what happens when I'm no longer useful to him.

Still, I jerk my face away. "What are you doing here?" My keys remain clenched in my fist, and I imagine jamming the one into his neck. "What if I hadn't been alone?"

He walks away from me, over to my small window overlooking the street. "Don't worry. I keep close tabs on your boyfriend. I know everywhere he goes... *and who goes with him.*"

His voice hardens on the last phrase, and my pulse ratchets up again. "He's not my boyfriend," I argue, protective fear swirling in my chest.

"Your fuck buddy, then." He returns to where I stand fighting for control.

"You being here is dangerous... for my assignment." I'm grasping at any reason to keep a safe distance between the two of us. "Anyone could see you."

"I want to be sure you're still focused on the job." A click of metal, and I gasp, drawing away from the point of his knife against my cheek, biting in to the soft skin at the base of my eye. "Keeping your eye on the prize."

*Eyes you own.* "The job was to reconnect with Logan." Acid rises in my throat as I say the words. "Find his weakness or distract him with our past."

"He's a sexy beast, I'll give him that." Blix leans closer so his breath is on my face. "Don't. Forget."

It takes everything in me, every ounce of strength I've mustered over the last several years to push back, but I do it. I force calm into my voice, cocky assuredness. "You're worried the tables will turn?" I even manage a smile. "That he'll distract me instead?"

I feel it the moment Blix's composure changes. "Sneaky bitch." His teeth clench, and he's back in my face. He's so close I can make out the furrow of his brow, the cruel line of his mouth. "You're too fucking good at this. I should cut your eyes out so I know you're telling the truth."

Panic flares to life inside me, but I beat it down. "You're smarter than that," I say, impressed by how casual I sound. "Why would you ruin a valuable asset?"

"What makes you so valuable?"

"I look innocent. People trust me." I do a little shrug as if it should be obvious to him. "Who would suspect me of working with you?"

Quiet fills my small apartment. The second hand on my old-timey clock beats loud in my ears. Will he relent or is my time up?

He takes a step back, and I allow myself to breathe. "Fuck up this job, and I will cut out your eyes. I'll use my knife and dig them out slow. I'll scrape the bones so I'm sure you feel it." The casual way he describes it, the undertone of pleasure, summons the ghosts of the men I've heard him torture. Their screams echo in my ears, and my throat closes.

"Have I ever let you down?"

"I can think of a few times."

It's why I'm standing here taking this shit.

"Neither of those times was me letting you down. It was the others."

"Others exploiting your weakness." He's back, and I feel the anger rising in him again. I struggle to hold on a little longer. "It won't happen again," His voice is cold, and he clutches my cheeks between his fingers and thumb. The pressure of his grip is painful on my face. "If it does I'll handle you. And I'll handle your little brother. I'll start with him so you can hear the consequences loud and clear."

He releases my face with a push that sends me staggering back, arms flailing, against the wall. He's to the door in two paces, and when it slams shut, my knees give out. I slide down the slick, white wall until I'm sitting, my face pressed against the backs of my hands.

My shoulders shudder as tears flow freely down my cheeks. My throat closes, and I fight the vomit. I touch my closed eyes. The sounds of torture are in my memory, and I'm racked with the same fear that gripped me every one of those nights. It's so strong.

I went to Blix at a time when I couldn't think about the future. I'd lost everything. I was losing my vision. I wanted to die. I actually hoped one of his jobs would kill me. None did, and I've lived my life as his slave ever since.

Now the cost of my hopelessness is Cam. He's in danger, Logan is in danger...

My hand falls open on the wood floor at my side and the ring of keys tumbles onto the floor with a *clink*. In that moment, an idea cuts through my desperate mind. A solution. A way out of this nightmare.

The only question is when. The answer...

Tonight.

## Chapter 10: Debts

*Logan*

We're in the war room, that damn letter is in the middle of the table, and the four of us—Rowan, Sir Reginald Winchester (his great uncle), Freddie (his second in command after me), and me. We're the same team that brought Zelda home last year, minus only one member, Rowan's younger brother Cal.

"I'm glad to see we all appear well-rested and ready to meet this new challenge," Reggie says in his usual, superior tone.

"You look better, Logan," the king says, giving me a nod. "I hope this means you were able to regroup while we were away."

Discussing my private life is something I don't do. "It took me a day or two to relax, then I... found something I thought I'd lost."

Rowan's brow rises, and he smiles. "Good work. Now to get our minds back on the current situation."

"What's the latest news," I take my seat and frown at the offending missive.

"My spies have reason to believe Blix Ratcliffe returned to Monagasco last week," Reggie starts. His words make my scalp tighten. "We have verified proof he left the Caribbean, and a few strategically placed moles followed him from the market yesterday."

"But we've only just returned." The surprise in Rowan's voice echoes my response.

"How did he get into the city?"

"He's modified his appearance somewhat," Freddie answers, taking two glossy photos from the manila folder beside his laptop. "Our trackers captured these images, which we blew up. Charting the structure of his bones, the color of his eyes, we've established a positive ID."

I lift them and study his face. It's true. The dead blue eyes are the same. "His hair is dark," I note.

"It helps him blend in with the locals," Freddie says, pointing to the next one. "He's added a prosthetic to his chin."

"I actually think this a good sign," Reggie interjects, drawing our attention.

"In what way?" the king demands.

"If he'd known you were in Tortola, he wouldn't be here." The grand duke leans back in his chair, stretching his legs. "It would've been far easier to make a move on the family there, where protection is less… organized."

He nods toward Freddie's workstation just as our partner slides another printout across the space. "They followed him to this condo building, but it's unclear if he's staying there or if he was making contact with one of his associates."

"He has associates in the city as well?" My eyes flick to Freddie's, and all I can think is who might have been following me these last few days. I hadn't even considered covering my tracks.

"It's fair to assume someone like him never acts, or travels alone," Freddie says.

Reggie cuts in, sounding bored. "Of course he has associates. What do you have so far?"

Freddie pulls up faces on his laptop. "I've circulated photographs of all the men involved in the kidnapping of Zelda who are still at large."

Blix's head, with his now-dark hair and cold blue eyes is first on the screen. Next, is the giant gorilla-man with hands the size of dinner plates.

"He'll be difficult to hide," I note.

"I'm not sure he's trying to," Freddie muses, pulling up another photo of a man I don't recognize. "This is one of the two new associates our trackers were able to photograph."

Rowan steps forward. "New ones?"

The new man is lean with medium brown hair. He's average height and could easily blend into a crowd. His only distinguishing characteristic is the ink rising out of his collar along his neck. Still, his hands are fisted, and from his side-glance and the set of his jaw, I can see he's a cruel motherfucker.

"We believe his name is Taz," Freddie continues. "He appeared on our radar with the body in Miami. Police found his fingerprints at the victim's house and at the warehouse where they recovered it."

"He doesn't care about leaving behind evidence," Rowan says, his eyes never leaving the man's face. "Not a good sign."

"We also have reason to believe he's been with Blix since the beginning, but we're still piecing together his story."

"You said there were two new associates," Rowan presses.

Freddie's thin lips disappear with his frown. "We don't have a positive ID on the second," he says. "It's possible he's deep undercover."

That's not good enough for me. "Why are you sure there's another?"

"Four people are on the manifest coming from Miami. All were on the same flight. All arrived at the same time. It's not a coincidence." He glances up, dark eyes determined. "At least we're not treating it like a coincidence."

Rowan pats his shoulder. "Good work." My eyes remain on the three faces on that laptop as Rowan continues to the door. "I'm confident none of those men will get anywhere near Ava."

"No one will," I confirm.

Our steely eyes meet, and he's as serious as I am. "I know I can trust you."

\* \* \*

It's dark when I leave the palace on my motorcycle. Rowan was reluctant but willing to let me slip out for a few hours—I didn't have to tell him much, just that I had made plans with someone before I knew they were home. Freddie was more than willing to take my place as Ava's shadow. He's the only one the king and I trust for the job. He'll keep her safe, but won't make her feel afraid.

Now, on my bike winding through the glittering streets, my insides are a twisted knot of concern and dread. I had no idea the threat had grown so high. What the fuck am I going to do with Kass? How am I going to keep tabs on her and protect Ava? The question has battered my mind since this morning, but now it presses so hard, my forehead aches.

I'd have to discuss it with her tonight. Now that we're involved, she's not safe. My being in a critical position makes Kass a liability Blix would be all too happy to exploit. I can just see that fucker rubbing his hands together at the prospect.

My fists tighten on the grips of my bike at the thought. I'll break every bone in his body…

Cool air pushes against my face, and I do my best to calm my raging insides. I don't want to be angry when I pick up my girl. Instead, I look up at the twinkle lights draping the colorful awnings of the cafés and restaurants along the streets.

Music is in the air, and tourists mix with locals at the small tables. Their lives are carefree. They're oblivious to the dangers someone like me lives with. They laugh and share wine, coffee, dinner, or pastries. They kiss and make memories in this beautiful city by the sea.

It's October, and the number of tourists has tapered off, although it hasn't disappeared. The days will grow a bit cooler, and the rain will increase. I slow to a coast when I reach Kass's warehouse apartment, and once stopped, I smell the weight of the water in the clouds obscuring the moon. It's a dark night outside of the cheerful lights of the busy streets.

Concern tightens my brow, and I wonder if it would be possible to take Kass to the palace for the night. The loud *clatch* of a metal door draws my attention, and I look up to see her emerge from her building.

In spite of everything, my insides release when I see her. Desire, longing... something like love replaces all the rage I've been wrestling with on my drive.

She's dressed in tight jeans that show off her slender figure, a long-sleeved, filmy black shirt with a low V-neck. A gold necklace peeks out of the opening, and those glasses are back. Her lips are deep red, and she crosses the narrow sidewalk to where I'm parked as if she's drawn to me.

"You're too good at this," I say, shaking my head. "I would never have figured it out."

"The glasses help," she says, giving me a little smile. "They help the dark shapes have a little more definition."

"But it's a dark night," I say, sliding my hands around her waist and pulling her to me.

With her tall boots and my position still sitting on the bike, she's closer to my height. She places her hands on my chest and runs the tip of her finger along my chin.

"And you're sitting right here under this bright streetlight." She smiles, but her beautiful blue eyes that don't quite meet mine tell me something is troubling her.

Her eyes. They're the only way I understood what was happening when she told me she'd lost her sight. They focus somewhere along the tops of my cheeks, never quite connecting with my gaze. While it hurts losing the connection we used to share when our eyes locked and we could read each others' souls, all that fades away when I hold her, kiss her, see her entire body light up with her laughter... or bloom with ecstasy when I make her come.

I still see her soul.

I lean forward to kiss the side of her jaw, speaking right in her ear. "What's wrong?" I'm rewarded with a little melt, but she shakes her head.

"It's nothing. Just... dealing with my business."

I pull back to study her face, and she isn't smiling. "You never told me where you went. Where did you live when you were in the States?"

She shrugs. "I was along the coast. You have to be when you're working in shipping."

"So New York?" She certainly looks like something you'd see walking Fifth Avenue. "California?"

"I wish it was somewhere that glamorous," she smiles. Still, it doesn't reach her eyes. "I was stuck in south Florida. Stripped down Ft. Lauderdale to be exact."

A flash goes off in my chest, and for a moment I pause, holding her. "Did you fly out of Miami?" I ask, thinking about Freddie's presumption. The second associate.

She nods. "It's the closest international airport."

"Alone?" I press. I have to be sure before I go back and tell them we're good. Blix is only traveling with one new associate.

Her head tilts to the side. "These are odd questions." Her eyes blink as they drift around my face. "Of course I traveled alone."

I'm simultaneously relieved and alarmed by her proximity to that bastard, even if she had no idea. I don't want her within inches of him. My decision is final. I'll discuss her with Rowan and Freddie tomorrow. I'll ID her as the fourth Miami passenger, and we'll figure out a plan to keep her safe.

"Are we going to the café?" she asks, and I can tell she's surveying my body language as much as I am hers.

"Yes," I turn in the seat as she holds my arm, climbing on behind me. "I think we both need a drink."

"Not too much for me," she says, leaning forward so her lips graze the skin of my neck right at

the back of my collar. The sensation registers straight to my dick.

"We might have to make a little pit stop along the way," I turn to kiss those lips. "I've missed you."

Her smile grows, but so does the distance in her eyes. "Even after last night?"

"Especially after last night."

She gives me a nudge. "Let's check in with Cam first and maybe we can leave early."

I like the sound of that, although the smell of rain in the air is growing stronger. I'm concerned I might have to cab her back before our date is over. As much as I'm committed to keeping my word to Rowan, to keeping Ava safe, I'm frustrated at not being able to stay with Kass tonight. Now that I have her in my arms, I never want her leaving them.

With a roar of the engine, we shoot off into the night, headed to the little café down by the waterfront. It takes a matter of minutes to arrive at our destination. Everywhere in town is close enough to walk, but I love the feel of Kass behind me on the bike, her body pressed close to mine and her arms tight around my waist.

They're just finishing a song when we walk in. Our names are on the list at the door, so we don't have to pay the cover charge. Still, I give the doorman twenty Euros. Kass is focused on the front where her brother sits on a stool between two other guys all playing guitars and harmonizing.

It's been years since I've seen Cameron, but I recognize the kid I met six years ago. He's grown into a good-looking guy. He shares a family resemblance to Kass. They both have those vivid blue eyes only his complexion is darker. He's got the rock-star hair hanging to his shoulders, and all the swagger of a front-man.

Kass made it sound like he was just getting started in the music business, but an appreciative band of females swaying on the dance floor directly in front of him makes me think he's been at it longer than his sister knows. With every smile, his groupies swoon, and I can't help wondering how much of what's happening Kass is able to perceive.

She's standing at the edge of the tables, where a wooden railing parts over a short staircase leading down to the open floor. I step up behind her and place my hand on her waist. She does a little jump, then relaxes into me. I don't like how tense she is tonight.

"I told him this was a bad idea," she says, turning her face to speak close to my ear. "I'll have to apologize. He's very good. It sounds like he has a fan club."

She nods toward the front, and I smile. "He's got a small mob of females hanging on his every word."

"That's good." Her tone is resignation, and I try to understand. Is she feeling some form of empty nest syndrome? Is she sad her little brother is not so little anymore? It seems unlikely.

For a moment we listen to his rich baritone singing a popular song I recognize. His voice is strong and full, and he's not a bad guitarist. When he gets to the part about having his heart broken, a pair of thong panties flies on the stage at his feet, and I can't help a chuckle.

"What happened?" Kass turns to me, confused. "Why are you laughing?"

"Your little brother is causing panties to fly."

"What?" She's still confused, and I decide to spare her the details in case she is feeling nostalgic. "Would you like a drink?"

She considers my question far longer than it deserves. "Maybe just a soft drink for now."

"I'll be right back."

In the time it takes to order a scotch for me and a soda for Kass, her brother is on a break and standing with her in the same spot at the edge of the dance floor. She tells him something that provokes an embarrassed smile, and she reaches out to tug the side of his hair. I glance up to see his groupies shooting daggers at her with their eyes. I have no problem shutting down their jealousy.

Walking up to the pair, I touch Kass's arm, and Cameron looks up at me with a carefree smile. It reminds me of his sister's back in our early days, and I want to see her smile like that again.

"Logan?" he says, holding out a hand. "Damn, you've grown!"

I laugh and pass the soft drink to Kass before shaking his hand. "I was about to say the same to you." My voice is noticeably deeper, more serious than his youthful one.

"But I grew up," he says loudly. "You're a fucking mountain!"

"Cameron," Kass's voice is quiet but scolding.

"Sorry, sis." He throws an arm around her shoulder and drags her head to this lips for a quick kiss. "My language is fucking awful since you left. It's why you need to move back here. Keep me straight."

She gives his side a gentle punch, and for a moment, her tension slips. I see the genuine love she feels for him warm her face. It slips away just as fast.

"I wish I could, but you know how my job is."

Her words hit me like a freight train. I hadn't considered she might be leaving. After last night I'd stopped thinking of her as someone who could disappear from my life as quickly as she'd reappeared in it.

Now I'm desperate to get out of here. We need to talk. I need to know what her timeline is, how much longer we have. How much time I have to change her mind.

Cam is still talking. "Just don't do like you did last time. Disappear without a word. I was fucking frantic until you finally called and told me where you were."

"I'm sorry," she says, reaching out to touch his arm. "It seemed better that way. I didn't mean to make you worry."

I can't take my eyes off her. Why didn't I follow up when she mentioned her business outside her apartment? I'd been too enraptured by the mere sight of her. Now the emotions that keep bubbling up in her eyes are filtering through my chest. *She'd better not fucking disappear...*

"So you liked the set?" Cameron asks us, but I'm finding it difficult to concentrate on his words.

"You're amazing," she tells him, "And Logan says you have a little fan club. Did someone throw panties at you?"

"I thought you couldn't see!" he cries, embarrassed again.

"Logan told me," she answers, and his eyes fly to me

"Dude!" he cries. I shrug, trying my damndest not to bring down his happy mood. "They just like the music is all," he says as if we don't know better.

Kass leans in close and squeezes his arm. "Use protection. You can't afford to be a father right now."

"Jesus!" he hisses, and it reminds me how young he is. The other two guys are on the stage, and one of them calls to Cameron. "Saved by the bell," he mutters, leaning down to kiss his sister's cheek. "Thanks for coming out."

He turns to me and holds out his hand for another shake.

"Hey, thanks for stopping by, and Logan? Do me a favor…"

"What's that?" I ask, holding his hand a beat longer.

Our hands release, and he scrubs it through his hair. "Convince her to move home."

"I'm on it," I say with the same level of conviction I used when I promised Rowan I'd protect his wife.

He's back onstage and the trio starts in with a more lively song. They have a drum machine, and the girls start dancing, waving their arms and letting their skirts flip up for his benefit. It's a great gig for a good looking kid his age.

Kass turns to me and pulls my arm. She has my complete attention as I lean down. "Can we go now?" The heaviness is back, and I'm ready to get to the bottom of it.

"Of course." I take her glass and mine and place them on the edge of the bar.

She's holding my arm, her body close at my side, as we make our way through the café that's grown more crowded since we arrived. I like having her near me this way. It's where I want to keep her always.

Outside she waits as I ready my bike. It hasn't started to rain, but a fine mist is in the air. It coats her cheeks, making them glow in the lamplight.

"Rain," she sighs, lifting her face to the sky.

I can't help myself. I straddle the bike and pull her to me. "We need to talk," I say, sliding my hand over her damp skin and cupping the side of her face before giving her a lingering kiss.

Her hand moves to my neck and she holds me, opening her mouth to deepen our kiss. My tongue finds hers and the smoky scotch I drank mixes with the faint sweetness of her. She's delicious and sexy, and I want her with me tonight. I don't want her in any position where she might slip away like Cameron said.

"Ride in front of me." My voice is thick, and I help her straddle the bike snug against my chest.

I take a slow speed, extending the time we're together, knowing I'll have to head back to the palace soon after we reach her apartment. The noise prevents us from talking, but my face is at her temple. I can't stop kissing her as we ride. I'm intoxicated and desperate for her. I breathe in the clean scent of her perfume mixed with the metallic flavor of rain wrapping around us. I kiss her head, and she tightens her grip on my arms.

When we arrive at her apartment our hair is wet along with our clothes. I don't pull up at her door. Instead I guide my bike into the shadows, down the alley where we're hidden from sight.

She sits straighter, arching her back against my chest and turning her head so our mouths can meet. She cups my face, and I hold her stomach, moving my hands under her wet shirt, higher to the lace of her bra.

Her skin is hot, her nipples peaked and straining beneath the fabric. I pull it down, squeezing her breast before pinching the beaded tip. She moans into my mouth as our tongues entwine.

I've pushed her bra completely up, kneading and teasing her breasts. She sighs and moves against me like a wave, her hips rock and her ass scrubs against the aching bulge in my jeans. I want to fuck her hard.

Our mouths part, and I exhale a groan. "Jesus, Sass." I release her breasts to quickly unfasten her jeans. My arm is a band around her waist, and I lift her against me so I can slide my hand down her bare pussy and sink my fingers into her throbbing core.

"Logan!" she cries, rocking her hips against my hand. "Oh… yes…"

I can't take it. I lift her off the bike and move us so her back is against the alley wall. She's feverish as me, her hands moving over my shoulders and biceps as I frantically unfasten and lower my jeans.

A slight lift and a drop, and I sink deep into her clenching insides. We both groan, and I can't stop. I'm driving faster, claiming her hard and furious. I hold her hands against the wall above her head, palm to palm, and our fingers twine. Her legs are tight around my waist, and she's meeting every thrust I make, gasping and moaning.

"Logan," she cries, and I feel the tremors of her orgasm start. It only makes me move faster.

"Come for me." I lean into her, my mouth at her neck. "Come…"

I give her a kiss, a gentle bite, and she shudders. My hands go down, and I hold her hips, working her clit against my waist. It only takes moments before she shatters, jerking and arching her back to pull me deeper.

Her nails cut into the skin on my arm, and I hold her securely as she rides out the waves of her orgasm. My eyes close, and I don't hold back. I release with a shout, riding the intense pleasure as her inner muscles massage and milk me.

She's coming down, and I hold her so close. I vaguely feel her fingers on my neck, her soft lips kissing my cheeks, my beard. I can only hold her tight against my chest, my head resting on hers.

We stay that way several long moments, pressed against the damp brick, sharing our breath. I feel a drop of rain against my cheek, and I know the clock is ticking on my ability to stay much longer. I have to say this before I lose my chance.

"I don't want you to leave." It's a low rumble right at her ear.

She starts to move, and I relax my hold, allowing her to stand on wobbly legs. She reaches down to straighten her clothes. I quickly do the same.

"I don't want to leave." Her voice is resigned. "But I have commitments. Old debts I have to repay."

"I can pay your debts."

Her head shakes and her eyes don't rise from my chest. "You can't. I have to do what I can to make things right."

I don't understand what she means, but my phone buzzes. I can't stay any longer. "Let me walk you to your apartment."

We leave the bike at the corner, and I go with her to the metal door. Once we're inside, we climb the narrow flight of stairs. Again, I'm frustrated by the lack of security and poor lighting, although I suppose the amount of light makes no difference to her.

We reach her door, and she hesitates. For a moment she wavers, but then her jaw sets and she pushes the key in the lock. I glance around the tiny apartment. Against one wall, her queen-sized bed is neatly made, and against the other is a small table with two chairs.

"Very clean," I say, and she seems to relax.

"I don't need much room."

"I want you to lock these bolts after I leave and don't go out again."

Her slim brows pull together, and she purses her lips. "You're worried I'll go out again?"

"Just... Don't." I say, and she shrugs. I'm not finished. I gather her in my arms. "And don't leave

Monagasco without telling me." Her chin drops, but out of habit, I duck my head to catch her eyes. "Promise me, Sass. I need to know you'll be here tomorrow."

She blinks rapidly, not returning my gaze. The sadness is back. My phone buzzes in my pocket, and I know it's either Rowan or Freddie. I've got to return to the palace. "Please," I urge, tightening my hold around her body. "Say you'll talk to me before you do anything."

She slides her hands up to touch my cheeks, and when she speaks, her voice is soft. "Promise me you'll always remember our night on the beach... or me in your bed that first morning. Or tonight in the alley... Remember me loving you."

My chest aches and my phone buzzes again. "Say you'll be here tomorrow."

She rises on her tiptoes to kiss me. I kiss her back, pushing her lips apart and claiming her mouth. My hands move into her hair, and I hold her to me, attempting to transfer all the strength of my feelings into her heart.

Another buzz, and I have to go. "Lock the door," I say, firmer this time. "Be here in the morning when I come back."

She nods touching my hand, sliding her fingers through mine.

It's not complete relief, but I'll take what I can get for now. I kiss her hand and step through the door, waiting on the other side as I hear the bolt click into place, the chain slide across its metal track.

Tomorrow I'll have more time. I'll make her tell me everything, and we'll see what debts can't be repaid.

## Chapter 11: Failure

*Kass*

I rest my head against the door listening to the sound of Logan's footsteps growing quieter as he descends the stairs.

*Oh, God...* Tears fill my eyes. It's very possible I'll never see him again. Still, I have to follow through. I have to do what I can to stop the chain of events my coming here set in motion.

My body is sore in the most wonderful way as I peel off my clothes to shower. At the same time, my heart is broken. "Oh, Logan," I whisper, wishing with every ounce of strength I possess I could change my life, go back in time and make different choices.

But I can't.

I have to focus on making this right.

Going to my dresser, I feel inside for the soft twill of my black pants. My system for keeping types of clothes in separate drawers helps me find what I need for tonight—long black pants; next drawer down, long black sweater; two drawers up, heavy canvass belt. I step into my black boots and pull a stocking cap over my pale hair. A small dagger is in its custom leather holster in the top drawer.

Lifting it, I slide the steel weapon from its sheath. It's a double-edged, pointed knife that fits in the palm of my hand exactly the way I was holding my keys this afternoon.

Blix calls it a push dagger, and ironically, he gave it to me when I first started working with him five years ago. He had thought I was too petite. He said I was too beautiful, and he worried one of the guys might try to rape me.

I was able to see the strange weapon when he gave it to me. I remember the night he showed me how to use it. My eyesight had only just begun to fail, and it was easy to hide from him. Now my fingers touch the braided leather handle, and I see it in my memory. From tip to tip it's only two inches long, and carved into the blade are the words "Best Pal."

"Keep it in your belt when you go out with them," he'd said, showing me how to clip the sheath inside my waistband so only the flat handle extended above my pants. "If one of them tries anything, wait until he's on you. Then jam it straight into his neck, front or back, and he'll go down."

At the time, the idea had nauseated me. Now I savor the thought of using this little tool. Without hesitation, I clip the holster inside the front of my pants and start for the door. I order an Uber car, so I don't have to bother with carrying money, and I give the address of a drugstore near the edge of the city.

Blix is hiding out at an abandoned villa. I can't see it, but from what I understand the exterior looks like a dilapidated old ruin with ivy and vines covering the turrets, and arched window frames extending over black holes.

The driver lets me out and I wait until I hear he's gone. I had listened closely on the plane as Blix gave Taz and Dev directions on how to find him. He didn't care that I was listening. He still thinks I can't get around on my own now that I'm blind. He's so stupid. I know to walk three blocks east and then five blocks south and I'll be there.

While I changed at my apartment, I heard the downpour release outside, and I hoped Logan made it home before it started. *Logan...* The memory of his strong arms, his embrace, his kiss, filters such sadness through my chest.

I love him.

I have to let him go.

The rain has subsided, but the air is still heavy and smells of the sea. The streets are quiet, but I use my clicks to avoid walking into light poles or benches. Echolocation opened the world to me, especially since a cane would be a death sentence. Talking signs are another useful invention, helping me in the crosswalks without anyone's notice. I count each block until I reach my destination. The reduced noise of traffic tells me I'm far from the busy center of town. I'm in a place were only homeless people or criminals would go, and I carefully proceed forward, off the pavement and onto what feels like vegetation growing over sand.

I continue walking, and I have to trust it's dark enough for me to stretch out my hand. More clicks, and I start to get the echo. A tall structure is ahead of me, and it sounds like stone.

"This must be the place," I whisper to myself.

Sure enough, in five more paces, my fingers encounter a wall covered in ivy. I place both hands on it and follow the perimeter, careful of where I place my feet as I search for the door. It isn't long before I come to an opening.

*Click click*, I hear the hollow of a large, empty space. It's the way inside, and I slide my foot forward to be sure there isn't a fallen rock or hole to greet me as I enter. Solid floor is under my feet, and as I step inside, I smell moldering wood. A drop of water lands on my cheek, and I pull back, flicking it away in disgust.

"No telling where that's been," I mutter, looking up. I can't see it, but I'm sure the roof is full of holes, or missing.

My boots crunch on sand, and in another step I kick what sounds like a board across the smooth floor. It's helpful, because it allows me to hear how open and empty the room is.

"Now what?" I wonder, moving my head as if I'm looking around. "Blix!" I shout as loud as I can. "Blix are you here? It's me Kass!"

For a moment, I wait. In retrospect I took a big chance coming here. Who's to say he's hanging around waiting for someone to find him? Still, it's after eleven. Where else would he be?

"Blix!" I shout again. "I need to talk to you. It's me Kass!"

The space seems quieter as the echo of my voice disappears. I'm breathing fast, inhaling the pungent scent of mildew, the earthy smell of plants growing over ancient rocks, the fresh scent of rain.

The complete and utter insanity of what I'm doing here tries to invade my mind. Fear rises in my stomach and my resolve slips. I fight my survival instinct pushing me to run away, to get as far as possible from Blix and his horrors. I fight my nerves telling me I can't see, I'm not strong enough.

I'm here for Cameron, and in a way, I'm here for Logan. I can't do what Blix wants me to do, and after his surprise appearance in my apartment today, I know the only way out is to do what I'm doing right now. I will be strong. I will get close enough, and I will finish this job my way. I'll stop him… even if it means—

"What are you doing here, Kass?" Blix's voice echoes in the darkness.

I don't jump. I don't scream in terror. I center my thoughts, control my breathing.

"I need to talk to you." My voice is clear as a bell in the darkness.

"Is that so?" He's moving closer, but I don't hear footsteps. It's unnerving to have him approach without warning. It reminds me of old stories about spirits or ghosts haunting abandoned castles. He's a demon. "It must be very important for you to come here. Why are you dressed all in black?"

"So no one would see me come in, of course." Cocky is my best attempt at confidence. "I've always followed protocol."

"Protocol says you should call before showing up unexpectedly." He touches the side of my cheek. "Otherwise, you might find yourself shot."

"Shot?" Again, I'm doing my best at confidence. "That isn't your preferred method of dealing with intruders. It's over too quickly."

He actually chuckles. "You know me so well."

My insides are tight. I'm in physical pain from the fear gripping my muscles, but I hold my shoulders straight, my face level. My fingers tingle, and in my mind's eye, I see my hand moving fast to my waist, curling around the short handle of the knife. One swift uppercut, and the blade will sink deep into his neck, ending his life. I focus all my energy on making it happen. I just have to get close enough so I don't miss.

"Why are you here? What couldn't wait until tomorrow?"

With a measured inhale, I allow a trickle of the nervous energy coursing through my body into my voice.

"I-I screwed up. I didn't know what to do, so I came here. I knew you'd tell me what to do."

As anticipated, his voice flat lines. "What do you mean, you screwed up?" He's back at my side, and I know he's on the brink of clicking into torture mode.

"I got too greedy. I wanted Logan to spend the night with me, and I guess... I guess I pushed him too far. He said we shouldn't see each other anymore."

I'm blinking fast, wringing my hands together, waiting to see if he'll take the bait. He's quiet a moment. I can't see his eyes, but I know he's sizing me up, gauging my body language. My one advantage is Blix truly thinks my mental strength disappeared along with my sight.

He takes a step back. Another breath passes then he chuffs out a disgusted laugh. "More like he realized what a pile of shit he stepped in getting involved with a blind girl." The words sting, but I go with them.

"Maybe that's it." I shake my head. "All I know is he changed. He doesn't want me, and I need you to help me fix it."

"What the fuck do you expect me to do?"

"Well..." My heart is lodged in my throat, but I push through the pain. "I thought maybe... maybe you could coach me. Tell me what to do to get him back."

"I don't know what you're thinking—"

"You're a man..." I lower my voice and step to where I feel his body heat radiating. Reaching out, I slide my hand up the front of his shirt. He flinches, but doesn't pull away. I keep going. "You're powerful like he is." Another step closer, and my face is at his shoulder.

"I'm more powerful than fucking Logan Hunt." Blix's voice has grown thick, and I'm betting everything on that one time he told me I was beautiful.

"Then it should be easy for you," I whisper, allowing my lips to touch the side of his jaw light as a feather. "Teach me."

Everything stills. The air is razor sharp, and I'm holding my breath. The rhythmic tapping of rain begins on the roof above, and my hand starts to move. I slide my palm down the front of his shirt to his belt, over the buckle to the distinct bulge I feel in his jeans. *God, give me the strength to go through with this.*

I slide my hand up and down the bulge once... twice... and I hear his breathing change. Closing my eyes, I move my hand from his dick to my waistband, ready to close my fingers over the handle of the dagger.

I'm there, I'm clutching the handle, I see it happening...

Then the world tilts.

Blix pushes me back and spins me around, jerking my back against his chest and holding me by the throat. I try to scream, but he's crushing my larynx, forcing my head against his shoulder in the process.

"Did you think I wouldn't have you watched?" His other hand rips my shirt up and jerks the punch dagger from its holster. "You fucked Logan Hunt like a cheap whore... And now you're trying to fuck with me."

He pushes the razor-sharp tip against my neck, right at the base of my jaw.

"No!" I scream, but I can't move. He's got me by the throat with the point of my blade cutting into my skin.

"Tonight I watched you myself," he hisses in my ear, little drops of spittle landing on my cheek. "I watched him finger-fuck you on that motorcycle. I watched him slam you against the wall like the lying little slut you are. He followed you indoors where I'm sure you sucked him off."

My entire body is shaking, and tears are coating my face. "You're wrong," I gasp, flailing for anything to get the upper hand again. "He followed me inside, and he told me it was over!"

His grip on my throat grows tighter and he uses it to jerk my head back against his shoulder, punctuating each word. "Stop. Fucking. *Lying*!"

A cough rips through me. My eyes heat and my nose starts to run. "I'm not lying," I gasp. *Oh, God, I've got to kill him…*

"You're not lying?" He mocks me. "Then what the fuck were you planning to do with the knife?" He jams the tip of the blade further into my skin.

"*Ow!*" I cry as it pierces my skin. Hot blood runs down my neck, and a violent shudder moves through my torso. "You told me to carry it for self defense!"

"Bull. Shit." With a violent push he throws me to the ground.

My hands flail as I grasp thin air, trying to protect my head from smashing into the concrete. The rest of me hits the floor, and a sharp rock or piece of wood, I can't tell which, jams painfully into my hip.

"Oh, god," I cry, curling into a ball on the filthy marble.

Blix crosses the space to where I'm lying. I don't have time to block him before pain explodes through my torso. He kicks me so hard an *Oof!* flies from my body. I hear the sound of another kick coming just in time to roll, absorbing the force of the blow.

He takes a step back, and I clutch tighter, waiting for what's to come, wondering how long I'll hold up before he kills me. Blix seems to be wondering this as well.

"What shall I do with you, little bat?" His tone is morphing, turning cruel.

I've heard it so many times, I can still see how his eyes are changing. All humanity is leaving his body, and what's coming next will make me wish I was never born.

A hissing noise comes from the area around his waist, and my arms are jerked back, causing me to yelp. Both my hands are in his vice grip and cold rope is looped and tightened around my wrists... tighter, cutting painfully into my skin.

"You're something of a special case." He finishes and shoves me back against the hard floor. I bend my knees and draw them up against my stomach, ducking my head. "What would a blind girl find most terrifying? You're clearly not afraid of the dark... or of losing your sight."

Shudders ripple through my torso, and I couldn't speak even if I had something to say.

"Ears..." Blix continues. "Yes... Silence. Darkness. Trapped in the prison of your own body until you die."

He leans down and touches my earlobe with his blade.

"No!" I jerk, drawing my shoulder up to protect my hearing.

"Burning oil." He bends down to speak right at my shoulder. "I'll slowly fill each one and let it scald away whatever's left inside your head."

Tears flood my eyes, and as much as I don't want to picture what he's saying, I can't escape it. The burning, the silence, the pain. Darkness and no sound... Vomit rises in my throat. Fear beats like a drum loud in my chest. I'm shuddering and crying shaking my head. *No... no... NO!*

My hold on reality slips. My breathing is frantic,

ragged pants in and out as another second passes... then another. I'm flailing down a spiral of panic and fear and loss and grief... pulling myself together with the last shred of hope, I inhale slowly, then let out a loud scream. *"NO!"*

Silence follows the brief echo of my voice.

The space is empty.

Far above is the shimmer of rain on the roof. I strain against the rope holding my wrists together, but it's a waste of time. More silent seconds pass, and I realize... *Blix is gone. I'm alone.*

I unclench my eyes and try to see in the darkness. It's futile, but I'm sure of this one fact. He left me here. *But why?*

A drop of water hits my cheek. I'm trembling as I struggle to a sitting position, hands still tied behind my back. I inhale a shuddering breath, my face slick with tears, and I try to figure out what happened. I don't have to wait long.

*CRASH!* The noise from behind makes me scream. I try to turn, when another *CRASH!* blasts at my left. Glass shatters across the floor. I yelp and struggle away from the noise. I don't know what's happening. I don't understand the shouts of male voices surrounding me in this huge, empty space.

High beams of flashlights streak the darkness, swirling up and over, all around until they land on me.

"I've found one!" A male voice shouts, rapidly closing the distance between us. "Female, blonde, looks early twenties..." He jerks the hat off my head.

My insides collapse at the voice that joins him. "Stand down, soldier. I've got her."

"I'm leaving her with Hunt." The man says, releasing me as he narrates his progress. "I'm moving to the back of the structure."

The sound of heavy boots recedes behind us. I'm still on the dirty floor. My hat is gone, my knife is gone. I'm bound. Blood is on my neck, and I'm in Blix's secret hideout.

Another crash further away, and more soldiers invade the abandoned villa. They're moving up and down, searching every inch, but I know they won't find him. Something or someone tipped him off, and he's long gone, leaving me to face the consequences of being found here.

## Chapter 12: The Whole Truth

*Logan*

My stomach is tight. A tornado of rage and confusion batters my insides, and I'm doing extremely well not to shove my fist through the wall.

I left Kass at her apartment with a promise not to leave. Now I'm standing here in this crumbling ruin searching for the worst monster I've encountered in my career as a guard... and I find her sitting in his lair.

*Did he kidnap her? Did he somehow know we were coming, and he left her here to send me a message?*

I'd like to believe that, but the timeline makes it impossible. She came here on her own. It's the only explanation. The burning question is why.

No one knows where this place is. I had returned to the palace to relieve Freddie, and he was with me when Reggie's email came through. One of his spies had made contact with Taz. They were gambling, drinking, and swapping stories. As with the island where they took Zee, the thug let it slip that "not all abandoned buildings are truly abandoned."

It set us off on a desperate hunt, a race against time. It wouldn't be long before Taz sobered up enough to realize he'd fucked up. Once that happened, it would be seconds before Blix would know we were coming for him. He'd slip through our fingers again, and he'd be more on guard then ever.

Rowan stayed with Ava, and we called in soldiers to cover him at the palace, then Freddie and I set out with a specialized team trained in search and recovery. We started at an abandoned warehouse near the shipyard. Freddie reasoned they had used cargo ships before, so maybe they would try it again. It was a dead end.

The Villa Auvergne had been our second stop, and here is Kass; Blix long gone.

A shudder jerks her small body, but she doesn't make a sound. She sits completely still, waiting, her blue eyes staring at the floor in front of her. Her cheeks are slick with tears, and I fight everything in me wanting to comfort her.

Rain drums harder against the roof, high over our heads. A lone drop of water hits the back of my hand. Another hits her cheek, but she doesn't brush it away. She sits as if she's in shock.

Blood is on her neck, and her hands are bound with that same fucking yellow nylon rope. Blix favors tools you'd find in a tackle box, and the horrific remains of his last victim trickle through my mind. Nylon twine lashed over and over around the victim's neck. The tips of every finger clipped off with skinning sheers…

Freddie's voice breaks my macabre reflection. "It's completely deserted. He knew we were coming and ran."

My eyes remain on the small woman sitting on the floor shivering.

"He must have left her behind," Freddie says going to Kass. He pats down her arms before moving to her waist. "What's this?"

In one swift move, he whips a holster from her waistband. She flinches back as if he might strike her, but Freddie doesn't even notice. He's back with me shining his light on the triangle of leather.

"Cold steel," he muses. "It's the holster for a punch dagger."

We both look back at her shivering, eyes fixed on some point on the floor.

Freddie returns to her, speaking loudly. "What are you doing here?"

Her eyes slide shut and she shakes her head slowly. A lone tear slides down her damp cheek, and I steel myself. I won't let it tear me apart.

"Answer me!" Freddie barks. "Who are you working with?"

Silence again, the noise of rain. We wait, and I refuse to interrupt this. I won't act like I know her when clearly I know nothing.

Another minute passes, and finally she shakes her head slowly. "No one." Her voice is thick and broken. "I'm a dead girl."

Freddie looks at me, but my eyes are fixed on Kass. I hadn't told any of them about her. I never had a chance. Rowan knows I had a date tonight, but he doesn't know with whom. Nothing connects me to her. I'm free to walk away and let her face justice.

My feet move. I'm walking, but I go straight to where she's sitting, pulling a knife from my pocket as I move. I kneel beside her and grasp the thick rope binding her wrists. Her chin drops, and it takes me a moment to saw through the cords. With a pop, they fall away, and I see the raw marks where they tore into her delicate skin.

My jaw grinds. I'm angry and confused. Still, I move her hands into her lap. She's silently crying as I grasp her arms and lift her to her feet. Her knees give out, and I lean down, picking her up. Her face presses against my neck, and I feel her tears on my skin. I pause a moment to breathe through the pain before heading to the broken-down wall where we entered the villa.

"Let's go," I nod as I pass Freddie.

He's silently watching the whole thing. "Where?"

"We'll take her to Occitan," I say, stepping over the pile of stones into the darkness and rain. My partner's right behind me.

\* \* \*

Kass sits on a small cot in the service room near the back entrance of the royal family's ocean estate. I'm not comfortable taking her to the palace, and this is the closest secure area to the villa where we found her. I don't trust her now. As for the other feelings still alive in my chest, I'll deal with them later.

The housekeeper Nesbit brings a bowl of water and a cloth. Freddie leans against the opposite wall, arms crossed, his dark eyes trained on her. I sit in a chair to the side of the narrow cot my fingers steepled at my lips. We wait as the woman dips the cloth in the water and uses it to clean the blood off her neck.

Freddie breaks the silence. "I've alerted Reggie we have a captive. None of his spies have information about a female working with them."

"I can confirm she was with them on the flight from Miami." My voice is level, angry. I watch as Nesbit finishes cleaning the blood then rinses the cloth.

"How?" Freddie asks.

I wait for the housekeeper to rise. "If that will be all, sir?" Nesbit asks with a slight bow.

"For now. Thank you," I say, and she leaves the room.

Freddie shuts the door behind her and looks at me, waiting. It's late, and my eyes are tired. My whole body is tired. The rain has grown stronger, and flashes of lightning are followed by loud peals of thunder.

With a measured breath, I start the interrogation. "What is your relationship to Blix Ratcliffe?"

Kass looks down at her wrists, now wrapped in clean white bandages. I'm not sure how much she can see, but the room we're in is white walls and dark furniture. Freddie is darker than I am, so I'm pretty sure she can at least make out there's two of us here.

"Nothing now," she says in a broken voice. "I'm as good as dead."

"Let's back up to before now." My voice is sharp. "Tell us why you accompanied him here. What was your assignment?"

Her eyes slide closed, and again, a tear slips down her cheek. "My assignment was to reconnect with you."

Pain slices through me like a knife. Freddie's eyes dart to mine, but I hold it together. "And once you'd done that?"

She takes a breath and continues. "Establish a relationship that would compromise your position. At an appointed time I would distract you so his men could kidnap the queen regent."

"What the hell?" Freddie pushes off the wall. "This fucker has no idea. There's no way anyone could compromise Logan..."

His voice trails off, and I feel his eyes on me. My eyes are on Kass's wrists, and I can only imagine the pain her words inflicted is all over my face. My armor is down. It was a brilliant plan, and it would have worked perfectly.

"So what happened?" Freddie says, his voice lower. "What went wrong?"

Several seconds tick by. I count the drops of rain hitting the window, not sure I want to hear her response to his question.

"I couldn't do it." Her voice cracks. "When he told me it was time, my only choice was to kill him. I was determined to do it... But he's too strong for me."

Freddie walks to the door. "We have this threat neutralized. I'll call Rowan while you finish up here."

He's gone, and it's only her, me, and the storm raging outside. I stand and pull the chain on the small lamp on the desk then I go to the door and switch off the stark white light. We're bathed in a soft, yellow glow.

I pause before leaving. "Freddie will let you know what the king decides, whether you'll be detained or... something else."

My hand is on the doorknob when she speaks, her voice high and shaky. "I'm so sorry, Logan."

The things she said before I left her apartment earlier this evening are in my mind as she finishes.

"I never wanted to hurt you."

At that, something in me clicks. I'm not hurt. I'm destroyed, and I want her to feel the pain she's caused me. Pushing the door closed, I turn and cross the room to where she sits. Grasping her upper arms, I jerk her off the cot.

She gasps, and her lips part. Small hands clutch my biceps, and I give her a shake. "Your *only choice* wasn't killing him." Rage seethes through my tone. "Your *choice* was to trust me." I give her another shake. "Your choice was to *tell me* what was happening."

Tears streak her cheeks, and she blinks rapidly. "I couldn't take that chance, not with you." She hiccups a breath and closes her eyes. "I've listened to him with his prisoners. I've been outside the door when he tortures them. It's horrible. I would never let him do that to you. I couldn't let him hurt you like that."

"So you did it yourself." It's a statement of fact.

Her head moves side to side and more tears fall. "No, Logan."

My jaw is clenched and my words are a low growl. "Yes, Kass." I'm still gripping her arms, but she bends her elbows, reaching for me.

I'm furious. I'm doing my best to hold a protective shield between her and my heart, and the sight of her pale hand reaching for me splinters it. My hold on her falters, and she moves forward, burying her face in my chest, small hands clutching my shirt. For the space of a heartbeat, I keep my defenses strong. Until I feel her body shudder, and my arms go around her.

"I'm so sorry." Her voice is soft, muffled against me, and my arms tighten around her slim body.

I hold her through the tears. I hold her, allowing the depth of the pain she has inflicted to be soothed momentarily. I drop my face to her hair and inhale deeply the clean, sweet scent of her fragrance. *God help me*, I'm being torn apart.

"I can't let this go." Forcing my resolve in place, I move her back so I can see her face. "Blix is evil. You worked with him. You were in his inner circle. Are you still?"

She shakes her head no. "He'll never trust me again."

"How can I ever trust you again?"

"You can't." No irony is in her tone. She's not pleading or crying. It's a simple acknowledgment of fact.

I go to the chair and drop heavily. My fingers scrub my eyes, and I try to make this make sense. "How did this happen? The Kass I knew would never get mixed up with men like this. Shit, you were a fucking virgin. I'm supposed to believe you've changed that much?"

She sits on the cot, and the sadness is back. "A lot can change in a year. A lot can change in less than a year."

"It's time you told me the whole story."

She presses her lips together before starting. "In the winter after you left, I was diagnosed with... this blindness. I was devastated. My aunt tried to comfort me, but I wanted to die."

Standing, I go to the small desk holding a crystal decanter. I pour us each two fingers of scotch. "Here," I say, nudging her hand with the tumbler.

She takes it and lifts it to her nose. "Expensive."

"You're at the royal estate in Occitan."

She does a little nod and takes a sip, flinching slightly at the burn.

"Please continue," I say coolly, sitting and taking a sip from my glass.

"I was very young... You were gone—"

"Are you attempting to blame me?"

"No." She's quiet a moment. "I only meant, I didn't have anyone else. I didn't believe I ever would, so I got into... risky behavior. I took jobs for the thrill of it, hoping I'd be caught. I never was. I guess I look innocent. No one suspected me of anything."

"Glad to know I'm not alone." It's a shitty thing to say, but my insides are dark. My whole world has turned to shit.

She doesn't skip a beat. "A friend of mine knew a guy."

"Isn't that how they all start?"

"I don't know about all." She takes another sip of her scotch. Another wince. "He said I could make a lot of money carrying drugs from one place to another. I didn't have to touch anything. I didn't even have to speak to anyone. I carried them in my purse, then I left my purse at the designated drop. I did it twice, and then I met Blix."

"It only took two times?"

"I think he liked me." She shakes her head and tilts her glass side to side a little too fast. "He wanted me to work directly with him. He wanted me to go with him to Miami, but I said no."

My insides twist tighter and tighter with every word, and it all comes out as cruel commentary. "Why? You were an adrenaline junkie. Why not go with him."

"My aunt was killed." Her voice shakes and my stomach churns. "I couldn't leave Cameron. I suddenly realized what I was doing, and I wanted out."

She falls silent. I don't speak, and the noise of the rain surrounds us like a blanket. It drowns out the silence with the deluge of water washing in, whether it's cleansing, I can't tell.

I break the silence. "Let me guess. He wouldn't let you out?"

"I'd kept my blindness from him. He had no idea until the first time I was cheated. I was supposed to bring back ten grams of pills, and I was short by twenty."

I'm confused. "Twenty pills?"

"Yes. It felt like the right amount, but when Blix counted, I was short." She finishes her glass of scotch, and I take it, pouring us both a refill. "No more for me," she says shaking her head. Her eyes are tired. My eyes are tired, but I have to hear this. I hand her the tumbler of scotch and sit back with my own.

"Go on," I say.

She nods, wiping the back of her hand over her nose. "He said he would cut off a digit for every pill—all my fingers and my toes."

"Jesus," I groan.

"I was terrified." She tilts the crystal tumbler back and forth then takes another sip. "I told him everything. That I was blind, my aunt had died, my little brother needed the money... He was repulsed. He didn't like that I was disabled."

"Asshole."

"He was right. Being blind is a deadly handicap in the drug world." She takes another sip. "So he moved me to Miami to handle his logistics. Only Davis knew I was blind there. And when Davis started to steal—"

"You were back on the hook again?"

"Davis took a very long time to die." Her knees bend and she wraps her arms around her legs. "I had one choice. Do what I was told or follow in his footsteps."

"So you came after me." Placing my tumbler on the desk I push off my knees to stand. I walk around the narrow space fighting the urges pulsing through me. "I've wanted to nail this guy for so long now. I get so close... And he's always five steps ahead of me."

"He owns a lot of eyes," she says softly. "And ears."

Turning, I look at her. She's more relaxed thanks to the scotch. I confess, it was part of my plan. Her pale hair hangs around her like a cape, and she's pushed one side behind her ear. Her red lipstick is smeared on her full lips, and she's so fucking beautiful. Even tired and battered, my body longs for hers. I want to hold her.

"How did he know about us?" I have to know how much she told him.

The saddest smile touches the corner of her mouth. She seems to be studying her fingers as she tells me. "I had a picture of us. I don't remember who took it, but your arms were around me, and you were hugging me so tight. I was smiling, and there was just so much warmth and joy and... *love*... in that scrap of paper. I can still see it. I used to look at it at night before I'd fall asleep."

"Jesus, Sass." I toss back the rest of my scotch and consider a third.

Clearing her throat, she shakes away the nostalgia. "He took it from me. He's always looking for new weapons."

I've heard enough. I'm exhausted and I'm not ready to forgive her. I'm angry and tired and betrayed and so fucking torn up inside. I stop when I reach the door to the small room.

"I'm locking you in." She doesn't respond, and I keep going. "The windows are sealed, and the grounds are monitored by security cameras. You have a bathroom just there — the door beside the closet. I'll be back in the morning."

She only does a slight nod. "I'll be here."

"Get some sleep." It's the last thing I say before leaving. I pull the door shut and lock it.

It's pretty damn familiar to the way I left her in her apartment earlier this evening. Only this time, I know she's not going anywhere. This room only has two keys, and I have both of them.

## Chapter 13: Confrontation

*Kass*

Logan leaves, and I melt into a defeated puddle on the narrow cot. The scotch took the edge off the pain, but I'm still throbbing from the way he left me. He's so angry, but more than that, I hurt him. Pain spilled from his voice like acid on my shredded insides.

Tears pool in the corners of my eyes. I don't want to cry. I don't deserve to cry, but I can't stop them flowing from my eyes.

"Oh, Logan," I whisper, holding the thin blanket over my mouth. I don't want him to hear me. I don't want anyone to think I feel sorry for myself.

A long time ago I thought I was a good person. I took care of my brother, I listened to my aunt, I followed the rules. Good people don't do what I've done. When life turns to shit, good people rise up and make noble choices. They don't make deals with the devil and put their loved ones in danger.

*Cameron...* I scrub the heels of my hands over my face. He's out there unprotected. Blix will kill me when he finds me, or manages to lure me out of this safe house. He's a master at getting what he wants, and the best way to get me is to go after Cam. Logan is far away. I don't have a phone... *Oh, God! Please, please protect my little brother.*

Pain, fear, despair all twist into a tight ball in my chest. Bending my legs, I press my forehead into my knees and repeat the words like a mantra. *Please please please...* As if I deserve any divine favors.

All I can hope is Blix will think they're watching Cam, waiting for him to make a move in retaliation. All I can hope is maybe they are.

\* \* \*

The creaking of my door rouses me. I can't believe I fell asleep. I'm still clenched in a fetal position, and my last thought is still on my mind. *Cameron...*

"I brought you breakfast." It's Nesbit, the woman who washed my neck last night.

Her voice is stern, and I don't move. I only listen as she puts a tray on the desk where Logan sat. I'm not hungry. I don't deserve food, but the delicious scent of toast and bacon and coffee make my stomach growl loudly. I'm so embarrassed.

"Sit up and eat," the woman snaps. "Do you need help?"

She grasps my shoulder, and I flinch. I push against the cot and slowly rise to a sitting position. No telling what I look like, considering I cried most of the night—when I wasn't begging for divine intervention.

"Here," she says, raking fingernails through my hair several times. I sit like a child allowing her to repair the damage. "That's better."

I'm so thirsty, it's difficult to speak. "May I have something to drink?"

"Of course. I have coffee and juice..."

"Coffee please." My head aches from crying and from the scotch. I'm not used to alcohol. When my vision failed, I backed off anything that could impair my ability to be independent. Alcohol is a distinct liability when I'm alone.

Nesbit rattles the cup and saucer, and I hear the metallic stirring of the spoon. If I tried harder, I could make out shadows of her progress around the room, but I don't want to try. I only want to know my brother is safe. After that...

"Is this her?" An equally angry (if somewhat softer) voice enters the room.

"Yes, your highness," Nesbit answers.

My skin prickles. A young, female voice and that salutation can only mean one thing.

"You're the one working with Blix?" She's speaking to me, and her voice has grown louder, challenging me. "Do you know who I am?"

Since I'm sitting, I can only bow my head. "Your majesty." My voice breaks. Porcelain touches my fingers.

Nesbit hands me the coffee. "Drink this."

"Thank you," I whisper just before taking a sip.

The coffee is comforting and delicious. An undeserved wave of relief moves through my insides. I realize this young queen is standing over me, watching me, and I lower the cup. I don't know if there's a table nearby, so I hold the saucer in my hand and wait.

She starts to pace. "Are you aware of what Blix Ratcliffe does to the people he takes?"

"Yes." My moment of relief is replaced by a cringe of shame.

"You do?" Her voice is different from anger. It's more... outrage. "You're aware he tortures his victims? You're aware he cuts off pieces of their bodies and sends them to their loved ones?"

She gets louder as she speaks, and I cower more. I'm very, very aware of how Blix treats his prisoners — and anyone who crosses him.

"Answer me!"

"Yes, your majesty. I've heard what he does."

"You've heard about it?"

A cold knot has settled in the pit of my stomach. Davis's screams are in my ears. "No, ma'am. I've been outside the door. I've heard them."

It's quiet a moment. The only sound is the soft click of her heels on the wood floor. "Do you know me?"

I'm confused by her question. "I think you're the queen regent." I've never seen her, but I don't know who else Nesbit would call *your majesty*.

"But do you know me? Have we ever met before?"

"N-no... of course not."

"Of course not." Her voice is sharp. "Have I ever done anything to you? Have I ever hurt you?"

"No." I shake my head, keeping my eyes down.

"You don't know me at all. I've never hurt you. Yet you would help this devil, this heartless, soulless bastard... Why? I want to know why."

I'd thought it was impossible to feel worse than I did last night. My head is pounding, and my bladder takes this opportunity to remind me I haven't gone to the bathroom since last night.

"I'm so sorry," I whisper, holding the cot for balance as I rise. I try to make out the room, but the sun is low and shapes are fuzzy. "I'm so sorry, but... I need to use the restroom."

"Here." Nesbit steps forward and takes the cup and saucer. I hear her set it to the side before she grasps my arm. She's not gentle in the least, but she guides me to the door leading to the small room.

The light clicks on, and she walks me to the toilet, placing my hand on the roll of paper before she returns to the door.

"I'm standing outside if you need anything," she says.

I can't speak. I only nod and slowly remove my panties before reaching out to sit. My insides are raw. I can't take any more of her questions. She doesn't understand—this was never about her. None of this has ever been about her. It's always been about protecting Cam, paying for my debts, trying to get free of my bad choices.

Tears are in my eyes as I reach for the paper. I never thought of her. She's right. It was easier to trade her anonymous life for mine. Looking at it now, I realize it wasn't a fair trade. Our lives aren't equal. She's more generous than I am.

My clothes are back in place and I feel for the little lever to flush. Fingertips on the wall, I go to the sink and wash. No clicks. I don't care to see this place. I'm broken and tired and utterly worthless. I've lost Logan...

The door opens, and Nesbit speaks to me. "Do you need help?"

People always think the blind are helpless. "No."

I make my way slowly to where she stands and stop. I don't know if I can pass her. She takes it as a signal to help me and grasps my forearm again, leading me to the cot. I'm too tired to fight her.

Nesbit positions me in front of the cot, and I slowly take a seat. I sit on my bed and look at the floor. A clink of dishes and what sounds like metal hitting porcelain fills the air. Nesbit is preparing a plate. I should tell her I can't eat. My stomach is too tight, and I feel sick.

The queen is still in the room, but she doesn't say a word. I have to guess she's watching all of this. I'm bracing for the continuation of her wrath. She has every right to say these things to me. I don't know her, and I was ready to deliver her to the worst human alive.

"Have to eat something." The older woman takes my wrist and turns my palm up then puts a plate in my hand.

I release a breath and try not to cry. Jesus, the worst thing I can do right now as cry like I have the right to self-pity.

More time passes. I'm uncomfortable and miserable and this plate is in my hand. I don't know what to do.

"You're blind," the queen finally speaks. She's still angry, but her tone is different. The sharp edge is gone.

I move my eyes in the direction of her mouth. I can just make out she has dark hair. "Legally blind," I clarify.

"What does that mean?" she says.

I strain my eyes around the room. The sun has risen higher and more light filters in through the windows. I don't see another shape, which leads me to believe Nesbit has left the room.

"The woman is gone. It's only you and me."

"Nesbit," the queen says. "She's the housekeeper here at Occitan."

"You're standing near the door," I say, trying to make out more. "You have dark hair."

The sound of footfalls brings her closer to where I'm sitting. "So you can see me?"

"It's like a thick fog all around," I explain, thinking of the last time I said this, sitting in the bed with Logan. His warm hands on my waist, our bodies humming and satisfied from making love. Blinking fast, I won't allow tears.

"How long have you been like this?" she asks.

"It's been growing for a long time, but I didn't know it. It suddenly grew much worse and quickly deteriorated over the last five years."

"So you used to see?"

I nod and look down. "Yes, your majesty."

She's quiet again, observing. I hear a car outside and wonder if it might be Logan.

"Is that how he got you? Did he somehow use this to make you help him?" Her voice is challenging. She needs to understand, but I don't know how she ever could. How could a lady understand the cruel twists of fate that would lead one to choose a life of crime?

"No, ma'am." My eyes are on my hands. I slide a finger over the bandages at my wrists, thinking of that nylon rope. "When I lost my sight, I became very depressed. Then my aunt died."

Warmth swirls at my side and she sits beside me on the cot. "Your aunt—did you live with her? Not your parents?"

"My mother died shortly after she had my brother. It was a hard pregnancy, and she never recovered. I don't know my father."

My hands are covered by cool, slim ones, and she gives them a squeeze. "Why were you working with Blix?"

Why is she doing this? I'm not sure what to make of her kindness. She knows I'm one of the bad guys.

"I... I helped a friend. Well, not really a friend. I helped a guy I knew move drugs around. He paid me a lot of money for my help. Enough to take care of Cameron and me for a month."

"Cameron is your brother."

"Yes, your majesty."

"Please call me Ava."

I'm pretty sure I'll never be able to do that. She doesn't give me a chance to object. "So you did drugs?"

"No—I wasn't a junkie." I hesitate. Just because I never took drugs doesn't make me somehow better. "I moved them from place to place. My... friend said they wouldn't bother me because I'm blind, and I guess I look... innocent."

"You're very beautiful." Her voice is gentler. "Is that what led to Blix? Did he make you swallow balloons?"

Shaking my head, I think of the mules who swallow heroin wrapped in latex. One weak link and as much as two kilos could dump into their bloodstream. For comparison, twenty milligrams is an average bump. Basically, it would be a gruesome way to die.

"He said I was too valuable. I only carried them on my person. Then one of his connections thought he would trick me by switching out the pills. He was stupid."

"Did Blix hurt you for it?"

That night lingers in my memory. It doesn't take much work to remember Blix's hand clamped over my wrist, the knife pressing into my knuckle. "He threatened to hurt me, but instead he dealt with the man and moved me to Florida."

Her voice is grim. "I can't believe he's capable of mercy."

"He's not. He made me earn back the missing pills. It was thousands of dollars. Then it happened again. Only the second time, it was one million."

"That's how he got you to do this?"

It's difficult for me to take that easy way out. "My bad choices led me here."

She stands and walks around the room. I'm still holding the plate in my hand, and I lean forward to set it on the desk.

"You need to eat something," she says gently.

I'm so confused by the change in her. I don't know if it's rude, but I have to ask. "Why are you being nice to me?"

"Earlier when I said you don't know me." All traces of anger are gone at this point. She's speaking as if we're friends. "Before I came here, my sister and I lived on the street. We had to steal money for food. We broke into boathouses to sleep when it rained. My sister robbed casinos…"

My brother had told me a little about this new queen, how she was a true Cinderella story. At the time, I didn't really care.

"Basically, it would be a cruel hypocrisy if I sat here and tried to judge you. I've never had any disabilities. You might say I had an edge… although, you wouldn't really know me if you did."

I'm not sure what that means, but surging to the forefront of my mind is the problem I prayed all night about. Could this woman standing here be the answer?

"I have no right to ask this, but you see, I must." My hands are clutched together in my lap.

She walks back to where I'm sitting. "What is it?"

For a moment, I bite the inside of my lip and press my eyes closed. I don't matter, but this… I have to ask this favor. "My brother Cameron… He's alone, and Blix knows how much he means to me. I'm so afraid he'll—"

"You don't even have to ask." She sits beside me again and covers my clutched hands with hers. "I overheard Logan speaking to the king, my husband this morning. It's why I wanted to come here and confront you myself."

"I don't understand. They let you come here to see me? Without trying to stop you?"

"Rowan knows my freedom is important to me. Anyway, I wasn't afraid to see you. I thought it would make a difference, and I see I'm right."

"But... what about Cam?"

"They've assigned two men to stay nearby. They're watching him. Hoping Blix does make a move on him."

Relief washes over me so strong, I'm again fighting back tears. It's what I'd hoped for last night, and I'm so relieved and grateful. At the same time, hearing her say Blix might try to hurt my brother sends my panic levels rising again. "They won't let him..."

"Logan seems very determined to keep your brother safe. He seems very concerned about keeping you safe." Again her tone has changed, and she seems to be thinking, evaluating my response to her statements. "I like Logan very much. He saved my sister from Blix last summer..."

I'm doing my best to maintain a neutral expression. I've done enough to hurt Logan. He's strong and perfect and still protecting me, and I can't see how he'll ever forgive me for betraying him — even if I couldn't go through with it.

"Since he's my personal guard now," she continues, "I've decided it would be less stressful for him if I spend a few days here at Occitan. I'm not being completely unselfish. I love being here. It's more relaxing than the palace. Perhaps we can get to know each other better... since we have so much in common."

I study my hands. "I don't have anything in common with you, your majesty."

She stands and touches my shoulder. "You have more than you know." She pulls the door open. "I'll send some clothes for you to wear. The rain has finally stopped. Let's take a walk along the beach."

I don't know if I'm allowed to say no, so I shrug. "Thank you."

"I'll send Logan to escort you down."

## Chapter 14: Struggles

*Logan*

Waves crash under a grey sky. The air is cool, and both the queen and Kass are dressed in long-sleeved sweaters as they walk along the secluded beach at Occitan. I follow from a distance, keeping them in my sight.

A small outcropping of rocks protects the cove from the brunt of the ocean's waves. The water is usually calm here, more like a lake. Not today. October is our stormiest month, and the wind whips through in occasional, violent bursts.

Ava's dark hair curls in long spirals around her slim shoulders. She's tall and confident, and with her sapphire-green eyes, she's a striking beauty. It's easy to see why the king and the people fell in love with her, why they were willing to overlook her checkered past and make her their "Cinderella queen."

Still, my gaze is drawn to Cassandra.

For all Ava's elegant grace, the petite drop of moonlight walking by her side has my heart and my insides tied up in knots. I watch the two of them growing closer. Kass is hesitant, but Ava acts as though she has her sister back.

It's impossible to deny how much Zelda and Kass have in common. It's also easy to see why I developed an attachment to Ava's sister. It's an easy reach.

Like Zelda, Kass is a survivor. Her bad choices have been motivated by the curveballs life has thrown at her, and her determination to survive. She's mixed up with criminal subculture and dangerous men, but purity shines out of her eyes. Her heart is not black and hard, and I understand now she had to keep going or risk losing the only family she has left.

Intellectually, I understand her reasons. At the same time, she made me a target. She used our love as a weapon against me. The night we met at the casino, I fucking believed the universe had brought us together again, and it was all a lie. Every time I touched her, kissed her, loved her... Every time I wondered at the amazing twist of fate that I had her in my arms...

Shit. I'm getting fucking pissed all over again.

Fuck the past. I don't believe in types. I don't believe in soul mates. We have moments in our lives that are golden. Perhaps we try to recapture those moments with different humans who remind us of the ones we shared those times with. Or we stop being pussies and move forward, make new memories with new people.

I have to put all that shit behind me and *Do My Job*.

With a crash salt water breaks over my feet, and I swear, walking further up the dunes. I've taken my eyes off the queen. She squeals, and adrenaline spikes in my veins. I race forward.

"Your majesty," I say, looking around, my hand moving to my gun holster.

"Logan!" Ava laughs, falling on my arm. She's laughing so hard, her green eyes dance. "I'm sorry! I stepped on a crab. It's so overcast, they're all out scavenging."

Kass moves away, dropping her hand and walking ahead of us. Beneath the black sweater, she's wearing a beige dress Ava must have loaned her. It has a long, flowing skirt that whips around her sexy legs. The wind blows hard, and I can see the shape of her breasts beneath the thin material of the top. Her pale hair flies around her in the breeze, and my fingers curl. I want to thread them in her hair. I want to slide them down her body and love her.

Fuck that. I shake away my residual desire when I notice the queen's eyes are fixed on me. Clearing my throat, I pass a hand over my mouth. "The king asked us to be extra vigilant."

She smiles and narrows her eyes. "Is Rowan the only reason you're staying so close?"

She's onto me, but I'm not playing into any romantic notions. "My job is to keep you safe. As long as the threat level is high, I'm afraid I have to stay with you. I'll try not to make you uncomfortable."

"You never make me uncomfortable." Her hand is still on my forearm, and she starts to walk. I stay with her, and we follow in Kass's footsteps on the sand.

Looking up, I watch Kass go toward the breakers then step out of them when they rush in deep around her ankles. The hem of her dress is wet, but it still moves up and around in the breeze.

"I like her," Ava says, her voice thoughtful.

"We're treating her like a suspect until we're sure she's no longer a threat. It would be careless to do otherwise."

Ava exhales a short laugh. "She's not a threat. She tried to kill Blix herself."

"So she says." I can't shake how easily she lied to me before—and how easily I believed her.

"I believe her," Ava argues. "I'd like to stay here while we have her in custody. She makes me feel less... lonely."

"Are you lonely?" I hadn't considered the possibility, but it makes sense. She's an outsider here, and her sister is far away.

She doesn't answer immediately. Her hand leaves my arm and she walks toward the line of water racing in and out with the wind.

"I have Rowan, and you or Freddie is always nearby." Her nose wrinkles with her smile. "Sometimes it's nice to have another woman to talk to."

I shrug. "I see no reason why we can't stay here. It's a secure location, and it's not hard to get to the palace quickly if needed."

Her eyes move over my shoulder, and her expression changes. Pink touches her cheeks and she smiles. "It's Rowan," she says, passing me and jogging up the beach toward the house.

I watch her go, and wait until she's folded in the king's arms before I turn back to see Kass still playing at the edge of the water. She drops to a squat right where flat, wet sand meets the softer, drier part. Her fingers lightly touch the dunes, and she rocks back to sit. She's a safe enough distance that she won't get wet, and I continue walking to where she sits. We can't leave her out here, and I'm confident Ava is safe with her husband.

Walking toward her, I watch as she bends her knees and places her cheek on top of them. Her eyes close against the wind, and she's so different than she was only twenty-four hours ago. It was clear she was happy with me those few days, even if it was a lie. *Her choice*, I think, steeling myself as I get closer.

"Rowan's here," I say, and she does a little jump, lifting her head. "I'm sorry—I didn't mean to startle you."

"The king is here?" Her legs drop and she starts to stand. "Does he want to... hurt me?"

"Ava likes you, so there's little chance anything bad will happen to you."

She's standing beside me, and the wind swirls jasmine all around us. Her hair flies forward, and she catches it, pushing it back, but not before it touches my cheek. Every little touch, every scent is another twist of the knife still buried in my stomach.

"She's too nice to me. I don't deserve it."

I can't argue with her there. "You remind her of her sister."

"Zelda," she nods. "You helped rescue her from Blix."

"It was a scary time. A lot of bad things happened to her while we searched."

Kass's slim brows pull together, and she almost seems like she'll cry. "I hate to be the cause of her pain. I hate that I'm a part of this. I thought I could get free of him, but I never will."

"You could have talked to me about it. I would have helped you."

"Now it's too late." A frown tugs at the side of her mouth, and she starts to move past me, turning her face to the ocean to hide her sadness.

My hands are on my hips, and I hold myself back, grinding my jaw against the pull of wanting to hold her. *Her choice*, my brain demands.

I see the driftwood partially buried in the sand in front of her, but I realize a second too late she can't see it. Her ankle turns, and she starts to fall. One swift move, and I scoop her up, into my arms.

"Oh!" she cries, gripping my biceps.

Her soft body is pressed against me, and her face is right at my chin. Her breath comes in quick pants, causing her breasts to rise and fall just beneath the thin material of her dress. With her sweater pushed back, I can see she's not wearing a bra, and all the lust I've been fighting shoots straight to my cock.

I know she feels it. Her lids lower, and her eyes are trained on my mouth. Her lips part, and I can just see the tips of her white teeth when she speaks, low and breathless. "Thank you."

Desire overrules my brain, and I don't stop myself. I pull her to me, covering her mouth with mine. It's not a gentle kiss. It's rough and punishing. It's all the anger and the hurt and the worry she's put me through these last days.

She meets me with equal strength. Her mouth moves with mine, and she tastes like mint and cool water. A little noise aches from her throat and fuck me, my dick gets harder. She's soft in my arms, and my stomach fills with warmth, desire, possession.

How can I still want her so badly? She used me.

Breaking our lips apart, I look up at the sky. It's thick with grey, swirling clouds. It mirrors the storm in my chest.

Kass's forehead drops to my neck. She's panting, and I feel her beaded nipples against my chest. I want to pull them into my mouth and suck them until she moans. I want to lower my pants and lift her skirt. I want to shove her panties aside and fuck her right here on this beach. I want it to be hard and angry. I want her begging me to forgive her, begging me for more.

I can see the whole thing, and it takes all my willpower to step back.

"I'm sorry." I hold her arms until I'm sure she has her balance, until I'm back in control. "I'll escort you to the house."

"Yes." Her voice is breathless.

Every touch is electric. Our chemistry is impossible to deny, but I can't be with her if she's not going to tell me the truth. I can't let her tie me up in knots yet never let me inside her walls. It kills me because I want to take care of her. I want to protect her—it's what I do—but I can't force her to let me.

Once she's clear, we walk side by side the way we came. I keep an eye out for debris or other hazards she can't see, but I don't touch her. We don't speak. I'm still recovering from the intensity of our connection. The way she crosses her arms over her stomach, I assume she's sorting out her feelings as well.

Another gust of wind sweeps around us, and my skin is sticky with brine. I taste the salt on my tongue.

"It's going to rain again," I say, looking out at the churning black waters.

She doesn't respond. Instead her smooth brow wrinkles. "Ava said you're watching Cameron."

"I sent a team of guys in plain clothes to his apartment last night. They're watching him."

She nods, pulling her full bottom lip into her mouth a moment. When it slips out, it's glossy, and I look away to block the images of me kissing her again.

"I can't tell you how much it means to me," she says, drawing me back. "I was so worried about him last night. He is the only thing..." She shakes her head and looks down. "He's been the only thing keeping me going for so long."

"You make it sound like something changed."

Her bare feet make soft squeaking noises in the damp sand, and a ghostly white crab scurries away from our path. It's as pale and ethereal as this beautiful girl at my side. This woman who holds my heart in her hand.

"When I came back…" Again, she's choosing her words. I want to stop her and make her tell me what she's holding inside. "I've been thinking about everything that went before." She looks ahead of us, far in the distance. "I wish…"

The squeak of footfalls in the sand, the sound of breakers crashing on the shore. She doesn't finish her wish, and we're back at the boardwalk leading up to the enormous estate. I see Ava with Rowan on the back porch. His hands are on her waist and her hands are on his chest. He says something and she laughs, rising on her toes to kiss his cheek. On her way down, he catches her, covering her mouth with his.

It's everything I want with Cassandra. Following her to the house, I watch the movement of her hair down her back, the graceful sway of her hips, her small feet, and I make a decision. I won't give her up without a fight. Maybe our reunion was staged as a way to break me, but maybe I can take what Blix intended for evil and turn it into what I've always wanted.

## Chapter 15: Dirty Hands

*Kass*

It's raining again. Time passes, and Blix is still in hiding. We remain at Occitan in a holding pattern, waiting. I'm not included in any of the discussions of what they're planning or how they're searching for him. It stings a little, but at the same time, I don't want to know. If Blix does try to contact me or worse, somehow kidnap me, the less I know, the better.

Ava and I are on oversized loungers on the back porch. They're covered in thick cushions, and she's holding a deck of cards she shuffles over and over. I wonder if she wishes I could play. I suppose I could if I held them close to my face, only I wouldn't be able to see what's on the table.

Letting it go, I lean my head back against the thick cushion and listen to the rain fall. We're far enough away that it's ambient back noise combined with the crashing surf, and I'm wrapped in a soft, cashmere sweater she gave me.

The muffled slap of shuffling cards fills the air. "When it rained, Zelda and I would search for unlocked boat houses to hide from the storm."

I turn my head in her direction. "You would stay in them all day?"

"Oh, no." More shuffling. "During the day we wandered around, doing our best to stay inside malls or drugstores. Places we could hang around unnoticed."

"It's strange to think of you that way." I try to picture this elegant lady as a street urchin.

"You remind me of her." She's smiling.

"Your sister? How?"

Another shuffle of cards. "You're brave. You're a fighter. But your vulnerability makes you accessible."

"You mean my blindness." A frown pulls at the side of my mouth. "I'm not helpless because I'm blind."

"That's not what I meant." She rotates in her chair so it's facing me.

I'm quiet a moment, thinking about what she said, where we are, and what's happening. "You're too kind to me. I should be locked in a dungeon for what I've done."

She's dealing the cards, laying them out on the table between us. "Logan is one of my husband's most trusted guards. He vouched for you."

That revelation hits my chest like a fist. "Why would he do that? I betrayed him."

"Probably because he's in love with you." She says it so casually, as if the suggestion doesn't crush me and make me hope and make me despair all at once.

The noise of rain surrounds us. The waves batter the shore. Cards flick against the table—*one, two, three*. She's playing Solitaire. I can tell by the way she repeatedly deals herself three cards then puts them away.

"And anyway, you didn't actually do anything."

"I almost helped Blix capture you."

"You almost got yourself killed."

I remember Blix's plans for me—hot oil, darkness, silence, imprisoned in my own body. "He wanted to do much worse than kill me."

"Which is why you're here. Logan was pretty adamant the night he found you."

"No," I shake my head, everything in me rejecting his forgiveness. "It's not fair to him."

"I don't think he cares." She leans closer, voice softer, and I can feel her looking around us. "He can't keep his eyes off you."

Heat floods my cheeks. "But I hurt him."

"Only because you didn't have a choice." Three more cards. She's back to casual, oblivious to my inner turmoil. "The way he looks at you sometimes could set the house on fire."

I lower my face to my cool hands and shift in my chair. "I wish I could see his eyes," I say quietly. "Where is he?"

"Oh, he's somewhere around here watching you instead of me." She laughs, but I'm not sure she's right. I can't imagine what Logan sees when he looks at me now.

"Damn," she sighs. "I lost."

She pushes the table aside and leans back in her chair. She's a filmy haze, but I can tell she's facing me. I don't know if she's studying me or looking at something else.

"It's easy to understand. You're very beautiful," she says, and I have my answer. "Do you know that?"

"It's been a long time since I've seen myself clearly." I turn the statement over in my mind a moment. I hadn't intended the double meaning. "I don't know what I'm like now."

"What's the hardest part about being blind?"

Her change in direction diffuses the conflict in my chest. I think about her question and rotate toward her. My legs are bent, and I look into the wind, listening to the noise of the surf.

"I've mostly adjusted to this way of life."

"Mostly means not entirely."

Nodding, I rest my cheek on the tops of my knees so I'm looking in her direction. "I miss being able to read people's expressions. Words and tone of voice can be so different from how people really feel." She makes a noise of assent, and I slide my hands down my shins. "Also, shaving my legs."

I see her dark head rise in my peripheral vision. "Wow. Shaving?" She exhales a short laugh. "I would never have thought of that."

We've moved onto easy ground, where my anxiety feels distant. "What's the hardest part about being queen?"

"Queen regent," she corrects me. I hum a yes and wait for her answer. "I miss being bad."

Not what I expected her to say. "I have no idea what that means."

"Well..." she's looking around. "I was brought to this country by the men who tried to kill my husband."

I'd heard this about her. Cameron had filled me in on the whole twisted tale. "You didn't know they were planning to kill him."

"Still, I knew they were planning to betray him." She hesitates a moment. "Money can be a powerful motivator."

I don't answer right away. It's possible I misjudged Ava Wilder... Westringham Tate. "How would you be bad?"

I hear a door closing behind us followed by footsteps moving toward the outer edge of the patio, giving us space. Ava leans closer and whispers, "What's something Logan always carries?"

"A gun?"

"Something else. Smaller."

I retrace the few days we were together. "He has two phones…"

"Stay here." She's up and walking away from me before the words register in my brain.

Waiting on the lounger, I don't look over my shoulder, but I listen as she greets the sexy guard who has my emotions so tangled. His deep voice squeezes my insides. I can't make out what they're saying, but Ava's voice is teasing. She does a little laugh, and I hear her returning to where I wait. She's moving quickly, and she pats my legs, causing me to sit up so she can sit close beside me on the lounger.

"Give me your hand," she whispers. I hold it out, and she places it on top of a small rectangular shape. "It was in his breast pocket." Her voice is giddy, and I can feel the excitement buzzing around her.

"What did you do?"

"I picked his pocket."

My eyes widen and she flips our hands, leaving the small phone on my palm and taking hers away. "You can give it back to him."

"But… How?"

"It's simply a matter of distraction and redirection." She's smiling, bouncing lightly on the seat.

"Everyone says you're beautiful." I turn slightly and hold up my hand toward her cheek. "May I? It helps me see you."

"Really?" She guides my palm to her cheek. "How?"

I drop the phone in my lap and slide the tips of my fingers lightly over her high cheekbones down to her full lips. "What color are your eyes?"

"Sort of a bluish green?"

"And your hair is long and dark." I move my fingers to the soft waves on her shoulder. "That's your secret weapon. You're very beautiful."

"It evens the score." Her mood changes so suddenly, I'm confused.

"You seem... angry?"

A sharp exhale, and she stands. "Beauty hurts me as much as it helps. It makes me a target. It's why Zelda got mixed up with men like Wade Paxton. She tried to protect me."

Chewing my lip, I think about this. "It's what brought you here... and now you're with the king."

"I'm going inside to check on dinner."

"I'm sorry—"

"Nothing to be sorry for. I'll be back in a little while."

She leaves, and I lean back against the cushions. I feel guilty... but how could I have known she would react that way? I can't seem to win in this place. Everything feels wrong, and my heart hurts. I wish I could go somewhere else. I wish it would stop raining. *What do I really wish?*

"Are you all right?" The lovely, low voice is like hot caramel through my insides, and I have my answer.

"Logan." I reach out my hand.

He hasn't spoken to me or come near me since our walk on the beach when he kissed me—that amazing kiss on the beach. Ava's words drift through my mind, *The way he looks at you...*

Insecurity rears its ugly head. *I betrayed him.*

Seconds pass and he doesn't take my hand. I lower it only to find his larger one is waiting below. Our palms touch, and his fingers close over mine.

I have no right to feel this way, but I miss his arms so badly. I don't deserve him, but it doesn't seem to matter. I start to move when I feel the weight in my lap and quickly catch the small phone.

"Ava wanted me to give you this," I say.

"How did she—" He makes a noise, and I sense him looking after her the way she came. "Little thief."

"She gave it back." My voice is quiet, and in defending her, I feel somehow like I'm defending me. Ava isn't truly bad is she? Am I?

Logan sits beside me on the chair, and I crawl into his lap. I hear him inhale sharply, as if I've surprised him, but just as fast huge arms encompass my torso. I can't deny this, and I can only hope, beg from somewhere deep in my soul that he might forgive me.

After all I've done, what's left for me if I lose Logan? I'll never return to Miami. I'll never help Blix again. If we're able to find him and arrest him—or kill him—could I possibly have a second chance? I want to say all these things out loud, but I feel like I don't have the right.

I close my eyes and rest my face against his broad chest. I listen to his heart beating in time with mine. His strong breath swirls in and out, and his hand touches the back of my hair. Electricity hums beneath my skin with every touch, and I'm willing to do anything to earn his forgiveness, even if I don't deserve it.

"Talk to me." His voice vibrates against my cheek. "What are you thinking?"

I take a deep breath of his warm scent mixing with the clean smell of ocean rain. It makes me want to cry. "I'm so dirty."

"You came clean." Our voices are quiet. We're in this intimate space.

"I did bad things."

"You'll never do them again."

"It's too late. The game has already started."

My eyes squeeze closed, and my grip on his shirt tightens. He continues holding me, stroking the back of my hair. I remember holding his body against mine, lying in his bed and tracing my fingers along the lines of his muscles. I remember him making me coffee. I remember the bookstore. The book he bought.

"We never read the book." I lean back as if I can see him. I long to touch his face, read his expression. I want to know if his dark brow is lowered. I want to see his blue eyes watching me the way Ava said he does, full of desire.

"I read it," he says. "That night I read it."

"Did you find a favorite verse?"

"I found two."

"Tell me one."

A warm hand touches my cheek. A large thumb tugs on my lower lip, not too hard. "If your eyes are opened, you'll see the things worth seeing."

I want to pull his thumb between my lips, touch it with my tongue. I want to kiss his palm, but I never get the chance.

With a deep exhale, he moves me off his lap and stands. My heart stills, but he walks away, leaving me on the chair silently aching for him.

## Chapter 16: Bait

*Logan*

Back in the war room, Reggie is sharing the information gathered by his network of spies.

"He's gone deep undercover," the grand duke says. "One report says he's somewhere in Tunis. He could be as far as Morocco."

"Would Fayed help us?" Freddie looks to Rowan.

Prince Fayed Patel is a longtime friend and friendly rival of the king's.

Rowan shakes his head. "If we involve more people, he'll only sink further into hiding. We have to draw him out." He stands and walks around to the laptop. On the screen is the map of our region with little red points on all the possible locations.

"We have to give him what he wants."

Apart from money, Blix only wants two things, and one of them the king would never risk.

"What exactly do you mean?" I say, locking eyes with Rowan.

His brow lowers, and my stomach tightens. "We have to send Kass back. She can't stay at Occitan." I'm ready to fight this when he continues. "She won't be unguarded. We'll assign someone to watch her, but she has to appear to be on her own. It's the only way to break this holding pattern."

He's right. I know he's right, and I'm mad as fuck. "Let me do it."

Reggie leans back in his chair. "If you guard her, we might as well keep her at Occitan." My attention is diverted to him, and I realize he's in on the plan.

I look to Freddie, and his lips are pressed into a line. His eyes are trained on his computer screen.

Stepping back, I can't fight the rage firing in my chest. "You discussed this without me."

"It came up when we were discussing our options," Rowan says, his voice calm. He's attempting to placate me. "No one is going behind your back. You were working."

I haven't left Ava's watch since she came to Occitan. I tell myself it's my job. I'm simply doing what I've been assigned. Still, I haven't slept a night at my apartment in a week. I've eaten every meal, showered, and slept here. When Ava takes personal time with the king, when I would normally have my leave, I go to Kass.

She often falls asleep on the patio, and I watch her through the night. Her hair is spread behind her and the tension leaves her face. Those nights, it's difficult not to touch her, kiss her.

She likes to walk along the shoreline, and I follow her from afar. It's too chilly for swimming, so she pulls a pashmina tightly around her body. I ache to replace it with my arms, but I don't.

I believe her when she says she had no choice before, but I'm still angry she didn't tell me the truth. She's still vulnerable as long as Blix is a fugitive. So I maintain the distance. Only twice I've broken it. The last time nearly made me forget everything.

She reached for me, and I couldn't hold back. I stretched my hand out, almost daring her to find it. She did, and I held her in my lap, stroking her hair. My eyes closed and I remembered every night she'd slept in my bed with her face nestled against my chest, allowing me to care for her the way I always want to do. The Cassandra-shaped hole in my heart was momentarily filled, but even then she was guarded.

I want to tell her not to be ashamed or afraid because I already know everything, but if I do that, I'll remove the option for her to trust me. It's an important gesture I need from her. She has to meet me halfway. So I continue to wait.

Now Rowan is telling me to send her back into danger, and he won't even let me follow.

"I can't agree to this." My fists are clenched. "It's too risky. He could take her and disappear. If he captures her, he will hurt her. She betrayed him, and we've seen what he does to people who betray him."

Heat burns around my heart. Protective rage at the possibility of Blix touching her piques every muscle in my body.

"It's a risk we have to take, but we won't take it lightly," Rowan says.

"How will you guarantee she won't be hurt?" I've lost all vestiges of rank or subservience, but Rowan is not offended.

"Freddie has an idea for planting a tracking device under her skin. It would be a tiny chip emitting a GPS signal."

"Is it safe?" I look to Freddie.

"So far it's only been tested in animals." My stomach turns, but in his voice is the enthusiasm of trying out new technology. "Still, the results have been positive across the board."

I'm out of my chair, pacing the room. "This means you'll tell her she's to be used as bait?" It's ironic, considering the man's preferred method of torture.

Reggie's bored tone enters the conversation. "Of course not." He lifts a small vial containing what looks like a tiny SIM card. "We'll inject it beneath her skin under the guise of being a vaccination of some sort."

"So you'll lie to her."

"For her own protection."

I don't like it. I stand and go to the window, clenching my jaw and thinking of all the arguments against this plan. The second hand on the large clock in the back of the room ticks low and loud as the room falls silent. When I turn to face them again, three pairs of eyes are on me.

Again my body is tight. "What do you want me to do?"

"Give her a reason to leave," Reggie says flatly. "Ideally, to leave and return to her previous occupation."

My stomach roils and my voice rises. "Let me get this straight. You don't want her to go home. You want her to go to Blix. The man who we're pretty sure was ready to kill her at their last meeting?"

"Not necessarily go to him. But perhaps be open to contact from him," Reggie speaks slowly, as if I'm too thick to understand. I want to pop him in the mouth. "She cooperated with him before because she thought she'd lost everything. Perhaps if she feels that way again—"

"No." I cut him off. Anger is burning in my veins. "I won't do it. We can send her out, but I won't hurt her. She's been hurt enough."

"Just think about it. If she ignores his calls, we won't have any way of tracking him. We need her to talk to him, help us draw him out."

The grand duke always has a twisted approach to capturing suspects. I think back to his idea for luring

Wade Paxton, the prime minister who wanted to assassinate Rowan. From a certain angle, his methods work, but as long as I've been in the picture, there's always been collateral damage. I think of Ava being shot, Zelda being kidnapped...

"You're assuming she will accept his calls." My tone is sharp. "I'm not convinced anything would make her go back to that life."

"It's worth a try," Freddie says quietly. "We won't lose track of her. If he somehow does take her, we're never more than five minutes away."

I don't like their level of certainty. I don't like that they're willing to dangle her like a fish on a line hoping to jerk her back before the shark devours her.

Rowan steps forward. "Let us have a moment." Freddie and the duke rise at the king's command. When the door closes behind them, he turns to me. "Your concern in this case seems more than professional."

"Your majesty," I do a slight bow. "I'm sorry. I just... I can't agree with this, not after what happened last time."

"Because you're in love with her."

I can't answer. I won't lie to him, but I'm not ready to own these feelings just yet—not after what she did. Instead I go to that damn window. The view is of a line of cliffs curving around the sea. Whitecaps are visible below, and it's a majestic view of our small country.

"I know this is asking a lot—more than I'm willing to risk." Rowan's voice is quiet, calm. "However, after our success in Tortola, I have the utmost confidence in this team, in you." His tone turns grave. "We have to stop this madman before he strikes us again."

He's thinking of the threat to Ava. I can only think of Kass. Ava at least is protected by his hunger for money. Kass has nothing to keep her safe.

Except one thing. "I have to be the one to guard her. It's the only way I'll agree."

"How long have you known Cassandra?"

I'm uncomfortable opening up, but in this case, I overcome my innate reluctance. "We met before I joined the guard. She was the last person… she's been a memory ever since."

"And now he's using her against you."

"He tried." Our eyes meet, steel against steel. "I know his game now. I won't let him succeed at it."

"You cannot be detected or we'll lose everything."

"I won't."

The king nods. "Do what you have to do."

## Chapter 17: Leaving

*Kass*

*Hiraeth: Longing for home.*
    Occitan is a beautiful place. I love the proximity of the beach. The royal life is elegant and luxurious, and I have everything I could ever want. Ava is charming, and we're becoming friends, which is strange but nice. She's warm and funny and unexpectedly edgy...
    And I want to go home.
    I'm one step up from being a prisoner in this plush holding cell. I go from day to day walking along the beach, talking to Ava, waiting... always waiting for the men to say they've found Blix and tell me my fate.
    They watch me, and I know most of them don't trust me. Ava has decided to forgive me based on her past indiscretions. I'm not in chains, so the king must agree with her. Logan is never far away, but despite what he says, he holds himself apart. No one else is allowed or wants to get close.
    I think about Cameron. I think about rebuilding my life. In the time I've spent here, I've thought about what I could do to make amends and how I might find a job that would make me useful. I worked as a waitress before things went bad, and I do speak several languages. I've lived in America. Perhaps I could get a job as a translator. Or maybe I could teach blind children. I could embrace my life as it is now without having to worry my weakness will be exploited. I have

dreams... I know I can be something better, something good.

The only thing that makes me hesitate is the thing that will break my heart. If I leave Occitan, I'll say goodbye to Logan. It paralyzes me. It holds me in this fancy prison, and freezes my insides when I try to go. Even with this distance between us, being here and knowing he's close gives me strength. It gives me hope for a life where I'm not only good, I'm happy. Is it to much to wish for?

He held me last time so close in his arms. He wanted me to talk, but I couldn't find the words. He said I was his, and it was a little piece of heaven. If I go... the next time I reach for him, I'll find nothing. Can I face that? Alone in the dark?

Sitting on this patio chair, my mind drifts to my tiny apartment. I wouldn't be entirely alone. I'd have my brother. Cameron and I have texted a few times. His security detail is apparently keeping him safe. He's well and even seeing someone.

Luc and Henri must have noticed I'm gone, and while Luc might not care, I'm sure Henri misses his daily pets and treats from whatever store I've visited that day. I do have a small world outside this place. I have to be strong enough to return to it and start over.

"Here you are!" Ava cuts through my melancholy reflection. She dashes out onto the patio and grabs my arm, pulling me to my feet. "Come meet my sister!"

My heart stops. "She's here?"

"She's on Skype."

Digging in my feet, I pull my arm out of her grip. "No... I can't, Ava."

"What?" She catches my wrist again. "You'll love her. You're so much alike!"

I pull back again. "Blix kidnapped her and hurt her. I worked for him. She's not going to want to see me. Or if she does…" She'll hate me.

We stand for a moment facing each other. I hear the change in her breathing. "You're wrong," she says, touching my hand. "Forgiveness is a gift. The bigger the gift, the more you're willing to share it."

"I don't know what that means."

"It means you've both made mistakes, but they're in the past."

I'm tired and sad, and I don't feel like arguing. I only shake my head. My past is too close to the present.

She takes my arm again. "At least come and see my baby niece. She's adorable."

Reluctantly, I follow her into the house. "You forget I can't see," I grumble.

We cross the large living area to the smaller office in the back corner. I've clicked my way around this place enough to have a good feel for the layout, and while I might classify the office as "smaller," it's much larger than my tiny apartment.

We're about to enter when a male voice intercepts us. "Excuse me, your highness."

"What is it, Freddie?" Ava tries to keep going, but he stops her.

"The king asked for you."

"Oh…" She lets out a sigh and touches my hand. "Would you tell Zee I'll be right back?"

"Of course."

The two leave me alone, and I hear the happy echoes of voices inside. I start to enter until Logan's voice stops me. Why is he here?

"She's grown," he says, an undeniable warmth in his tone.

"She misses you." The female voice on the computer is equally warm. It sparks an uncomfortable, sick feeling in the pit of my stomach. "She says *Ga*. You know what that means?" Her voice goes to a breathy sing-song. "You're looking for Logan, aren't you?"

"Your majesty—" he begins, but she interrupts him.

"Just because you're in Monagasco, nothing has changed."

My throat tightens at that. What does she mean, *nothing has changed*?

"It's true." He sounds... guilty? I don't understand.

"Then no more of this *ma'am* and *your majesty* business. It's Zee and Logan. Yes?"

A brief pause, before he answers, and I hear him smile. "Always."

The tiny voice squeals. "See? She misses you!" Zelda says, and he laughs.

"I think she does."

"Please come and visit us soon."

"I'll see what I can do." Logan's voice is loving and warm. It reminds me of how he sounded those few heavenly days I was in his arms... before I hurt him. Before I lost him.

I have to get out of here.

"I'm back!" Ava calls, passing me at the door and quickly running toward the voices.

The sisters squeal and laugh and make all sorts of baby noises. Ava's niece responds with cute little coos and attempts at saying words.

I'm standing in the doorway dying inside. A knot is in my throat and it twists into a ball of sadness and loss in my stomach.

I can't take anymore. Ava is wrong. They're all wrong. Logan is clearly in love with this woman and her baby, and I'm only a cheap substitute. I'm a damaged version of the clever, smart survivor they all love and miss. I'm the rotten apple, and I've got to go before I ruin everything.

Unshed tears sting in my eyes as I flee. Using my hands and my memory, I navigate my way through the living room, headed to the kitchen and the small bedroom where I spent my first night here. All the clothes and sweaters I've worn over the last several days were borrowed. I'll have to wear this outfit home, but I can return it once I have my own things.

"You're here!" Nesbit startles me when I enter the kitchen. "I believe the king wanted to see you. Stay here while I fetch him."

I freeze in place, nerves tingling. I can't imagine why Rowan would want to see me. I don't have permission to leave. Perhaps he'll say I have to stay. Then my prisoner status will be confirmed. "Of course."

She leaves the room, and I wait wondering, listening to the noise of an oven fan, a pot boiling on the stove. The kitchen smells like tea and nutmeg. She's baking some kind of spiced bread, possibly pumpkin.

Voices appear in the passage, and I spin toward them. "Ah, Cassandra." It's a voice I've only heard one other time.

"Grand duke," I say, stepping back to curtsey.

"Yes, we can dispense with the formalities. The king can't make it right away, but you remember Freddie?"

"Miss Kroft," Logan's friend is beside Reggie. He was with Logan the night they found me.

"Did I do something wrong?" I can only see their shapes, looming over me in the hazy kitchen.

"No," Reggie says. He pauses as if choosing his words, "We don't' want to alarm you, but it seems you might have been exposed to a peculiar strain of virus while you were in Miami. The news has been filled with precautions about it, and considering your close proximity to the queen—"

"A virus?" Of all the things these men could have said, that was not what I expected.

"It's a nasty thing. Attacking babies," Reggie continues. "However, we've been able to get our hands on the vaccine for it. Would you mind if Freddie here gives you a quick inoculation? It should only take a second, and you'll be all set."

My head is spinning. I want to leave, and he's talking about me being sick? Babies? "Is Ava pregnant?" I can't help frowning.

"Not that I'm aware, but all women of childbearing age..." Reggie is holding my arm. "It will protect you as well."

"I'm not planning to get pregnant," I say, my lapse in birth control drifting through my mind. It's followed closely by the only person I ever want touching me that way... and the painful idea I've lost him forever. If I even had him at all.

"You can never be too careful." Reggie grasps my upper arm.

Instinctively, I try to pull away from him. "Will it hurt?"

"It shouldn't," Freddie says, touching my shoulder. The grand duke releases my arm, and my anxiety eases. Freddie is somehow gentler. "It needs to go in your hip."

"I'll stay out here," Reggie says.

I don't like this. I feel like I'm being ambushed, but I don't know how to escape it. I don't want to make Ava sick. "We can go in my room."

Freddie follows me inside, and I stop in front of the narrow cot. I don't know why the small space is comforting to me. Perhaps with the world so large and virtually unknowable, having a tiny area where everything is familiar gives me peace.

"Feel this," Freddie says, taking my hand. He places my fingers on a cool, metal gunlike device. "It will be quick and hopefully painless. Okay?"

"Okay." I appreciate his kindness, and I unfasten the button of my jeans, sliding the side down a bit.

The cold metal presses against my skin, and my insides squeeze. My heart beats a little faster and I hold my breath. No matter how brave I am, nothing is worse than the half-second before a shot.

A flush of air and a pinch at my side. "Ow!" I cry out of surprise… or habit.

Freddie's dark head pops into my peripheral vision. "Did that hurt?" He's scrutinizing my expression.

I give him an embarrassed smile. "Not really. I'm sorry."

"Good." He leans down and seems to be examining the site. "I can't see a thing," he says as if to himself. He takes a moment and I'm pretty sure he's doing something with his phone. "Yes…" he mutters.

"So, no Band-Aid, no sucker?" My voice is a little more sarcastic than I intend. All of this has me feeling like a lab rat, and I'm still miserable about Logan.

He only laughs. "Sorry. Fresh out."

My pants are fastened, and I straighten my shirt when hear him start for the door. I make a quick decision to stop him.

"Freddie?" He pauses, and I can tell he's facing me. "Can I ask you... Am I allowed to leave?"

He's quiet several seconds, and I hold my breath. I'm Blix's accomplice. They're not going to let that go. Bracing myself, I'm ready for him to laugh in my face. Instead, his voice is thoughtful.

"What are you planning to do?"

"I'd like to return to my apartment. Can I do that?"

I don't hear any noise of texting or gesturing to unseen company lurking around my door. Yes, as much as I hate to admit it, being blind does limit me in certain ways. It forces me to trust people I barely know.

"It might be dangerous," he says.

"I know. Still... I have to take that chance. I can't stay here. I have to try and start a new life."

He takes a few steps to the side as if he's thinking, considering my statement. "Aren't you afraid?"

"Yes." My voice doesn't waver. "But I don't belong here. I miss my family."

He releases a sigh and crosses to where I'm standing. "You're not a prisoner. If you want to leave, no one will stop you."

"Really?" *Can it be that easy?*

"The queen regent vouched for you. She won't allow any criminal charges to be brought against you." His tone is academic, as if he's sorting out a problem, and I try to understand this gift. I think about what Ava said earlier about forgiveness. "Are you planning to betray her trust?"

His question brings me up short. "Of course not! I would never do that." He has no idea how much I mean those words. "I hope I never see... or *encounter* Blix again."

"Here." Freddie catches my wrist and places something on my palm. My fingers close over it, and I recognize the item at once. It's my old holster. Only, it's no longer empty.

"A dagger?"

"I don't like giving you a weapon," he says. "I'm afraid it will be taken and used against you. Still, you had this when we found you. I assume it means you know how to use it."

My fingers move to the top, and I feel the hard metal of the handle. "Thank you," I say softly.

"Good luck, Kass." He leaves without another word, and I wait, allowing the sensation of freedom to wrap around my shoulders.

I slip the tiny weapon into the waistband of my jeans.

It's time to move.

Holding my oversized phone a millimeter from my face, I locate the symbol for my Uber app and select my old address.

* * *

Stepping out of the car on the narrow street, I feel like a lifetime has passed since I've been here. It's all so familiar, but I've changed. I'm out in the open, honest and free — for whatever that's worth. I'm terrified, but I have to take this step.

I walk to the door of my apartment and locate the buzzer. It's not too late to let Luc know I'm back, and I buzz the familiar rhythm we've worked out to let each other know it's us. The code was actually Luc's idea. He'd forgotten his key once, and I'd buzzed him in without even thinking. It was my first day here, when I was still working with Blix, and I knew my boss was the worst thing I had to fear.

Luc had yelled at me. He'd stated the obvious—I'm blind—and went on to lecture me in French about rapists and thieves and gypsies. He'd emphasized it was more his safety he was worried about than mine, then he dragged me downstairs and we agreed on a special "top secret" sequence of buzzes that only he and I would use. Once I'd done it correctly and agreed not to open the door for strangers ever again, he stomped up the narrow staircase and returned to his apartment, slamming the door.

It was the longest conversation we'd ever shared.

Nothing has changed tonight. The door releases as soon as I've finished with our secret code. I step inside the dim entrance and squint into the hazy fog out of habit. I can't see anything in this amount of light.

Still... I'm waiting, hoping...

Another second passes...

*Click click click*, the sound of nails on hardwoods sketches up above. Tears sting my eyes.

"Henri?" I call, and I'm rewarded with a happy staccato of short barks. "Henri!"

I grasp the rail and jog up the stairs. When I get to the top, I slide into sitting, and the husky little terrier is on my lap.

Immediately, he sticks his tongue in my mouth, and I laugh. "So French!"

I catch his muzzle and move it away. He proceeds to lick the salty tears from my cheeks. I get a warm swipe of dog-tongue in the eye, and I squeal. In his happiness, he's moving too fast for me to catch him. The result is I'm covered in Henri slobber.

Leaning down, I hug his wagging body. "Je vous ai manqué," I say. *I've missed you.*

Our reunion is cut short by the noise of Luc's door opening. He calls his pet home, and at once the little dog pulls away, headed back to his master. I sit listening to him click across the hardwoods until the wooden door closes.

No word for me.

No surprise.

"Maybe I'll get a dog," I say, pushing off my knees and going to my door. I wonder what Henri would think of that.

Reaching up, I slide my fingers along the doorframe until I find my spare key. My apartment is also the same as when I left it, and I try to remember that night. Logan had walked me to my door after blowing my mind in the alley. The memory makes my stomach hurt.

He'd told me not to leave. He'd told me to be here in the morning. I left without even saying goodbye. Twice.

Going to my dresser, I slide the top drawer open and feel around inside for my nightshirt. I lift the thin sweater I'm wearing over my head and fold it carefully. Ava said it's white, and it's so soft and delicate, I can only imagine it's super expensive. Holding the furniture, I pull off the tall boots, and finally, I peel off the skinny jeans she gave me. I'm not sure if she wants them back, but I don't want to keep anything without permission, not even boots.

I reach around and unfasten my bra, deciding I'll keep the underwear. I'm sure there would be no misunderstanding about that. Our entire building shares heat, so my room isn't cold. I stand for a moment and slide my palms over my breasts. In the quiet, I remember Logan's mouth against my skin, the scruff of his beard against my nipples. They harden, and I slide my thumbs over them. Heat floods my panties, and I lower my arms, wrapping them around my waist.

"I did have you," I whisper to the air. "For a little while you were mine again." It was only a moment, but I believe it with all my heart.

Going to the bed, I push through the cool sheets and curl into a ball. With my eyes closed, I can see his broad shoulders. My fingers tingle with the memory of his chest dusted with coarse, sparse hair. It's painful and miserable, and I miss him so much.

I can only blame myself. I could have trusted him that last night if I hadn't been afraid. I wasn't only afraid, though. I was ashamed, and I couldn't share my guilt with him. I didn't want him to see me for what I had become, and now his warmth is turned away from me. Now she has it.

Pain like a knife pierces my stomach. I've only ever loved Logan Hunt. His dark hair and steel blue eyes, his cocky grin… that tall, lean physique that ran by me on the beach that day six years ago… he's lived in my memory so long, and he's only gotten better since we were apart. Now he's broad shoulders and massive arms. He lifts me as if I'm a doll, and he's so focused and commanding. The boy I fell in love with has turned into a man I can't live without. I don't know how I'll ever let him go…

*Then don't.*

The words appear like lights in the darkness. I don't know yet what that means, but I know he's here. As long as he's here, I have a chance.

"I still love you, Logan Hunt," I whisper into the darkness, closing my eyes.

## Chapter 18: Watching

*Logan*

I fucking hate this.

I barely even remember having feelings for Zelda, and I'm standing in Ava's office talking to her on Skype as if nothing has changed.

Granted, it's not all acting. I do care about Belle and I miss carrying her around the island. She's a beautiful little baby, and I can only dream that one day I might be lucky enough to have that for myself. With Kass.

The distance between guards and the royal family was much closer in the West Indies, but since I've reunited with Kass, I realize my feelings for Zelda were a clear redirect, a longing for something I'd lost. My mind drifts to images of Kass's body changing, her belly growing round with my baby, and I want it so much.

I want the woman currently standing behind me in the doorway listening to every word I say. It's tearing me up inside, but I focus on the infant with a halo of blonde curls just learning to recognize the faces that love her.

"Please come and visit us soon," Zelda says to me.

The warm breeze moves her blonde hair across her face, and she pushes it away. The baby pats her mother's cheeks with chubby hands, and I can see the crystal waters behind them. I'd love to share that happy place with Kass, show her she has nothing to fear.

Belle lunges forward against her mother's mouth. It makes me smile. "I'll see what I can do" is all I say.

I hear it the moment Kass leaves. She bumps against the doorframe before practically sprinting from the room. My jaw clenches because I know she can't see what's happening here. I know all she can hear are our words and the way we say them.

I fucking hate this.

I say a quick goodbye and leave just as Ava joins us, launching into an animated chat with her sister. I follow at a distance, not wanting Kass to know I'm right behind her. Reggie convinced the rest of the team it would compromise her less if she didn't know we're using her for bait. I think that plan is as wrong-headed as it can be.

Kass is strong and tough. She can play a part. I should know. We could tell her what we're doing. Instead, I'm being forced to hurt her in this shitty way. I know we're not together at the moment, but dammit. We were making our way back.

Now it's all shot to hell.

She's supposed to think I've moved on.

Mission accomplished.

I linger outside the kitchen listening to Reggie and Freddie's story about Zika virus. They don't name it, but they basically describe all the symptoms. It's not a completely far-fetched lie. Cases of the virus have been detected in Florida, but if Kass had the disease, we'd know by now.

Reggie exits the small room first and gives me an approving nod. He might be the king's great uncle, but I've wanted to punch him in the face for going on eighteen months now. He's not helping his case.

Freddie takes several minutes longer to emerge, and when he does, he catches my arm and pulls me deeper into the house, away from Kass's room.

"Give me your phone." I fish in my pocket and hand it to him.

He spends a few moments pecking on the screen while I wait, watching. Finally he hands it back to me. "There she is."

I look down at the device, and on the screen is what looks like a common map of the city with overlapping red, blue, and yellow dots flashing right near the shore, right where Occitan is located.

"Which one is Kass?"

"All three." He smiles with the pride of a techno geek. "We're tracking the GPS in her phone, which is the red dot. The blue one is a bug I slipped into her purse, and the yellow is the chip I just injected right below her skin."

My eyebrows shoot up, and I confess I feel an enormous weight lifted off my shoulders. "You've got her covered," I say.

"And you're determined to be there in person." He pats me on the arm. "I'd say the chances of us losing track of Cassandra Kroft are slim to none."

All three dots start to move, and my eyes flick to Freddie's. "Where is she going?"

"I told her she could leave."

Even with all this technology, his words send a blast of panic through my insides. "Have we checked her apartment? Is it clean?"

I'm moving fast to my room, Freddie's right behind me. "We can get someone there ahead of her. The guys watching her brother are the closest."

"Jesus, Freddie!" I snap. "What the hell. You should have told her she had to stay another night. Tell

Ava goodbye or anything."

"She was ready. If I'd told her to stay, she might have changed her mind."

It was the fucking Skype call that did it. My stomach twists hard, and I'm ready to punch all these assholes who don't love her like I do. To them she's a bridge to a goal, but to me she is the goal. She's all I want.

"Call the guys. Tell them to do a quick sweep, but let them know I'm on the way. If they need backup, I'm less than five minutes out."

"What about Ava?" Freddie calls as I grab the keys to my bike off the small table in my bedroom. "You're assigned to guard the queen regent."

"Rowan changed my assignment when he decided to use Kass as bait."

"I'll tell him you said that."

At this point, I don't give a shit. I'm shooting out in the night on my bike, doing my best to beat that fucking Uber to Kass's apartment. In the front of my mind is that stairway and the old man who didn't even care that he let me walk right into the building that first day. If Blix has anybody watching her place, she's as good as captured within the first twenty-four hours.

I have to cut the speed considerably as I maneuver my way through the narrow city streets. My only comfort is I'm pretty far ahead of the Uber, and Freddie said he'd send the boys from Cameron's watch over to check out the place. I don't like leaving her brother unguarded, but I won't risk anything happening to Kass.

It's after eleven when I pull the bike into that same alley where we'd been together that last night. The rain has left everything wet and smelling of copper and water. The air is cool, and the dampness makes it even cooler. There's no moon tonight, but I can still see Kass's beautiful body arched against my chest in the dim light of the alley. My hands covered her small breasts, thumbs circling, moving down her smooth skin. Moonlight glistened off her hair, and she was just so fucking mine. I have to shake the memory away and focus.

Checking my phone, I see the three dots are five blocks away. My bike is hidden in the dark alley, and I pause, unsure if I want to chance going to the front door. Blix has had long enough to recognize Rex and Stefano, the two guys watching Cam.

If they're keeping tabs on us at all, they won't think twice about them coming here to check on Kass's place. My appearance, however, moves her return to a whole new level. It gives everything away. Yes, I get now why Rowan doesn't want me here, but I'll be damned if I trust Kass's safety to anyone else.

I open the app and type a quick text to Stefano: *I'm in the alley. She's getting close. Finished the sweep?*

Pacing the narrow space by my bike, I wait for his reply. It doesn't take long.

*The place is clean. We're heading out the fire escape.*

I walk all the way to the back of the alley, where it ends in a wooden fence that would otherwise open onto the next block. Looking up, I can't see them, but I hear the groaning of metal and the crash of a ladder rolling up. Two sets of shoes click on the damp pavement, growing more faint as the guys blend into the night.

Walking to the front of the alley again, I'm only mildly appeased. All of this is happening too fast. I haven't had time to process what we're doing. I didn't have time to plan. I'm pissed that I was left out of the discussion, but I'm even more pissed I didn't get to see her once more before she left.

The hum of a car engine sounds on the street out front. I pull up the app, and sure enough, the three dots are right with me. My chest squeezes, and I place a finger on top of them. She's here. Leaning against the wall, I rub one hand down my face, pushing back on regret. I have to be here for her now. If this scheme works, none of that shit will even matter.

She walks slowly to her door, no doubt letting the car disappear. Her keys weren't on her when we found her in the villa. I'm not sure how she'll get inside. I slide to the front of the alley, pressing my back against the wet wall. She's pressing the buzzer. Seconds pass and the lock clicks loudly. He didn't even ask her to identify herself.

Now I'm really pacing. She could have been anybody just then, and from this distance, I wouldn't have time to catch an intruder before he was on the other side of that door. Without hesitating, I dash to the wooden fence. It's sheer planes with nothing to serve as a foothold or provide assistance getting over it. Stepping back, I leap, grasping the top of the boards. The wood cuts into my palms, but I use all my upper body strength, swinging my legs to the side and pulling myself over the barrier.

My muscles burn and my palms are bloody when I make it to the other side, but I'm unable to care. The fire escape is my next obstacle to overcome. The ladder has retracted three meters over my head. Pushing my wounded hands in my pockets, I walk up a block, looking around for anything I can use to pull that ladder down. It's late enough that most of the businesses are closed. I'm two blocks up when I come across a florist shop with a ladder propped in the alley along the side of the building. It's not ideal, but I'll take what I can get.

Pressing my back against the wall, I look down the street where I came. Only streetlights shine in rainbow puddles on the pavement. Grabbing the metal ladder, I hustle back to the fire escape. Once I'm on the landing, I kick the ladder back and aside, doing my best to hide it in the shadows.

It's only a two-story building, which makes it easy for me to access her room. Again, it's too easy. Anyone could do this, get here, hurt her... Without making a sound, I creep to the small window outside her bedroom and drop low, sitting in the dark shadows.

Her interior lights are off, and the streetlight silhouettes her body as she stands in front of her dresser. I watch as she reaches around and unfastens her bra. It falls away, and I have to swallow the lump in my throat as her lovely breasts are revealed.

"Kass," I whisper, just as I realize the window is lifted a quarter.

My breath stills, and I wait to see if she heard me. She never responds, and I let out a slow exhale. Her hands cover her small breasts, and she tilts her beautiful head to the side. I imagine my lips touching the skin just behind her ear. She would shiver in response. I would replace her hands with mine, caressing her breasts and tweaking her beaded nipples.

Her fingers would thread in my hair as her back arched against my chest. I know her so well. The light touches her fair hair, her dark lashes, and I see she's been crying. It twists that old pain in my stomach.

"I did have you," she says, the longing in her voice palpable. "For a little while you were mine again."

My eyes scan the space, and it's empty. *Who is she speaking to?*

She turns and goes to the bed, pushing through the sheets in only her panties. I want to meet her body between those sheets and hold her through the night. I watch her a few moments longer. I want to be sure she's asleep before I slip into her room to spend the night. I'm just about to enter when her voice touches me once more like a brand.

"I still love you, Logan Hunt."

Tightness seizes my throat, and it takes all my willpower not to answer. My lips are sealed, but my heart aches. I've never wanted to be free so badly. I could take her away from this place. We wanted to go to Campania…

My head is in my hands as I wait. Minutes like hours drift by and eventually I hear her breathing level out. I reach out and push the window open all the way, slipping through it into her bedroom. I'll crouch against the far corner out of her line of traffic and out of any chance of detection. I'll stay until dawn, when I'll slip out again.

"I still love you, Cassandra Kroft."

## Chapter 19: Explanations

*Kass*

*Close your eyes.*
*Fall in love.*
*Stay there.*
*~Rumi*

Logan's thumb slides across the line of my jaw. My eyes are closed, and his face is so close to mine, our noses touch. The heat from his lips causes mine to throb. His rich, masculine scent is all around me, and I know he's here. It's so intimate and perfect, my entire body lights up like a flare. I never want to open my eyes.

BAM BAM BAM! I bolt upright in my bed with a little squeal, dream shattered.

"Kass? Are you in there?" It's Ava. She's outside my door banging on it. "Kass! Let me in!"

I'm only wearing panties. "Hang on!" I shout, sliding out of my bed and grabbing a shirt from my middle drawer. What the hell is she doing here?

The long-sleeved Henley is over my head, and I swipe a pair of boxers off the floor. Pausing a moment, I turn my head around the room. It's bright from the morning sun, and I don't detect anything out of place. Still, his scent... It seems like...

I shake my head. "Vivid dream," I say.

Logan isn't here. Although, if Ava's outside... Quickly, I rake my fingers through my hair, hoping it doesn't look like a bird's nest. I slide the chain and twist the dead bolt open.

"Ava?"

Her voice is exasperated and she storms into my tiny apartment. "You totally disappeared! Worse—you ran off without even saying goodbye!"

She's fills my room like a glamorous tornado, and my mind scrambles for an explanation. I can't tell her the real reason I left—I couldn't bear watching the man I love falling for her superhero sister.

"I missed my brother," I stammer. "I missed my things... and my neighbor's dog, and I just... Freddie said I wasn't a prisoner."

For a moment, I wait for her answer. She takes a few steps around my tiny studio apartment. "I'm sorry you felt that way." She sounds hurt, and I feel awful, considering what else Freddie said about her not pressing charges. "I thought we were having fun. I didn't want you to feel like a prisoner, but you were sort-of... being watched. And protected."

I nod. "I know. I don't mean to be ungrateful—"

"Don't put it like that," she huffs, dropping onto my bed. "That makes it sound so formal—like we weren't even friends."

Pressing my front teeth together, I try to think of the right words. "It was a strange setup from the start. You know this."

"My whole life is strange," she sighs. "I don't even notice anymore."

Walking toward the sound of her voice, I take a seat beside her on the bed. I chew my lip a moment. "I've never really had a close female friend. I started working right out of school, and then my eyes... and then my aunt... I guess I'm not very good at this."

We're both quiet, and the noise from the street below echoes through my window. Vendors shout at deliverymen, and metal chairs scrape across flagstone pavements as the cafés set up for business.

"I've always just had Zee," she says. "I'm not very good at this either."

"No, you're great," I argue.

"But you were uncomfortable."

I can't argue with that. I'm not even really sure what I'd say other than it wasn't her fault. "I have an idea." Standing, I walk to the dresser and pick up my phone. "Remember how much you wanted me to meet your sister? I'd like you to meet my little brother."

"The musician?" She's looking up at me, curiosity in her voice.

"He's playing tonight at this little club down by the water—the Café Steele?"

"I've heard of it!" She stands then and walks to where I'm standing. "What time? I can meet you there."

"He usually goes on at ten."

We step to the door, which I realize now is still open. Ava strides out onto the landing, pausing just before she descends.

"What are you going to do today?"

I take a few steps in the direction of her voice, although I can't see anything in the hallway in this light. "I thought I'd see about finding a job."

"Let me know if I can help you." I hear her descending the staircase, and I reach out to place my hand on the bannister. Instead my fingers collide with what feels like a warm wall of granite covered in soft cotton.

"Oh!" I start to pull it away, but two larger ones I recognize at once cover it. "Logan..."

He doesn't speak. He only lifts my hand, pressing his lips against the back of my fingers just below my knuckles. My stomach tightens. His scent of clean ocean breezes, warm fires, and him is all around me. I recognized it in my room earlier, only now I can't remember if that was before or after Ava entered. Of course, he would be with her. I want to say more. I want to say anything to make him stay, but he releases me, heading down the stairs after his royal charge.

I'm still at my door, and I lean my head against the jamb. The downstairs door closes with a metallic slam, and my eyes close with it. My dream floods my memory, and I can't wait for tonight.

\* \* \*

The day passes quickly with me spending the entire time searching for jobs I might be able to perform. Most of the hotels are seeking maids and housekeepers, but that's no good.

"I can't see dirt," I mutter.

The Boulangerie down the block needs an experienced seller, and I wonder how well I can trust my fingers to differentiate between a cinnamon twist and a marble rye... or a donut versus a bagel.

"I can at least smell the difference," I say to my computer screen, which is practically touching my nose, the text blown up to a zillion points. "Then again, I'm sure customers don't want my nose on their pastries."

Clicking toenails sound on the landing outside, and I hear a throaty little bark. Picking up my glass of water, I walk to the door and open it.

"You might as well come in and view the damage," I sigh, returning to my seat. Henri hops up in my lap and greets me with his usual tongue-kiss. "I'm going to catch you before you get me one of these days."

Letitia Rousseau (whoever she is) seeks a trilingual personal assistant. "Must speak French, Italian, and English," I read aloud to the dog, who immediately begins wagging his body. "Will manage the daily demands of the family trips, various reservations, administration…"

Henri hops down, and I rock back in my chair trying to imagine organizing a family. "I wonder how many little monsters Letitia has," I muse. Henri barks twice. "Well, if that's the case and it's mostly phone calls and logistics, I have all the necessary experience."

My phone starts to buzz, and I pick it up, holding it to my face to read the screen. It's my brother finally responding to my earlier text.

*Royal command performance?* He teases. *The place is crawling with security.*

*I see you're keeping rock star hours.* I tease right back. *What time?*

*I'm at the café now if you'd like to come on over.*

Dropping in my chair I pull up my clock. "Shit," I whisper, hopping out of the chair. "Time flies when you're having fun."

*See you soon*, I text back to Cam then scoot Henri out the door so I can shower and change.

It's dark and the streets are already filling with the usual, nightly revelers when I step out to meet my car. I'm wearing grey jeans and a black silk cami under my burgundy leather bomber. My glasses are back on my nose, even though they don't help much at night.

I texted Cameron on the way to the café, and the minute I step out, I'm surrounded by toned, lanky arms. "Where have you been?" he cries, lifting me off the ground slightly with his hug. I can't help a smile.

"I kind of got tied up," I say, not really wanting to give him the whole story. "It was a job."

"I was worried." His arm is around my neck, and he escorts me into the bar. The doorman says something, and I feel him wave. "I don't like it when you disappear without a word."

"Sorry." I give him a nudge in the ribs. "From what I understand, you were pretty occupied the whole time anyway."

"Only briefly. Here," he stops at a high table. "I reserved this one for you and your disruptive guest. Half the crowd is undercover guards."

"I'm expanding your audience."

"So you're saying I'll get new fans out of this?"

"Only if you're good."

"I'm always good." A kiss to my cheek and he takes off in the direction of the stage.

I press my lips into a smile, thinking how I can't regret a thing when it comes to him. I'll do whatever it takes to shield him from my bad choices.

"Can I get you a drink?" A female is at the table, and I try to decide if I'll risk alcohol tonight.

I wonder if Cameron's security detail is somewhere nearby and who they might be. I'm jolted with the sudden thought, Do they have a guard on me? Why didn't I consider this before?

"Miss?"

"Oh!" I snap out of my light bulb moment. "Just a coke for now, thanks."

She disappears, and I move my head as if looking around. No dice. I can't see anything once the sun goes down.

A loud murmur moves through the room, and the flash of cameras registers in my limited vision. Within seconds, I know what's happening.

"I love this place," Ava says, joining me at the high table. She slides her arm around my waist in a hug before climbing onto a chair beside me.

"You made it!" I say, trying to calm my racing pulse. Logan is somewhere around here. I wonder if he'll join us at the table, and I try not to care.

"I love that jacket," she says, running a finger down my sleeve.

I pull back, unable to resist. "Hands off, thief."

"Rude!" she laughs.

Just as fast she catches my wrist, placing my tiny wallet on my palm. My jaw drops. "You're completely corrupt."

She only laughs more. "When I hugged you. I was testing your extrasensory abilities. I have to say, you failed."

"That's a myth. Blind people don't have any special powers. We just notice things differently than sighted people."

Warmth approaches from my right, and I know at once who's standing behind me. "I'll be in the back corner behind the bar," he says, and my heartbeat quickens.

"We'll be here," Ava calls happily and orders a glass of champagne when the waitress reappears. Leaning against my shoulder, her lips touch my ear as she coos. "Your little brother is hot."

I'm so distracted trying not to think of Logan being somewhere in the shadows behind the bar, I almost don't even register.

"What?" I blink back to my royal guest. "Oh! Cameron. He was always a cute kid."

"I can't imagine not being able to see him." Her voice is sad, but I cut her off.

"No, you're right! I can see him in pictures on my phone. I just have to enlarge them."

The music starts, and it's impossible to hear each other. Cameron's band has gotten electric since the last time I heard him. It's louder and less acoustic, and from what I can tell, Cam's out front more now.

"I thought he played the guitar?" Ava shouts in my ear. I wince back from the ticklish vibration of her voice.

"He's not playing?" I shout toward her.

"Nope," she calls, pausing for a drink. "Just singing and prancing around being all sexy."

That makes me want to laugh. I slip off the stool and realize I need to visit the ladies. "Do you need to use the restroom?" I shout.

A prolonged pause while I wait, then she cries, "Oh! I shook my head." She makes an embarrassed sound. "No, I'm okay. Are you okay to go alone?"

"We're never really alone, are we?" I think of the guards all around us here.

"Very philosophical."

I do a little wave and follow the noise of voices and the echo of glasses toward the bar area. Once I arrive, I walk slowly along the perimeter of the busy area where patrons sit with their backs to me. I can tell by the changing of the sounds I'm approaching a more secluded corner. I realize too late I'm on a fool's errand, considering I'm not familiar with the layout of this place.

"Are you lost?" The deep voice stops me in my tracks.

My insides go liquid at the sound, and I swear I wasn't looking for him. *What you seek is seeking you* drifts through my mind.

"I thought I'd visit the ladies', but I realize I don't know where it is." I don't have to speak so loud in this part of the club. It's easier to hear, and when Logan answers me, he's smiling.

"I can show you the way," he says.

He covers my outstretched hand in both of his like earlier, and I can't move. I no longer have to use the restroom. I'm convinced the only thing I need right now is him.

"What's wrong?" He stops and steps toward me.

"I guess I don't have to go anymore."

I lift my other hand and my palm is flat against his firm torso. My fingers spread like a starfish over his lined stomach, and my breathing picks up. All I can think about is my dream, last night, this morning. He kissed my hand. *Perhaps I haven't lost him?*

"Logan?" I tilt my head toward where I think his face should be.

He doesn't answer. He only touches the side of my jaw with the pad of his thumb. My eyes blink slower as a wave of longing begins from that contact point and ripples over my shoulders, down my arms.

"I want to see the things worth seeing," I say, desire vibrating my bones.

We're in a back corner of a noisy bar but at that moment, we're in a place all our own. His thumb slides under my jaw and gives it a little lift at the same time he leans forward. Electricity pulses under my skin with every beat of my heart. My eyes flutter closed as his warm lips cover mine. His beard scuffs my cheek as our mouths open, and when our tongues touch, my knees give out. I grip the front of his shirt as his other arm quickly sweeps around my torso, lifting me against his chest.

A little moan aches from my throat as he backs me against the wall, and all of it, all the chemistry, every moment, every desire we've ever shared blazes from my head to my toes.

I reach up to thread my fingers in his soft hair, and his mouth breaks from mine, moving into my ear. "I've wanted to do that for days." His low voice vibrates to my core, and I can only nod. "You have to get back. I have to guard Ava."

I nod again. "I know." My voice is breathy and cracked.

Two large hands cup my cheeks. He leans down and kisses me twice more, pulling my lip between his teeth on the last time. I'm running my hands down the front of his shirt, feeling the ripple of muscles under the thin fabric. I want to be with him, but he's right, I have to go.

So many things I'm ready to tell him. I want to tell him everything, but it will have to wait. In a hazy, happy dream, I walk to where I left my friend. I'm a little wobbly, which makes me want to laugh, and when I arrive at our table, I notice the band has taken a break.

"What took you so long?" Ava says, as I slip onto the chair beside her. "Your lipstick is smeared. Here, let me help you."

She reaches over and touches the side of my chin. She does it again, then she pulls back. "It's not smeared... it looks like your skin is irritated. Did you eat something?"

Ducking my head, I have to swallow my laugh when I realize what she's seeing. "It's nothing." I prop my elbow on the table and drape my hand over my face where Logan's beard scuffed my skin.

"Anyway, I had hoped to meet your sexy little brother, but he seems to have disappeared."

"What?" I frown, sitting up straighter in my chair as if it helps me see better. It doesn't. "Where did he go?" Just then my phone buzzes. "Hang on. This is probably him," I say, pulling up the large device.

I hold it to my face expecting a quippy text from Cameron, but I almost drop it when my eyes register the words. It's Blix.

*Thank you for always being so useful. While you distracted your guard, Cameron took a ride with Taz. If you ever want to see him again, you will stay calm. Leave the bar, and wait for further instructions.*

"Uhh…" I can't form words. My eyes close, and I lower my forehead to my hand. Stay calm? How the hell can I manage that?

My phone is in my hand, but I can barely hold it. The club seems to move out as if I'm trapped in a horror movie with a vertigo lens pushing everything away from me.

"Kass?" Ava shouts. "What's wrong?"

I'm fighting to hold it together. I'm fighting to follow Blix's instructions. It's the only way I can save my brother now.

"I think I ate something bad." I slip off my stool and stagger back. I've got to get out of this place before I break down. "I don't feel well."

"Your face was red just a moment ago…"

"Yes," I decide to use it. "I'd better go home. I'll touch base with you tomorrow."

She's on her feet and holding my arm. "Let me help you. We can drive you there."

Leaving with her probably isn't a good idea. It will seem as though I'm telling them what happened. "It's okay. I paged an Uber. I can't cancel it."

"You did? When?"

"Just a moment ago."

"I didn't even see…"

I leave her speaking at the table and go the way I came. The door is in the center of the back wall, and I'm moving towards it as swiftly as possible without seeming suspicious.

He's done it. Blix has always known my weakness, and he struck tonight in this place to send me a message. Cameron will never be safe. Not anywhere. No matter how many people are around him, no matter how many guards. Blix can get to anyone at any time, and I was a fool to think I could protect him.

Once outside, I hail a cab. It draws close to the curb, and I dive inside, telling him my address. I'm at my apartment in less than ten minutes, jamming my key in the outer door and then dashing up the narrow staircase. My ears are roaring with panic. All I can see is Cameron bound and gagged. He'd be blindfolded to keep him from seeing anything. He'd be afraid, but he'd pretend to be brave.

"Oh, god," I cry, pausing halfway up the stairs.

Only then do I notice the barking. Henri is barking repeatedly from behind the door of Luc's apartment. It's not like him. It's not like Luc to keep him shut up when I return to our shared dwelling.

Stomach tight with fear, I run up the final steps, pausing when I reach my room and feeling around the doorframe for my key. It's missing, and I reach for the handle. The door isn't closed. It falls open with a creak, and I know something is wrong.

Pain streaks through my chest with every heartbeat. "Hello?" I say into the darkness.

"You made good time." The voice sends ice through my veins. "Come inside and shut the door."

I do as I'm told. I'm not about to cross Blix this late in the game. Not when he holds all the cards. "What do you want me to do?"

His laugh makes me wince. "Right. Don't waste any time. Cut to the chase."

"I want my brother back." It's less demanding and more explanatory. Why wait when Cameron could be anywhere being subjected to anything.

"I want what I've wanted from the beginning."

"Money?"

He steps around in my apartment. "Wade Paxton died owing me millions. I ran around doing his bidding like a fucking dog, and I'm not about to give up what I was promised."

*Stay calm, focused, in control.* "I don't know how I can help you with that."

He's across the room in my face before I've said my last word. I'm too late to stop a cry from slipping out of my throat. He's too fast for me to keep from cowering away.

"You can finish your assignment," he snarls right at my temple.

My insides are breaking. Now that I know Ava, there's absolutely no way I can make this choice. I'm Solomon facing the prospect of cutting a baby in half.

"Logan knows you used me to get to him," I say. "He'll never trust me again."

"He seemed to be trusting you just fine at the bar tonight."

"Chemistry and trust are not the same thing."

He grabs my arm in an angry pinch. "Don't make

me spell it out. Fucking use the chemistry to get what we need."

Tears are in my eyes as much from the physical pain as the thought of betraying my friends. "Then what? How will seducing Logan bring you Ava?"

That question buys me time. He steps away from me to the other side of my room. "Your position has changed."

I go to my dresser and open the top drawer. The knife Freddie gave me should be inside, still in its holster. I drop my arms and pretend to be discarding my accessories. I'll place my glasses in their holder and take out the dagger.

"You've become friends with the queen regent. She appeared at the café tonight on your request to see your brother."

"It's true," I say. My earrings are off, and I'm placing them in the small drawer. My muscles are tense. If only I could manage to kill him…

"Tomorrow I'll text you the location of a pickup point. Get her there, and we'll take her from you."

I'm only half listening. I'm feeling the slick wooden base of the drawer, sliding my fingers under my bras and panties. Blix is back at my side, jerking my upper arm away from my mission.

"Looking for this?" He spins me around, holding me secure. The blade of the knife I was seeking is cold against my cheekbone. Its razor-sharp tip touches the soft skin under my eye, and I cower away. "Stop being a fucking amateur, Kass. I trained you better than this."

He shoves me back, and I lose my balance. I fall all the way to the floor, and my back hits the wall so hard, an *Oof!* flies from my lips.

"Tomorrow. I'll tell you where to bring her. Alone."

"But—" I start to argue it's too soon. I have no way of guaranteeing I can get Ava away from the guards. Logan will never go for this.

"Logan can make the choice — Ava or you."

"He'd never choose me over her. He's sworn to protect her."

Blix's laugh is curt. "For the first time, I realize how blind you truly are."

Desperation has me by the throat. I don't know how to get out of this. "No," is all I can say.

"You'll do it, or you'll be collecting pieces of your brother from the Mediterranean."

I turn my head and press my eyes against the backs of my hands. My stomach is a ball of thorns, and I can't stop crying. The door slams, and all I can say is "No no no…" *Not Cameron!*

I hear every step Blix takes down those stairs, and when the metal outside door slams, I slide all the way down, resting my cheek against the cold hardwood.

I have no way out this time.

## Chapter 20: The First Move

*Logan*

I'm not aware Kass is gone until Ava finds me in the back of the bar. "We should leave," she says, and I go to where she's standing.

"Did you meet Cameron?"

She sighs and shakes her head. "He left. Kass left. Nobody knows what's happening."

My instincts hit red alert. "What do you mean nobody knows? Where are Rex and Stefano?" I push through the crowd in the direction of the table with Ava right behind me.

"Kass went to the bathroom and took forever to come back." She gives my lips a suspicious glance. "When she got back, her skin was red and blotchy."

I clear my throat. "What did she say?"

"She said she was having an allergy attack and left."

My brow knits. "That's it?"

"Well..." Ava is studying me, and I know she's smart. If I give anything away, she'll demand answers. Rowan will have my head. "Her brother disappeared mysteriously. Then she got a text."

"From who?" I'm headed to where Cameron's guards were stationed earlier with Ava right behind me. Rex is there alone, and I signal for him to come to me.

"I'm sorry, sir." He looks down. "Stefano had gone to the loo, and I... I was..."

"What were you doing?" My voice is lower, a bit more sinister.

"I looked away." He glances to the side where a busty redhead is swaying to the music. She looks over her shoulder and waves at us, and I have to fight my urge to grab him by the collar.

"Did anybody see anything?"

Stefano returns to where we're standing. He's breathless and sweat lines the dark hair at his temples. It's the one thing that brings me down a notch. He'd better be sweating.

"His band mate said one of the delivery guys needed help. Last he saw, Cameron was following a fellow out to a lorry."

"Why the hell would he do that?" Rex snaps. "He's the fucking front man for the band!"

If Cameron is captured, I have no idea what Kass will do to save him. This time panic squeezes my chest. "He's young and friendly. They could have told him anything." I can't waste time here. I've got to get to Kass. "See what you can find out about that truck. Report back to me or Freddie."

I turn and Ava's so close, I have to catch her arms. "Your majesty."

She arches an eyebrow, and I'm pretty sure she knows this is more than a casual situation. "I'll return to the palace with Hajib. See what you can find out and let me know."

"I'll escort you to the car."

Hajib has been a longtime driver for the royal family, and he easily doubles as a guard. He's thick and stocky and served in the Moroccan military.

A strobe of camera flashes blind us as soon as we exit the café. Paparazzi are a fact of life for the royal family, and I hold out my arm, blocking her from them with my body.

She's in the car, and I lean down, speaking to Hajib. "Take her straight to the palace." He nods, and I straighten, ready to close the door.

Ava's hand shoots out and stops it. "I want to know she's safe. Text me when you find her."

"I will." She relents, and I slam the door.

I'm of little importance in the entertainment world, so as the car moves slowly away, the photographers move with it. For the first time, I'm not so annoyed by their presence. They're another layer of protection tonight, and Hajib won't be reckless or put Ava's life in danger. He'll deliver her safely to their destination.

That matter settled, I'm racing down the alley, headed to my bike.

Kass is in her apartment alone when I secretly climb the fire escape to check on her. The noise of her crying rips my heart, and I want to go inside, take her in my arms and comfort her. The only thing holding me back is the king's order to wait. To see if Blix comes to her or if she goes to him.

She's not sobbing or breaking down, but every few moments, she slides her palm across her cheek, wiping away a new flood of tears. As much as it hurts me, I steel my emotions. We've got to find out what she knows.

I've never been more frustrated with Rowan in the history of my career as a guard. Still, I can't jeopardize the case.

Freddie texted me shortly after I arrived. They're searching for her brother. His friends had to improvise their final set. They're pissed, but they're also worried.

*The consensus is he never does this*, Freddie texts. *Even the girl he's been sleeping with is worried.*

*Keep me posted*, is all I reply.

Based on what I'm seeing, how Kass is acting, I'm convinced Blix is behind this. *Dammit*, I swear in my mind. If I could only be sure she would work with us. Instead, I watch helpless as she walks around her apartment hugging her torso when she's not wiping away tears. I won't leave her. I won't let her do anything dangerous without me here to save her.

For the second night in a row, I have to lean back in the darkness and breathe through my urges. Last night I had to listen to her confess she loves me. Tonight I struggle against going in there and taking matters into my own hands.

The night wears on, and I start to nod. My phone buzzes, and it's the king. *Come in. I've sent Freddie to watch her while you sleep.*

My jaw clenches, and the last thing I want to do is leave. Leaning forward, I can see her cheek in the light of the streetlamp. It's no longer shining with tears, but a line pierces her forehead. She's stressed and it makes me worry.

*I can stay*, I text back.

*You can't help her if you're exhausted.*

Leaning my head against the brick wall, I know he's right. Two nights in a row is too long for me to remain sharp. I have to trust Freddie won't let her out of his sight until I return. It's one of the hardest things I've ever done, but I follow orders.

Ava meets me in the back foyer when I arrive at the palace. She's still wearing what she had on at the café. Her arms are crossed, and she's clearly angry.

"I've been waiting for your text," she says.

It's the first time I remembered what she said when we parted. "I'm sorry." I do a little bow. "I was distracted, and I forgot."

"Distracted? Weren't you sitting and watching her?"

"Physically, that's what I was doing." She's the queen, but she's still pissing me off right now. "I was also plotting out all the possible scenarios of what could go wrong and how to address them."

She lets out a heavy sigh and sits on the bench lining the wall. "If Zee had gotten a text like that and I was missing..." She doesn't finish. She only shakes her head side to side as if to say no.

It's everything I already know and why I was so hesitant to leave her tonight. "When you were with her, did you see anything unusual?"

Ava shoves a tangle of dark waves behind her ear and studies the floor in front of her. Then she shakes her head no.

Her response tings my instincts. "Try to remember. Anything could be a clue."

She only shakes her head again. "It was just the usual club crowd." Pushing against her legs, she stands with a deep sigh. "I'm going to sleep now... but I want to see her. She's my friend, and I want to help."

All the reasons she should stay here, especially now cloud my tired brain. "You need to stay put. If Rowan suspected that you put yourself in danger—"

Her aqua eyes flash. "I only said I was going to see her. I'll take my new guard."

Exhaustion is winning. Stepping back, I do a little bow. "I'm going to rest for five hours."

"Maybe I'll see you tomorrow."

I don't like the dare in her voice, but I have to let the king worry about her for now. Rowan is right. I need to rest.

## Chapter 21: A Plan

*Kass*

"I read the text." Ava's crisp tone cuts through my tired mind.

I have no idea what time it is. I didn't even bother changing out of my gown when she called to say she was out on the street at my door. I only knew I had to get her inside.

"What text?" My voice is thick.

I'm surprised I even slept last night. After Blix left, I had been overwhelmed by despair and fear. I can only see my little brother bound in a dark warehouse. I can hear the screams of the tortured men. The memories have my eyes heating with tears again, and I thought I'd cried them all away last night.

"You know what text." She pushes past me into my room.

I turn, closing the door and leaning against it. "You shouldn't be here. You need to stay at the palace where it's safe."

"Because what's happening has something to do with me."

I'm awake enough to start acting. "Ava, you're the queen, but not everything is about you."

She presses on. "Last night, after your brother disappeared. I didn't mean to spy, but your phone is huge. The font size is even bigger. It was pretty hard not to see—"

"You read my phone?" My voice rises, and she grasps my arm.

"I wasn't trying to read it. The point is it was a threat." I shake her hand away and stalk around my small room.

"You don't know what you're talking about."

"I know you can't do this on your own. Let me help you."

She has no idea what she's asking, and even if she did, there's no way I could allow her to be pulled into what I'm doing. I've been fighting hard enough to keep Cameron out of my mess.

"I think you should go now." I'm digging in my closet, feeling each item for a sweater… jeans…

My phone buzzes, and I drop everything to lunge for it. It's closer to her, and she snatches it up before I get there. She reads the text loud and clear, and my insides cringe.

*Follow Boulevard d'Italie into the mountains toward Menton. Will meet you on the old windmill road. Don't be alone.*

"Give it to me." I hold my hand toward her, but she doesn't do what I ask.

"What does this mean 'Don't be alone'?"

"Ava," I sigh. "You have to trust me."

She's quiet, and I listen to the creak of her shoes as she paces my hardwood floors. Her heels are quiet, which means she's wearing flats. The leather squeaks softly as she takes four steps to the right and stops. She turns and takes four steps in my direction. The closer she gets, the faint scent of her perfume grows stronger. It's freesia… or some small flower.

"Zelda did this," she says. "She believed getting us involved with Wade Paxton was her fault, and it was up to her to make it right. As if he wouldn't have found another way..." She stops, and I hear a tone of anger enter her voice. "She never considered my feelings. She wouldn't let me be a human who would be hurt by her choices."

Going to my window, I face the street, doing my best to discern meaning in the haze before my eyes. "I don't know your sister. I never met Wade Paxton. But I do know Blix Ratcliffe. He's a monster we can't stop."

"He almost killed my sister." Ava's voice wavers. "Now he's threatening my friend."

"You haven't known me long enough to feel an obligation to help me," I say quietly.

"You didn't know me at all when you tried to kill him the first time."

My failure at the villa is another reason to say no. "I couldn't betray Logan."

She crosses the room to where I'm standing, reaching down to capture both my hands in hers. "I'm sick of being locked away in the palace, unable to help anyone. That's not me. It's never been me." She pauses for a breath, but I know her eyes are on me. "I won't be innocent if I let you face him alone. Together we can do this. We can take him by surprise. Zelda and I always worked better as a team."

I'm still not convinced. Shaking my head, I go to the door. "I won't hand you over like a lamb to the slaughter."

"So I was right." Her voice is solemn, and I know she's not leaving now. "When he said 'Don't come alone,' it meant you were supposed to bring me to him."

"As if I can tell you where to go. It's ridiculous. I plan to tell him that."

"You're right. You can't tell me. Which is why I'm coming with you."

"Ava..." I growl, pushing her hands away.

"What happens to your brother if you show up without me?"

My throat squeezes tight. "I plan to offer myself in his place."

"Because he won't accept that." Her voice is rising, and I hear the frustration in her tone. "Stop being stubborn, Kass. Let me help you."

"You can't! You're not strong enough!"

"Let me get this straight. You think a blind girl with no weapons and only an argument that an insane man is making insane demands is somehow stronger than working with me?"

I'm growing weary of fighting. I'm running out of arguments. "He has helpers... thugs... who do whatever he says."

"Okay." She's walking around my apartment again. "What does he want? Ultimately, I mean. He doesn't want your brother. He doesn't want me. He's using us... What's his goal?"

It's possible I underestimated Ava's brain. "Money."

She stops short. "That's it? Money? He only wants money?"

I almost laugh at her incredulity. "A whole lot of money."

"At least when Zelda was taken, they wanted power."

"Money is power."

She sniffs, and I can almost see her shrug. "Either way. He has demands, and he won't do anything to jeopardize getting what he wants."

I don't answer. I don't like opening this door to her.

"Am I right?" she demands.

As much as I hate it, I tell her the truth. "You're right."

"Then we can do this."

I exhale a deep sigh and walk to the bed. "All right. I've told you my plan. Now you tell me yours."

\* \* \*

The streets are wet as we head out on Ava's silver Vespa. It's before noon, but it feels late without the sun shining down on us. I can tell by the shadows and the haze the sky is grey and lowering. The Boulevard d'Italie runs straight through the center of town, and as a result, we have to take it slow. Freddie is shadowing us, keeping watch over the queen, and as much as I'm glad he's there, I know it doesn't matter. We're headed straight into the snake pit.

She pulls off suddenly, and I sit back as she dashes up to the little coffee cart in the middle of the market district. A few minutes pass. I hear her ordering mixed with the sounds of couples talking, people passing, little dogs clicking by on the semi-crowded streets. We're pretending to be having a simple morning out. Ava hands me my latte, and as I sip it, she points to a flower vendor and exclaims about the beautiful arrangements.

Every muscle in my body is clenched so tightly it hurts. I don't even bother noting I can't see a thing she's trying to show me. This is crazy. This isn't going to work. *This isn't going to work.* The words are on repeat in my brain like a mantra.

My fingers tremble as I tap out the text. *We're on our way.*

Just before I hit send, I hold it close to my eyes to be sure I didn't make any typos. It's exactly right.

Lowering my phone, I look in the direction of her dark outline sitting on the seat. "No going back when I hit send."

"No going back," she repeats solemnly.

My thumb hesitates, trembling over the green arrow. "Oh, god, Ava," I whisper just as I let it drop.

The noise of a swoosh tells me the message has left my control. The clock has started.

"Let's go," she says, and I hear her determination.

I wish I felt the same, but Blix has destroyed my confidence with every man he tortured to death.

We're on the outskirts of the city now, and I can tell by the sounds from the streets around us when we begin climbing the mountains. Traffic thins, and the air seems cleaner. Damp hangs all around us, and our hair is getting wet where it extends out around our helmets.

"When will we know if he got it?" Ava yells back to me.

A seagull cries overhead, and my nose touches her shoulder. "We'll know. Is Freddie still with us?"

Her torso moves as she looks around us. "Yes," She shouts, and I have to believe Blix planned for her to be followed. She's the queen regent, after all.

Dread is hot in my veins. We're risking everything doing this. We're giving Blix exactly what he asked for, and I have no idea what he has planned once he gets it. Still, I'd run out of arguments. Ava is right. Alone, I'm no match for Blix, and offering myself in her place was a ridiculous idea. I don't bring anything to the table. After all, Rowan hadn't stopped me from leaving Occitan. Reggie practically helped me pack.

Blix would have simply killed Cameron and me and used some other method to capture the queen. Heck, it's possible he'll do that anyway. I'm in the midst of this macabre thought when Ava's body stiffens. For the first time since she showed up at my apartment uninvited, I feel a tremor move through her.

"They're here," she says, and fear flashes in my chest.

The Vespa engine continues its happy buzz, but coming up fast are the low roars of truck engines. I look down and back, and I can make out three black SUVs approaching us fast.

"Don't act like you know," I say in her ear.

She's already on it, accelerating her small scooter. Her breathing goes faster, and my fear intensifies as a result. Lowering my face, I press my closed eyes against her shoulder.

The noise of engines is all around us, loud and intimidating. Ava lets out a little wail and accelerates more on the Vespa. It's wide open, going as fast as it can, but we can't outrun these men. The black SUV swerves in closer to us, and we're right against the side of the mountain.

"Slow down!" I cry, gripping her waist. "You've got to stop!"

"I can't!" she shouts back. "They're right behind us!"

I look over my shoulder and my heart drops. A huge black vehicle is right on our tail. Any unexpected moves, and it'll roll right over us.

"What do they expect us to do?" I cry.

The truck that had been crowding us suddenly accelerates and shoots ahead of us on the narrow road. A junky old farm truck shoots past where the SUV had been, and just as fast, another vehicle shoots up to take it's place, matching our speed.

I hear the noise of a door opening. It's a sliding door. I didn't expect it, since the car beside us doesn't resemble a mini-van. Either way, the door is open, and

I can just make out the form of a man standing in the dark space.

Two arms like steel bands fly around my waist, and I'm jerked into the dark open mouth of the van.

"NO!" I scream, but my hands slip off Ava's waist.

For a moment, I'm suspended in thin air with only the man's arms around me. I flail, trying not to let my feet hit the speeding asphalt below. My hand makes contact with what feels like bungee cord as I'm dragged into the van and thrown against the opposite wall.

He doesn't give me time to react, he's back out the door, leaning into the brilliant space of light toward Ava still racing at the same speed on her Vespa. The SUV behind her is forcing her to keep the pace. As fast as he grabbed me, the man whips her off her scooter. Her scream is loud and strong, and tears spring to my eyes. Just as fast, they're back, and she's flying at me with her arms flung out like a starfish. She lands on top of me, and I roll with her until we're both in a heap on the floor of the strange vehicle.

The three vehicles slow, and I hear the Vespa continue speeding forward on its trajectory before flying off the side of the cliff. It's not long before the sound of an explosion echoes from behind us.

Ava and I are sitting on the floor of the strange, square-shaped vehicle clinging to each other. Our arms are around each others' waists, and I can feel her straining, trying to see anything.

"What's happening?" I say in her ear.

She rises on her knees, and her head moves forward and back. "The three vehicles are lined up. We're in the middle."

The centrifugal force tells me we're racing around the curving road of the cliff. "They're taking us to him. Then we'll find out if this is going to work or not."

## Chapter 22: Heartbreak

*Kass*

I'm sitting on a rubber mat covering the floorboard with Ava right at my side. Our arms are around each other, but we're equally defiant.

Truthfully, she might be a bit more defiant than me.

"Isn't this a pretty sight?" Blix's tone immediately makes me shudder. He's using his torture voice, which means his humanity is completely shut down. "Ava Wilder... The rumors do not exaggerate. You're as beautiful in person as you are on the lips of beggars."

I feel her jerk away. "Don't touch me," she hisses.

His laugh makes my skin crawl. "We have a stop to make. Then we'll see how serious your husband is about getting you back."

"The king doesn't negotiate with terrorists," she says, and I admire the confidence in her voice. I wish I wasn't so fucking afraid, but I know what he's capable of.

Every now and then the vehicle we're in will jerk to the right or left, and we take a little tumble before quickly righting ourselves on the empty floor. It smells like the inside of a gym.

"You're being very quiet, Kass." Blix is at my shoulder, but I don't move. "What could possibly be going on behind those empty eyes?"

My jaw tightens, but I don't answer. Nothing about me is empty, but I'm not about to feed the monster.

Ava is another matter.

"Aren't you the brave man, picking on a blind girl?" So much hatred is in her voice, I'm afraid for her.

"I'm the man who decides if you live or die. I'd suggest you shut the fuck up."

Ava's about to respond, but my arms tighten around her waist. I turn my head toward her ear and barely speak the words. "Stop talking."

She tenses, but I know she understands my meaning. Our plan hangs on Blix believing he's beaten us; that we're too weak and afraid to retaliate. And while I don't believe Blix will actually kill Ava—at least not until he gets what he wants—her taunting might provoke him to hurt her. I've seen it too many times... him sending messages coupled with body parts.

Silence closes around us like a shroud. The vehicle stops, and Blix moves in close to my ear. "Time's up, Kass."

His breath is like tiny bugs crawling on my skin, but I hold steady. I don't have the same level of confidence about Blix sparing my life. I've delivered the goods, but he knows I'm compromised. I've already tried to kill him once and failed.

The metal door behind us slides open, and Ava and I both scramble forward. Taz is outside the door. "Everybody out," he says.

We don't move. I don't move because I'm not sure where to go or what I'll be stepping into. Ava is having a hard time letting go of her innate defiance, but I clasp her hand in mine and scoot us toward the opening. Taz has never shown any compassion for my blindness. Thankfully, instead of taunting me, this time he only turns and walks away.

Ava takes the lead once we've reached the edge of the van and steps out into the cool, damp air. I hear her shoes crunch on gravel, and I slip my foot forward, feeling for the ground. If the sun were out, I'd be able to discern more about my surroundings, but as it is, I take Ava's arm when she offers it. The best course of action for both of us right now is to play like meek little lambs.

"Get inside." Blix shoves me forward, but I hold onto Ava's arm, dragging her with me.

A noise like a quiet growl comes from her throat, but I tighten my fingers on her arm. *Keep steady, Ava.* The air inside the structure is as cold and damp as the air outside, and I can tell by the sounds of the wind the roof is missing. It's darker in this place, which doubles my handicap, and it smells earthy and old like rotting wood.

"It's an abandoned mill," Ava says close to my shoulder. "It's completely empty except for us."

Heels click on the stone floor approaching us rapidly. My arm is seized in an iron grip that causes me to gasp. "This way," Taz says, ripping me away from Ava and pulling me behind him.

I stumble and do my best to stay on my feet. My hip strikes a wooden object that scrapes loudly across the floor. Taz continues dragging me faster, and I wave my free hand, hoping to ward off any more collisions.

"Duck," Taz orders.

I'm confused, and he doesn't give me time to process before my head slams into the stone wall. White light flashes behind my eyes, and pain splinters through my head.

"Oh!" I shout. Tears sting my vision, and I reach up to stop the bleeding.

"I said to fucking duck," Taz jerks me forward, and I almost miss the step down into the small room. Water is at my feet, small puddles on the floor.

I can't stop crying, and I feel the warmth of blood running down the corner of my eye, down my cheek. I reach up again to hold it. It isn't a large cut, but I know from experience facial wounds bleed profusely.

"Tie her hands." Blix is in the room, and I jump at the sound of his voice.

Taz turns me roughly, shoving my stomach against what feels like a solid piece of wood. I'm able to steady myself against it. It's some sort of desk, but he grips my elbows, yanking my hands behind my back.

My insides shudder, causing my shoulders to collapse forward. Taz has my wrists behind my back, and he quickly loops the rope over them, pulling the knot so tight, it's biting into my skin. I can tell by the echoes of his footsteps we're in a very small room.

I'm in darkness, waiting for what happens next. My mind keeps pulling up Logan's face, but I push it away. I want him so badly, I can barely breathe. If only he could save me. If only I could let him know where we are. It's too late for that now. For five seconds, I allow myself to mourn the loss of him. I allow myself to be comforted by the warmth of our memories. Another set of footsteps joins us, and that moment is gone.

Feet shuffle, the noise of a body being thrown forward and hitting the stone floor joins us. A deep *Oof!* comes from the person who hit the floor.

"Why are you doing this?" My eyes fly open at the sound of his voice. It's Cameron!

"Cam?" My voice is shaky and high. "Are you okay?"

"Kass?" He moves fast as if he's sitting up, and all at once I hear the sharp smack of fist hitting face. Again he lets out a grunt and falls against the wall.

"Don't get up," Taz snarls.

"Don't hurt him!" I shout.

"Scan her." It's Blix again.

Taz is at my side, and I hear a high-pitched noise moving around me. It starts at my head, and I can tell it's a wand or gun—something like airport security would use. It's a steady humming around my shoulders, over my arms. He pushes me back and runs it down the front of my body, over my waist, at my ankles. Shoving me forward again, he comes up the back of my legs to my thighs, and when he reaches my waist, it lets out a shrill squeal.

"What's that?" Blix's voice snaps.

Taz moves it around my lower back to the right, nothing. To the left, another shrill squeal. He drops the gun on the desk in front of me and feels all around my side. I have no pockets, and he grips my waistband, ripping it down.

"Oh!" My stomach tightens. "What are you doing?"

Now Blix is with us. I catch the halo of a light being shined on my body. "Fuckers," he mutters. "Have you got your knife?"

"Wait!" I'm breathing fast. My entire body is shaking. "What's going on? What are you doing?"

Blix is back up at my face, speaking close. "Don't act stupid with me."

My entire body is shaking, and I scream when Taz touches my skin. "I'm not acting! What is it?"

"You didn't know you were bugged?"

I don't know what that means. Bugged? Flying through my thoughts, one thing stands out in my mind. "The vaccination!" I say, just as the pain rips through my skin.

"NO!" I scream trying to pull away.

"What are you doing to her?" Cameron demands.

Blix shoves my upper body down on the desk so hard my cheek bounces off the wood. He lays across my back so I can't move as Taz cuts through my skin roughly, not caring if he hurts me.

I scream again.

"STOP!" I hear my brother shout.

"Shut up," Blix presses his forearm against my cheek, grinding my face into the wood.

Tears flood my eyes. Warm blood runs down my leg, and the pain causes my knees to buckle. "Please stop," I beg. My face is hot. Snot is on my nose and in my mouth.

"Got it." Finally Taz stops.

More pain rips through my side as he jerks my pants up, over my injury without even covering it. My body goes instantly lighter as Blix rises off me. He takes the thing Taz dug out of me and slams a piece of paper in front of my face. I slide off the surface, collapsing all the way to my knees then my butt, leaning against the front of the desk on the opposite side of my injury.

I can't stop crying.

"Kass? You okay?" Cam's voice breaks with worry, but after that manhandling, I can't seem to pull it together.

With a sharp bang of the knife, Blix steps away from where I'm leaning. "That will give him something to think about." He moves around the small area. "It seems I have too many hostages. Get rid of that one."

He goes to the door and leaves us alone. I hear the shuffle of leather, and I know Taz has taken out his gun.

"ME!" My voice is sandpaper, but I manage to push myself up. I'm leaning forward in the darkness in the direction I know he's standing. "Let it be me!"

I hear him cock his weapon, and I brace myself for the impact. I wonder if he'll kill me all at once, or if it'll take some time for me to die. The loud *POP!* makes me scream and fall back.

I wait… nothing happens. No impact. It's silent. He didn't shoot me.

My world crumbles all around me, and I fall forward onto the wet floor screaming at the top of my lungs. "NO! NO NO NO!" I scream until my throat is raw. I scream to fight back the spiraling agony shredding my insides. I scream because all of the mistakes I've made have led to this.

I scream because if he didn't shoot me…

Cameron is dead.

## CHAPTER 23: DISCOVERY

*Logan*

My eyes spring open, and I sit straight up in the bed. Despite the overcast skies, I can tell I've overslept. I had intended to be back at Kass's apartment before ten. Grabbing the white plastic clock off my nightstand, I see it's after eleven.

Dropping the device, I jerk back the covers so hard, my sheet rips at the corner. I hustle to the shower, spinning the dials and stepping to the toilet to take care of my morning wood as the water starts to warm. I make quick work of cleaning up, using my hands and not even bothering with a washcloth.

All told, I'm out of my apartment, on my bike and headed to Kass's place in less than twenty minutes. Mist hangs in the air, and I'm glad I didn't waste time with the blow drier. My hair is already hanging in damp waves around my face when I reach my destination.

Pulling straight up to the front, I decide I'm going to level with her. I'll tell her I'm keeping an eye on her and ask her straight out what she knows. She's got to start trusting me at some point, and I feel more confident than ever today is the day. She can't get her brother back without help, and I'm the man to help her.

Swinging off my bike, I stride up to her door and hit the buzzer. Several moments pass as I wait for her voice to crackle through the ancient speaker. I study the building's façade. Ironic how colorful it is, considering she isn't able to see it. The thought sends an ache through my arms. I miss holding her. I want to lift her against my body and carry her into the sea, let the salt-water wash away our past then make love to her. I press the buzzer again a bit longer this time.

More time passes, and still no response. A hint of worry nudges my insides. "Where are you?" I say, stepping to the side and looking around.

She doesn't drive, so I can't use a car to let me know she's here. Taking out my phone, I pull up the app Freddie installed and look for the dots. Only the yellow one lights up, and it's nowhere near here. It's east of the city in what looks like the cliffs. My brow lines, and I'm about to punch up Freddie's number when the metal door scrapes open. It's the old man.

I take two steps toward him, and he glares at me. He's dressed in a different tweed suit this time, but his wool driver's hat is the same. His short-legged dog is wearing a small Burberry blanket on his back.

"It's you," he snarls through a thick French accent. I'm happy to speak French to him, but I never get the chance. "I know you from the papers. You work for the king."

"Oui," I say, offering our native tongue.

He doesn't take. "The other one she let in is bad. She's going to get us both killed."

Ice is in my chest. "What other one?"

"His eyes are dead. His heart is dead. I lock my doors. All the locks."

My jaw clenches along with my fists. "When did he come to her?"

"Her first night. Then again..." His face is lined like a tree trunk. "I was hard with her. I shouted and told her not to let any man in. I let you in, but she doesn't listen."

And to think I discredited this guy. "Did he come last night?"

"You were here last night." He tosses his thumb over his shoulder. "Out back, watching."

"I'm trying to keep her safe." It's as much as I can give him at this point.

"The queen was here this morning. They left together."

I waste no time contacting Freddie now. "Thank you, sir," I say, but he's not finished.

"She cries too much." I pass my hand over my mouth, unable to answer him. Still, he continues. "Get her to where she doesn't cry so much." He takes a step away then pauses. "Henri would like that."

"Henri?" I glance around.

"*Allons*, Henri!" He gives the leash a little flick, and his dog perks up, happily following his owner as the old man shuffles up the street in the direction of the café.

For a moment, I'm lost in thought. I had completely misjudged this old man, believing he jeopardized Kass's safety with his carelessness. Now I realize he's seen everything. He's had his eye on her from the beginning.

I can't lose time on this. For now, I have to reach Freddie. My finger slams down on the green dot to place the call.

"Logan!" Freddie's voice is breathless when he answers. "I lost her." He's shaken for the first time since I've known him. "Them. I lost them both."

I'm on my bike, switching the phone to Bluetooth and inserting a headphone in my ear as I kick the motorcycle awake. "Tell me what happened."

"They left together... on Ava's Vespa—"

"Shit," I exhale, twisting the handle and roaring the engine as I start down the winding street. "Where were you when they were on Ava's Vespa?"

"I was right behind them. I was with them the whole time."

Freddie's an experienced guard. He's been with me since the days I was training in Morocco. His specialty is technology for a reason, and I blame myself for this screw-up. The only reason Freddie was guarding Ava was because I wouldn't leave Kass's side.

Until last night.

"We're in a situation of increased danger," I say, doing my best to keep the fury out of my voice. "You don't let them choose such an insecure method of transportation at a time like this."

"They were only riding… having coffee… looking at flowers." He sounds legitimately stunned. "They rode into the mountains, and before I could stop them they were surrounded."

Fire is in my chest. "Who was it? Did you get plate numbers?"

"I took photos with my bike's camera. I have to get back to the palace and analyze them, run them against our databases. We can still find her on GPS. Kass's implant is functioning. I'm heading to the palace now. I'll send you the location."

"Don't waste any time." I'm doing my best to maneuver the crowded streets, but it's got me at a snail's pace. "Where were you exactly when you lost them?"

"She turned off at Route de la Turbie. They were on the Boulevard d'Italie climbing into the cliffs when they were surrounded. I was completely cut off."

I wish I had asked that question first. I would've taken another route. "Any clue where they were headed?"

"None, but we have the signal. I will find her."

"Does Rowan know what's happening?" I've finally reached the outskirts of the city, and I'm turning my motorcycle north into the hills leading to the cliffs.

"I wanted to tell him in person."

*So he can kill you*, I muse. Shaking that thought away, I push on. "Let the king know I'm tracking them. As soon as you've found her, report their movements to me."

"Her Vespa went over the cliff. She wasn't on it. Neither of them was, but at the Col de Guerre, the SUVs split up. They went in three different directions."

"This is why we have a tracking device. I need you to hurry. I'm at the bluffs."

"I'm at the palace now."

I lean into the wind as the bike climbs higher into the mountains. The air is heavy with rain, but I won't let it stop me. I only wish I had a car. So many choices would be different in hindsight. I can only push through the regrets and focus on finding them before Blix does anything lethal.

I reach the Route de la Turbie and follow the Boulevard d'Italie into the higher elevations. I can pick up speed on the straight ways, but when I reach the hairpin curves, I have to drop my speed all the way to a crawl. Otherwise, I risk going over the cliff along with Ava's Vespa.

Deep green trees surround the road the higher I go. I'm in the high altitudes, but deep in the forest. As more time passes, I get further away from signs of life. Still, I'm making progress. Between the speeding up and slowing down, my arms are weary, and it feels like

I've been out here for hours. The sun is overhead but still behind a dense layer of clouds, and I'm starting to wonder where the hell Freddie is. I'm ready to pull the bike off to the side and check the app myself, when my earpiece crackles to life.

"Logan—you there?"

I barely resist the urge to shout at him. "Of course, I'm here. What's taken so long?"

"I don't know if it's the altitude or if he has her inside a steel container. It took some time to locate her signal."

"Am I headed in the right direction?" I don't have time for explanations or technical details.

"You're close. Slow down and look for a road to Roquebrune. You'll follow a tunnel straight through the hillside."

I'm not far from the turnoff, and I know the tunnel well. "Roquebrune isn't large enough to hide them." The medieval village is perched on a rocky outcrop overlooking the sea. "I was here two years ago for the tennis masters. Ava will be recognized at once."

"You're not going to Roquebrune."

I'm trying to understand. "Is he taking them to Italy?"

"Tell me when you're through the tunnel."

The road is straight here, and I'm way over the speed limit. "I'm approaching it now." A bit further, and I'm plunged into darkness. The road curves, but it doesn't take long for my eyes to adjust.

"Once you're out, look for the first road headed east. It comes up quick."

The tunnel is less than a mile long, and I can see the white opening rising ahead. I can't help it, I open the throttle even more until I'm devouring the distance. I've got to make up for lost time. If Blix is planning to leave the country, he's got an enormous head start.

Rain hits me in the face when I shoot out on the opposite end of the underground passageway.

"Shit," I hiss, flipping the visor down over my eyes. I'm thankful for my leather jacket, but the stinging drops hit my exposed skin like pellets from a gun. "How much further," I ask.

"Did you find the road? It's unmarked."

I ease off the throttle straining my eyes for the road. Trees pass. A cutoff fools me at first. I'm about to pick up the pace when I see it. Hidden in the trees, a very narrow dirt road. Tree limbs hang low over the entrance, and it's dark and undisturbed.

"I've found something, but it doesn't appear to have been used in ages."

"That's it. Take it."

Without question, I turn the wheel sharply, thankful for the shelter of the trees against the storm. The rain is picking up, but the canopy overhead makes it easier for me to go fast.

The road isn't winding. It's a straight shot east and somewhat south, in the direction of the sea, only at a higher altitude. I have no idea what I'm looking for.

"Will it dead end?" I ask my remote guide.

"No, but on the satellite image, I see a stone structure. It's ancient, and it's in an open location."

I'm about to ask more questions when the trees part, and I zoom into a clearing. Letting off the gas, I hit the breaks so hard, the back wheel skids to the side. My boots are down, and I'm able to brace the bike and catch my balance. In the center of the clearing is an enormous stone windmill—or what's left of one.

It's tall, wider at the base and rising to a narrow top, which is broken and missing. The wooden arms of the mill are rotted away, and only one remains at its full length. I can only hope the thunder masked the noise of my engine. I kill it and roll back into the low-hanging trees to hide and have shelter.

"What's happening here," I say, scanning the perimeter, looking for any signs of life.

"It's where Kass's signal is coming from."

Dread filters through my chest like acid. This place is grey and deserted. No cars, no lights, no signs of anyone. It could be the rain making it appear empty… or it could be something worse.

"I'm going in." I rip the helmet off my head and check the pistol in my back holster. Safety off. The knife in my boot is backup.

Clinging to the tree line, I make my way around the clearing, looking for any signs of guards or spies. I don't see cameras. I don't see anything.

"I don't like this at all," I mutter.

I decide not to waste any more time. I dart across the open space, glancing over my shoulder to be sure no one's closed in behind me. Nothing is there. The opening is much shorter than I am and curved. The white stone is stained, and the words *Pinot* and *Sicilia* are scratched in the surface.

Ducking into the narrow space, it opens at once to the large interior. Rough hewn blocks are exposed where the plaster has worn away, and it extends straight up to the broken ceiling. It's dark, and drops of rain fall to greater and lesser degrees all around me. I see the giant gear near the ceiling with a thick metal post extending down to another giant gear. The grinding mechanism at least is intact, even if the means of running it is gone.

"It's empty," I whisper. "No one is here."

"Impossible," Freddie's voice is equally quiet in my ear, as if he's looking through my eyes at this abandoned edifice.

*Should I call her name?* My boots make a shushing noise on the sandy floor. Little bits of gravel crunch with my steps. "There's got to be a mistake…"

Then I see it. Near the floor at the back wall is a small, black rectangle. The frame is painted aqua blue, and all around it is rotten wood and decay. My stomach tightens. Reaching around to my back, I pull out my gun, holding it right at my face as I carefully pick my way through the mill.

"I'm approaching a tiny room," I whisper.

It's completely dark inside except for white light filtering in through a narrow opening. Fumbling at my coat pocket, I take out my phone and switch on the camera light. Dust motes dance in the beam cutting through the darkness. It smells like mildew and musty earth. My throat stings, but I fight a cough.

The light only allows me to see a small circle wherever it hits in this space. Tension creeps up my shoulders when it hits a small, metal card table. Water puddles around it, and my eyes land on what looks like an electrical cord.

What appears to be the broken blade of a knife reflects the light back at me, hurting my eyes. I take a step forward, my heart beating faster.

"What is this?" I whisper, going to what appears to be a wooden desk against the far wall.

I'm breathing fast as I approach. A sheet of white paper is pinned to the grey wood by a jagged Bowie knife. Around the sharp tip is brownish stain, and a tiny square is trapped against it.

"No…" The word is out of my mouth before I even make sense of the ink on the paper. "Freddie…"

The words die on my lips as my mind decodes what I'm seeing, the writing on the paper.

*Stop wasting my time. The clock is ticking, and either I get my money or you get body parts. I'll send you the drop location, and remember, I make good on my promises. –B.*

My heart is lodged in my throat. Leaning forward, I try to calm my breathing. All I can think of is Kass.

"What's happening?" Freddie shouts in my ear. "Logan! Talk to me—what's going on? Are you down?"

"She didn't even know." My voice is practically feral. "He hurt her and she didn't even know why."

My body is shaking, and I have to rein in my fury against the king, against Freddie, against all of them, before I do something I'll regret.

"Tell me what's going on," Freddie orders. As if he has the right.

"I let you do this to her. I let you hurt her…" Pain twists my insides. "She can't even fucking see!"

Staggering back, my leg hits the metal card table. Turning, I grip it by the sides and hurl it with all my strength against the wall. I hear it collapse in a heap on the wet floor. My phone is on the desk, the light still shining on that fucking knife stained with her blood. My head feels like it's splitting in two. The black is taking over my vision. I'm raging and hopeless, one thought ringing clear in my mind: *I've got to find her.*

"Logan, talk to me." Freddie is in my ear, and I reach up to claw the earpiece away, but just as my hand reaches it, he stops me. "Send me a picture of the letter."

My stomach tightens at the request. "It has her blood on it…"

"Logan, think like a guard. We have to see it. We need to analyze it."

Rage burns red in my chest, but I go to the table. I push my wet hair out of my eyes and lift my phone to snap the photo.

"Sass," I whisper, reaching forward to pull the knife out.

I slip the weapon in my boot, replacing the smaller knife currently there. I put the letter and the tiny chip in my pocket, vowing with each step *I will break every bone in his body.*

I'm just about to leave, back to tracking, when a strange sound makes me pause...

## Chapter 24: Strength

*Kass*

I vaguely recall Taz jerking me up from the floor and carrying me to the van. Without care or ceremony, he throws me inside on the rubber-mat floor and slams the door. I close my eyes and beg for unconsciousness. My insides are flayed. *Cameron…* I can't even help him or retrieve his body.

A few moments pass and the door opens again. Ava stumbles as if she's being pushed into the vehicle as well. She crawls quickly to where I'm lying and puts my head in her lap.

"Kass… are you okay?" Her voice trembles and I hear her tears. "This wasn't supposed to happen."

She touches the wound on my forehead, which I'm sure is clotted and bruised. From there, she moves to my side.

"Your pants are soaked with blood." She tries to move my side, but I whimper and pull away from the pain. "I'm sorry!" she cries.

Two doors slam and the engine starts. We're pulling away from the windmill, leaving my little brother behind. I curl forward as my insides collapse.

*He's in there alone… He needs me… We can't leave him here… I don't even know where here is…*

"Can you talk to me?" Ava whispers, smoothing my hair away from my face. "Did they shoot you?"

"No," I whisper, tears flooding my eyes.

Ava thinks I'm answering her, but I'm crying for my little brother. I can't save him. I can't help him. I don't know if I'll ever be able to find him again.

Despair rolls over me like a tidal wave. More tears are on my cheeks.

"Kass, you've got to be strong," she whispers, wiping my tears with her hands. "Stay with me. Think of your brother. Think of Logan."

"Logan," I whimper, but I'm unable to find hope in even that warm memory.

"Yes, Logan!" She's whispering, but her voice is faster. "I know he's searching for us. Last night when he returned from watching you, he said he would only sleep for a few hours before he went back. When he sees we're gone, he'll search... He'll find us. They all will."

This information digs its way through the numb surrounding my brain. "What are you... What?" It doesn't make sense.

"Logan's been watching you every night since you left Occitan. He stays all night, but Rowan made him come in last night and rest."

*Every night...* I remember the certainty he was there. I remember smelling his scent. I remember falling asleep secure.

"He was there?" I whisper.

Blix shouts from the front. "Stop whispering or I'll gag you both!"

"She needs help," Ava's voice is less defiant this time. "Can you give me bandages, please?"

"No."

We're moving slower, stopping and starting, and the noises from outside tells me we're in a city. People are all around us, people who could help us, but they don't even know we're here.

"She's bleeding all over the floor," Ava argues. "If you're planning to hide us, whoever finds this van will know we've been here by the blood."

"This van can be washed out with bleach and a garden hose," Taz says, as if washing away blood is a regular occurrence.

It probably is.

Ava falls silent, and we continue on. She strokes my hair, and I vaguely wonder if I'm bleeding all over her. I wish I could see her face. I know she's thinking about our plan and wondering how it's possibly going to work now. All I feel is hopeless.

Blix takes an abrupt turn off the road and stops. His window lowers and he speaks to what I can only assume is Dev, the hairy gorilla who usually does his heavy lifting. I hear gates opening and we start to move again, slower this time. We go a bit further and stop for good. He kills the engine, and they're both out. The metal door slides open, and I'm roughly dragged out of the bed.

"Walk," Taz orders, and I do my best to limp.

My hip throbs, and I feel fresh blood oozing from the open wound. My head aches from where I slammed it against the stone doorjamb, but none of it matters. All the life drained out of me when they shot Cam.

"Take them both to the back," Blix says, sounding less like an animal now. I suppose his blood lust has momentarily been assuaged. His tone turns disgusted, and he's at my side. "Clean her up."

"What?" Taz is equally disgusted.

"I'll do it," Ava says, then quickly changes her tone. "Please let me do it. I'll be gentle with her."

"Gentle?" Blix's lip curls over the word. "Who the fuck said to do that? This bitch tried to kill me. She's only alive because of you."

"Please," Ava says again, even more demure.

A beat of silence passes. "Five minutes," he says to Taz. "Watch them."

"Right."

We're shoved into what I can only assume is a massive cargo hold. The noises and the echoes remind me of where I worked in Miami counting boxes and making sure the drugs passed through as they were intended.

Taz stands in the doorway of a small bathroom while Ava touches my forehead gently with a wet washcloth. She's so close to my face, I can see her clutched brow. I can see her full lips pressed together, the fine line at the corner of her mouth.

"Your hair has blood in it. I wish—" she says quietly.

"No talking," Taz shouts.

His loud voice sends a pain through my head, and I wince.

"Do you have any ibuprofen?" Ava is no longer demure with Blix's chief thug. "Different pants she can wear?"

"What the fuck do I look like? The corner drugstore?"

God, I hate his sarcastic mouth. Taz and I have never gotten along, but we've always co-existed because we had to. Now that I'm on the way out, he's lost even the smallest traces of human decency.

"So I clean her up, and she puts bloody clothes back on? I don't think that's what your boss had in mind."

He takes a step forward, and my insides cower. "You think you know what the boss has in mind? You have no fucking idea, queenie."

A knot is in my throat, but I feel Ava turn into a rod of iron at his sickening threats. It's as if his nastiness makes her stronger.

"Shall I ask him? Or shall I tell him you're trying to intimidate your queen."

"You think that means anything here?"

Her shoulders drop, and I'm growing weary of standing on my injured hip. Just as I'm about to say forget about it, the unexpected happens.

"Wait." Taz leaves us alone in the tiny bathroom.

Ava inhales a sharp breath and turns to me. My heart is beating faster. I can't see if we're alone, but I can tell by her enthusiasm we must be.

"You still with me?" She says in a voice one notch above a whisper. "I need you Kass. You have to help me."

Tears flood my eyes, and I shake my head. "We've got to go back there. Can you find the way back?"

"Where?" She pulls away to glance out the door.

"The mill... we've got to get back to the mill. Cameron—"

"Put these on her," Taz tosses something to her.

"They're huge." Ava takes my hand and puts it on what feels like cotton. "Sweatpants," she tells me.

"She can fucking go naked for all I care."

"Thanks." Her tone is sarcastic, but Ava takes my hand and moves me around to the opposite wall.

"What are you doing?"

"Don't look," she snaps. "Pervert."

"You think I want to see that?" Still, he shuffles out of our space.

Ava leans close to my face, and I see her eyes wide. "We'll go back, but I need you now. Are you with me?"

Even though pain floods my chest with each heartbeat, I nod in response. I'm still with her.

## Chapter 25: Searching

*Logan*

Pacing the war room, I watch as Freddie checks satellite clip after satellite clip. Rowan is in the adjacent room on the phone with border patrol, giving them the descriptions of all the vehicles. God knows where Reggie is, but I can only hope his spy network is proving useful.

"What are you doing?" I demand, my agitation getting the best of me. I can't stop seeing Kass wounded and bleeding.

"I went back through the satellite feed and captured the image of the square vehicle that took Ava and Kass, and now I'm using a macro to search it through the timeline for where it went after it left the mill."

"You're able to do that?" I confess, I'm impressed by this answer.

"It's military technology developed for missile tracking. Classified. Very new." He makes several clicks. "So far I don't have a match, but I'm hoping…"

"I've got something!" Freddie shouts.

"What is it?" I'm leaning over his chair, staring into the laptop.

Rowan quickly joins us, and our collective tension is palpable. "Tell me you've found her," the king demands.

The desperation in his voice compounds the anxiety I'm already feeling.

"Not yet," Freddie says, and our shoulders drop.

Rowan's dark head falls forward, but I take a fortifying breath. "What have you found?" I ask.

"I've got a trace on the vehicle. It's here." He points to a dot on the black screen. "They returned to Monagasco. I get as far as the *Cinq Mondes*, and they disappear."

"It's right on the water." I go back through my mind to all the possible hiding places along that stretch of road.

"Logan!" Freddie's out of his seat, racing for the door.

Rowan and I exchange confused glances before I take off after my partner. I'm just about to go through the door when he's back, coat in hand, and holding a rolled sheet of paper.

Rowan meets him at the door. "What do you have?"

"When we were searching for him last time, when we found Kass?" I'm with him, taking the paper as he puts on his jacket.

I scan the list of abandoned cargo holds dotted around the city. "Is something in that area?"

"Two large storage facilities are there."

"Let's go." I jerk my leather jacket off the back of the chair, list in hand.

He stops at the king. "Your majesty, It's my fault she was taken. I promise, I'll get Her Royal Highness back or die trying."

"Give me the list."

Reluctantly, I hand it to Rowan, grinding my teeth at the time passing. He quickly takes a picture with his phone and gives it back. "Go! Text me your first location. I'll send a team of men to the next place."

It's a good call. "Yes, sir," I say, headed for the door, Freddie on my heels.

## Chapter 26: Execution

*Kass*

The air is tight as a tripwire, and the men holding us pace in and out on a regular basis. Dev keeps saying it's dangerous to keep us here.

"This isn't Uranu," he says, whatever that means. "Anyone could find them, take a picture... The fucking paparazzi are all over the place here."

"Shut up," is Blix's standing response. He doesn't seem concerned, but Blix is a master of hiding his thoughts.

Still, I've been with these guys long enough to know if more time keeps passing, things will get ugly. I've never known Dev to be nervous. His hands are the size of my face, and he typically communicates in grunts.

"They've got eight hours to respond." Taz's breathy, nervous voice makes me think of a hyena. A spineless, lying hyena. "What then?"

Metal scrapes across concrete as Blix rises from his chair. "Then we incentivize them."

I know what that means, and my stomach sinks. Eight hours... It's the length of a workday, and it will go by fast. How much time has gone by already? It can't have been longer than a day... I can't tell since we don't have a window, and I can't read a clock. Less than twenty-four hours.

Ava is on a cot, but I'm on the concrete floor. The warehouse is cold and damp, and it smells faintly of gasoline exhaust. A loud drill clatters, and the sound of cranes lifting boxes never stops. Occasionally a strange beating noise I can't seem to place will run for about ten minutes then fade away.

In spite of the din, I managed to doze for a while. Now I'm awake. My hip still throbs, but my head has stopped hurting. We're all in one large room together, but Ava's too far for me to talk to her. I can't tell if they're worried about us trying to escape, or if they simply don't want to hear our voices. Not that we can accomplish much with me injured and blind.

The only hope we have is our plan. I'm not sure how we can make it work in our present situation. Still, I know our trigger word.

Blix is walking around, and I notice he stopped where I'm sitting. His feet are in front of me, and I can make out his dark shape looming above.

"You loved him?" he asks.

Occitan feels like a dream to me now. Logan feels like a dream. When my eyes are closed, I can see his smile clear as a bell. I can see his eyes, and even though his face has matured, it still smolders in my memory. I can feel his arms and his lips on my skin. I can feel his beard teasing my thighs.

"Not answering me?" Blix is waiting, but he'll only use whatever I say against me.

"If I didn't, I wouldn't have been any use to you." I say, not giving him anything he doesn't already know.

"You're no use to me now."

How many times have I watched him at this game? How many times have I wondered when it would be my turn to play it?

"I must be of some use or I'd be dead."

"*Touché*, Cassandra, although your usefulness will only cause you pain." He touches my chin, moving it roughly with his finger. I jerk my face away. "For a few moments, I actually wondered if it would be hard for me to kill you."

"Don't kid yourself. When the time comes, you won't even see me. I'll be meat for you to carve up for your purposes."

He exhales as if he knows the meaning of regret. "No one knows me like you do."

I'm about to respond when he turns and walks away. I listen to him take five steps to the left before stopping again. "Your majesty."

Ava's voice is as defiant as mine. "What do you want?"

He takes a few more steps, then a scraping noise like he turned on his heel. "So beautiful…" Shuffling noises come next then Ava inhales a sharp breath. "It would be a shame to ruin it."

Her voice is still strong. "I don't care if you cut me."

"It's easy to say until the cutting starts." He chuckles, and anger burns in my stomach. He's holding a knife on her, probably against her cheek like he always does to me.

Searching my mind, I try to think of anything to distract him. Ava beats me to it. "Beauty has cut me deeper than you ever could. It made me a target for abuse when I was a child. It drove us onto the streets. If you're looking for a way to hurt me, you'll have to do better than that."

"I know how to hurt you." He grabs her, and she emits a startled cry. "Your king won't want you once I've finished with you."

"Then his love isn't worth much." She's speaking as if he has her by the mouth.

Blix grunts, and she falls back onto the cot. I place my arms on top of my knees and press my forehead against them, willing myself to calm, focus. Ava is okay, and we know where the knife is. The ball is in her court now.

The men are speaking softly to each other. I take a deep breath and lean my head against the wall. Cam's death tries to creep into my memory. I've done my best to keep it at bay until I can finish our plan. Once we're out of here, we can go back to the mill, and I can recover his body, bury him… and mourn him. Tears threaten, but I'm able to hold them off when Dev rushes into the group.

"We got something." They all move quickly to him.

"What is it?" Blix's voice cuts through the chatter.

"The king," Dev says. "He replied to our demands."

"Read it," Blix orders.

I turn my head to where Ava's sitting, and I know she's on the edge of her cot. Anticipation and anxiety are so thick in the air I can taste them.

Dev is quiet, reading to himself at first then he swears loudly. "Motherfucker!"

"Give it to me." Blix takes charge, but his voice is on edge.

I swallow the knot in my throat. Whatever that message says is bad news for me. I wish with all my strength I was beside Ava so she could tell me what they're doing. Instead, I hear her speak, and fear paralyzes me.

"May I see the message?" Her voice is different now. It's innocent and strangely seductive. "Ooo, I never noticed your muscles. Do you work out? I bet you're ripped under this shirt."

*Oh, god, Ava, now is not the time to tweak his nose.* My brain is hot with fear.

"What the fuck!" Blix shouts. "Get your hands off me. Go back to your cot."

She sniffs as if he's offended her, and she walks away from the group toward the cot, taking a detour in front of me on the floor.

"Dear Sir," Blix reads loudly, derision in his tone.

He is not paying attention to Ava, which I realize is a great thing when I feel a hard object drop into my lap. Faster than anyone can see, I move my hand on top of it. She continues walking in the direction of that cot, and the men are none the wiser.

"He fucking called me *Sir*."

"That can't lead anywhere good," Taz taunts.

It's the push dagger. I don't know if it's my push dagger, but it's small enough to fit in the palm of my hand. If only I had my holster. If only I were still wearing my jeans. As it is, I'm in these fucking sweatpants with nowhere to hide it. I don't even have a pocket. My panties are gone... My only option is my bra, but I don't know if I can hide it there without attracting attention, much less get it out.

"He's not sending the money." Blix's voice has gone dead. "He says he's calling our bluff."

"Wrong choice, your majesty." Dev's voice drips with sarcasm.

That knot is in my throat again, and I don't have to be able to see to know they're all looking at me. I don't know what the hell I'm going to do now. I have a blade hidden in my palm, and my number just got called.

"Excuse me?" Ava's sassy voice breaks their focus on me. "Am I wrong or did my husband just refuse to negotiate with terrorists? It seems I told you that would happen."

"Is that right, queenie?" Taz starts to move in her direction.

*Ava, no!* I'm sitting in panic. Sometimes my friend is too ballsy for her own good.

"Won't negotiate with terrorists? Is that right?"

Sounds of a struggle then Ava gasps and whimpers.

"Don't hurt her!" I shout before I can think better of it.

*Shit!* Now all eyes are on me again.

"Taz!" Blix snarls. "Find a chair for the queen. She needs to witness how terrorists respond to a failure to negotiate." He's walking slowly to me, and I'm losing the ability to breathe. "Dev, get my kit."

Fear grips my chest. He's with me, jerking me to my feet. The small knife is in my right hand, and the pointed tip is digging into my middle finger. I can't hide it much longer. I need to get closer, close enough that I won't miss this time.

Dev leaves the room. Taz is getting a chair. Blix is so close, the front of his shirt brushes my left arm. It's now or never. *God help me...*

"DIE!" I scream, using my body weight for leverage as I rotate my fingers around the tiny blade.

No eyes, my aim is for the base of his neck. The satisfying *Chunk!* of metal piercing flesh fills my ears and warm liquid spills down my arm. I pull back to jab again, but I'm blocked.

Blix seizes my wrist. He's too strong, and he manages to squeeze the blade from my hand. It hits the concrete with a light tinging sound.

Gurgling is at my face, and vomit burns my throat. "Dev..." Blix tries to say, but his teeth are clenched together.

I got him right through the neck and into his jaw. Liquid bubbles in his throat, and I'm terrified. I got him, but it wasn't enough. He's still alive, and now I'm unarmed... And Taz and Dev are steps away.

Shushing noises come from my left. Ava races forward to grab the knife off the ground, but Blix is ready. Still holding my arm, I feel his leg move as he kicks her with all his might.

She yelps like a dog being kicked, and she lands with a hard thud. No more noises.

"AVA!" Tears are in my eyes, and as much as I try to fight them away, they spill down my cheeks.

He hurt her. More gurgling is at my ear. "Time to die, Kass." It's a snarling, wet sound through gritted teeth, and it nauseates me.

I try to jerk my arm away. I bend my knees and try to twist, but he has me. He whips me up and spins me around so my back is to his chest. Pushing me, he guides us to the cot. Blood is still pouring on me hot and sticky.

"JESUS!" Taz is back, running to where we stand. "What the hell happened to you?"

Blix's jaws are still clenched, but he grinds out a response. "Tie her up."

Taz takes me from his boss and pushes me onto my stomach on the cot. My hands are behind my back, and he grips my ankles. I struggle, trying to fight, but I'm hog-tied. I can't move. My wrists are behind my back, my ankles tied to them. I jerk, but it makes no difference. I can barely breathe, but I can hear Blix drowning in his own blood. It's the only thing that gives me hope. He's got to be weakening. He's got to pass out.

"Beautiful," he says through clenched teeth.

"Shit!" Now Dev is with us. "What the fuck happened to you?"

"I need fire," Blix says, and the momentary satisfaction I felt dissolves into panic. "Bring me a long, metal hook."

The tackle box hits the concrete. I hear it open, and I can see the scene in my mind's eye like so many times before. He's choosing the exact tool to inflict the most pain. A metal lighter scrapes, and orange flames appear in my peripheral vision.

"Where will you start?" Taz asks the question on everyone's mind.

"Ears," Blix growls, and I struggle against the rope. He knows the only thing I have left is my ability to hear. If he takes that away... "Only three things can cause permanent hearing loss in adults: disease, traumatic brain injury, or damage to the middle ear structure." I'm completely blinded by my tears as he continues. "Tie her hair back."

Taz jerks my head side to side as he pulls my hair into a knot. I can't escape. My wrists are bound to my ankles, and Ava is knocked out on the floor.

"Boss?" I've never heard Taz use such deference with Blix. It almost distracts me.

"What?"

"If you kill her, I'll never get to..." His voice dies out and my stomach roils. "I always wanted to try a blind girl."

Blix shoves off the stool and gets right in his face. "Blind-deaf girls still have warm pussies. You'll get to fuck her."

Bile fills my throat. If I wasn't sure I was in hell before, I'm convinced I've sunk to the depths now. Closing my eyes, I allow the tears to flow.

He pulls my earlobe taut, and I feel the heat approaching my skin. Hot metal sears my daith, and I shriek. I can't breathe anymore. I've reached the end, and with a final exhale, I release myself to...

Scream my ass off.

"NOOOO!!!!" I scream.

"NOOOO!!!!" I scream like it's the last thing I'll ever do, because it probably is.

I scream and scream. I scream so hard, I'll probably burst a blood vessel in my face.

I'm still screaming when the burning suddenly stops. I breathe hoarsely in and out. I sound like a wild thing, but I understand what's happening. Blix has fallen beside the cot.

"Boss?" Taz releases me to check on him, and I fall forward on my stomach.

Exhaustion hits me so hard. The darkness won't be held at bay any longer. It washes out my last ray of consciousness.

I'm drowning in what I'm certain is the end of my life...

I choke on a sob, and with the final strength in my body, I wish with all my heart for him. I hiccup a cry and say his name one last time.

*Logan...*

## Chapter 27: Recovery

*Logan*

Desperation sets in as we finish searching the third abandoned warehouse from top to bottom and find no trace of them.

"It's empty," Freddie says, returning to where I stand in the middle of the enormous, dark space, looking up at the grey sky visible overhead through the broken roof.

I let out a slow, measured breath. The king has his rejection of their demands set to go. He's convinced it will force them to make a move and blunder into the open, but I'm afraid of what will happen if he's wrong.

"What exactly did the satellite imagery show?" I demand, shining my light all around.

It's deserted, but clearly somebody's been here. We can tell from the abandoned shopping carts and the overwhelming funk of body odor.

"The king should be informed this one's a den of homeless people. Refugees most likely." Rex is beside me holding a cloth handkerchief over his mouth and nose.

"Ava will organize an outreach." I pat his shoulder, doing my best to keep our hope alive. "Come on. We have to find her so she can help them."

The evening is wearing on. It's not raining, but the low-hanging clouds makes it feel later than five. "What is the schedule on Rowan's email?"

"They gave us twenty-four hours from midnight

last night. He scheduled the email to go at five thirty. We can stop him if we think that isn't enough time."

Reaching up, I rub my fingers over my eyes. "Fuck," I growl. "What's left to search?"

Freddie is pacing, studying the face on his large smartphone. "It doesn't make sense. We've checked every abandoned site in the area. They have to be here!" His voice rises the more he speaks, and as much as I'm ready to shout myself, I need him to keep it together.

"So what's left?"

He stops and looks at me, his dark brow low over his dark eyes. "They wouldn't keep them in a warehouse being used... would they?"

"Let me see the images."

He quickly passes the device to me, and I watch as the black vehicle creeps around the outskirts of the city in the foothills before dropping down the Avenue des Guelfes.

"Central Export is right here." I point to the water's edge near the international heliport.

The muscle in his jaw moves back and forth. "It's too busy. Heli Air has hourly flights to St. Tropez. Anyone could find them there, and while they might get away with it because Kass is blind, Ava would yell for help."

Stefano has his phone out and starts to read. "Central Export specializes in food and non-food shipping to the African continent and the Caribbean."

Our eyes flash to each other's, and I'm moving before I finish saying. "MOVE!" I'm in the Mercedes with Freddie driving, Rex and Stefano are right behind us.

"We can't storm in there." Freddie is planning out loud. "They can't know we're coming. They have too many ways to escape. For all we know they could have a helicopter on standby."

"A helicopter is easy to track. They wouldn't get far."

"A cargo ship? They could already be gone in that case."

"No, they want the money." My bent elbow is propped on the window, and I pinch my top lip. "We've got to storm the place. We can't afford to waste time."

Kass is on my mind. I know she's been hurt once. I'm certain she's bleeding, in pain. My stomach twists, and I drop my fist willing the car to move faster.

"We need to get to her." It's a noise barely above a whisper, but I feel the car accelerate.

We have to go all the way up and around the university. We're on the border with France as we drive past the stadium. I check my watch. It's five thirty.

"The email has gone," I say, wishing I had my motorcycle.

Being in this huge vehicle we have to follow the wider streets, whereas on my bike, I could cut through alleys. I shift in my seat and rest my forearms on my legs.

"Come on!" I practically growl.

"Two more lights," Freddie says, and I hear the tension rippling through his voice as well.

I would say run the lights, but this is an incredibly busy area, filled with commuters to Nice and tourists catching helicopter flights further out to sea. If we're right, it's actually a brilliant place to hide two hostages. No one would ever think to look here. If we're wrong, we're losing valuable time, and I fucking know what happens when Blix is told no or made to wait. The gruesome package we received while searching for Zelda is at the forefront of my mind.

Finally we make it past the Avenue des Guelfes, and we're racing toward the shore where the shipping warehouse is across the street from the helipad.

"Which place do we search first?" He shouts, but I'm out of the car and racing toward the large, white airline hangar.

I push my legs so hard my thighs burn with exertion, and as I slam through the door, I sweep the area fast. An enormous black helicopter with white stripes down the sides and over the tail sits in the center of the enormous structure. A man in a dirty blue jumpsuit is at the back, and at the noise of the four of us stampeding in, he steps back, holding up a wrench.

"Que ce passé-t-il?" He's startled and wanting to know what's happening.

I explain in French we're searching for a party of men holding two women. He's confused, and I explain as best as I can without revealing the queen has been kidnapped.

"I've been here all day," he says in French. "No one like that has come or gone."

Stepping back, I face Freddie, Rex, and Stefano. "One place left."

We're out the door and headed back up the short distance to Central Export. A main office faces the road with a large warehouse rising behind it. The facility is blocked off from the main road by a chain-link fence, but no one appears to be manning the guard hut. Since I'm ahead of everyone, I race around the fence to the squat orange-stucco building. The windows are dark, and when I reach the glass doors they're locked. The front counter is empty.

"NO!" I shout just as Stefano joins me.

"Stand back!" he says, and I immediately comply.

He pulls what looks like a large pocketknife from his side holster, and turns it in his fist, lifting his blazer over his face just before slamming the tool into the glass. The door shatters at once, and we both charge through it, ducking under the steel bar on the inside.

The dark front office has two doors behind the counter, and we split up, right and left. Freddie and Rex are behind us. My door is bolted shut, but Stefano's opens easily. He flicks on a light, and I dash across looking all around the empty storeroom to verify no one is in it. A small bathroom is off the side, but the light isn't on.

"Look!" Freddie shouts.

He's pointing to heap on the floor that makes my insides clench. It's a pair of navy slacks I recognize as belonging to Kass. Even if I wasn't sure they were hers, they're soaked on one side with a dark stain that can only be blood.

"Fuck!" I shout, pushing out of the room and returning to the bolted door. "We've got to get this open!"

I step back and kick it with my booted foot as hard as I can. It doesn't budge. I push up on the counter and hit it hard with both feet. Still nothing.

From the other side of the door, I hear a noise that shrivels my insides. It's screaming. Nonstop screaming over and over. It's Kass.

"FUCK!" I shout louder. "Get this fucking door open! We're out of time!"

"Go to the back and try to get inside," Freddie shouts to Rex, who dashes for the broken glass doors. "You! A battering ram is in the trunk of our Mercedes."

Stefano is out the door, and I look at Freddie. The screaming has stopped, which is worse than hearing it.

Why did it stop?

"We've got to get in there..."

"Search for a key." He rips open drawers, shoving papers aside as I search the walls and doorjambs. The search is futile, but Stefano is back carrying a small red battering ram.

I'm the largest of the four of us, and I stretch out my hand. "Give it to me."

The two men flank me as I pull it back and slam with all my might against the plate at the door knob. It gives immediately and almost falls open on one strike.

"One more, and we'll be in," Freddie says as I'm pulling it back.

I let the ram fly with all my strength, and the door falls away to reveal a sight that sinks my insides. Ava is on the floor in a heap. Blix is sitting on the floor in a macabre state. His back is to the cot and blood soaks his neck and shirt running all the way down to his pants.

Gorilla Man and another man I recognize from the images on Freddie's computer stand over Kass, who is tied in a way that only makes me run harder. I grab Gorilla by the front of his shirt, and before he can respond, my fist makes contact with his neck. He falls back, most likely dead.

Freddie has the other guy, and the Bowie knife is out of my boot. I'm slicing through the cords, and as they snap, her feet fall, a little moan aches from her throat straight to my heart. Her arms go limp at her sides.

"Kass?" I say, petting her head.

I only get a moment to check on her when I feel that fucker Blix moving at my side. From the corner of my eye, I see as he reaches back then slams his fist into my leg causing an explosion of pain to rip through my calf.

"FUCK!" I yell, dropping to my knee.

I look down, and the handle of a punch dagger is sticking out of my leg. In that moment, Kass lunges past me. She's off the cot, grasping the handle of the Bowie knife. Sunlight blazes through the large warehouse doors as Rex slides them open to join us, and with a broken noise somewhere between a scream and a sob, Kass jams the blade straight into Blix's right eye just before collapsing onto her stomach.

"Jesus!" Freddie yells from behind me.

My rage is no match for hers, but when Blix makes another sound, my vision tunnels. Filling my mind is the torture he's inflicted. I see my beautiful Kass hogtied and bleeding, I see all the victims he's tortured and killed, and I remember my promise. Dragging him off the floor, I slam his back against the wall. His artery is cut, the knife still protrudes from his face, and that fucker refuses to die.

"Look at me," I say, boring into his remaining eye. No drop of humanity is left. He's pure evil.

"I see you, motherfucker," he snarls like a rabid dog. "I own you."

"You've never owned me." My fist is tightening on his neck, and he coughs up blood. "I'm the angel of death."

I might not have time to break every bone in his body, but I can get the one that counts. Lifting my right hand, I place it on the side of his head. Rotating the hand on his neck, I catch his jaw, and with one swift twist, the satisfying *Crunch* echoes up my arms.

His entire body goes limp, and I take my hands away, allowing him to fall into the heap of garbage he is. I turn away, and a flash of pain shoots through my leg.

"Shit," I hiss, reaching down to extract the push dagger from my muscle. I drop it on the floor and return to Kass. I'm injured, but from my time in the military, I know it's minor.

Kass is on the cot, her eyes still closed. Her beautiful hair is pulled away from her face in a crude knot, and her eyes are swollen from crying. A nasty purple gash is across her forehead, and she's wearing enormous grey sweatpants.

She's the most beautiful thing I've ever seen.

I sit on the cot and gather her into my arms, lifting her onto my lap. She begins to cry. "Is it over?"

Her whole body is shaking, and she grips my shirt. I have to blink a few times myself.

"It's over," I say, gently kissing her head, stroking my hand down the back of her hair. "I've got you."

"Logan…" Her voice breaks, and I feel her small body shudder in my arms.

I only tighten my hold on her. "Shh," I say, kissing her again. "Don't cry, my Sass. I've got you."

Freddie is across from me tending to Ava. She's not bloody, but she's wobbly. We need to get both of them to the hospital immediately. Stefano has Taz contained, and Dez appears dead on the floor. We're simply waiting for backup.

## Chapter 28: Nothing But the Truth

*Kass*

Panic strangles my throat. *Where am I?* The smell of bleach burns my nose, and a nonstop beeping is coming from somewhere above me. It's too dark to see forms, and my arm is restrained to the bed, which makes me panic even more.

"Let me out!" I try to speak, but my voice is gone. I try to sit up, but I can't move. A massive, dark form rises at my side, and fear floods my limbs…

Until he speaks, and I start to cry.

"It's okay, Sass." Logan's deep voice comforts me. His large hand smooths my hair. "I'm here."

"Logan…" It's all I can say.

His hand moves behind my neck, and I'm surrounded by his comforting scent.

"Where am I?" My voice is dry and cracking, and he moves away.

Cold filters around me without his presence, but it's only for a moment.

"Drink this." He holds something to my lips. "It's water. You're in the hospital."

"Oh!" I turn my head quickly straining my ears. "I can hear!"

It's a silly thing to say. Of course, I can hear. Logan and I have just been talking, but my brain is foggy, and I'm still piecing together where I am now and sorting through the macabre images in my brain.

"What..." Confusion is in Logan's voice, but just as fast he seems to understand. The cup is gone, and he's holding me again, wrapping me in those gloriously strong arms I love. I close my eyes and breathe deeply.

Anger simmers in the back of his voice when he speaks again. "You have a small burn on your ear... Is that what he tried to do to you?"

From inside the cocoon of Logan's arms, my voice sounds so small. "He was doing it... but you were there."

Even with Logan's arms around me and my face in his chest, a shiver moves through my bones.

His grip on me tightens. "He's dead, my Sass. You never have to fear him again."

I struggle out of his arms and try to push myself into a sitting position. Only my arm is still tied. "Why..." Then the realization hits me. *They think I took Ava... I'm one of the bad guys again.* I can barely say the words, "I'm a prisoner."

Logan slides off the small bed and moves around to where I'm restrained. "Not exactly —"

Just then the door opens. "*Excusez-moi,*" A female voice addresses us in French. "I need to check Miss Kroft."

Logan kisses my head and goes to the door. "I won't be far."

"Let me help you." The woman goes to my side, and I listen as she unfastens the buckles, releasing my arm. "We stitched your side and treated your head."

My head. I reach up with my now-free hand and touch the bandage. "I forgot..."

"We closed it with medical glue. It follows the lines in your forehead, so it shouldn't leave a noticeable scar." She's lifting the blankets near my hip, and I turn so she can access my side. "Yes." A smile is in her voice. "You're healing quite well. We can release you today if you like?"

Before I can answer, another voice joins her. "And how is Miss Kroft?" It's the grand duke.

"Healing quite well, your grace. I was just saying she could go home if she likes."

My brow furrows, *So I'm not a prisoner?*

"Let me speak to her, but yes, please start the release papers."

"Of course." The woman leaves us, and I sit up.

"Miss Kroft, I asked to speak to you a moment."

"It wasn't a vaccine." Unexpected anger fills my chest. Perhaps I have no right. Perhaps I was always a prisoner, despite what Freddie or Ava said, but still. "You lied to me."

"We needed your help—"

"You could have asked for my help." I lift the blanket to get up and stop when I realize I'm only wearing a hospital gown.

He seems to understand. "Yes, well. Perhaps this isn't the best time. However, I will say thank you. You helped us a great deal." The click of expensive shoes on linoleum tracks him to the door. "The queen regent brought a parcel of clothes for you. It's on the table there."

I don't reply. The door clicks shut, and for a moment I don't move. So many emotions rush in on me at once—I'm not a prisoner, Blix is dead, Logan is somewhere... Overriding them all, like a vacuum opening in the center of my chest, is the crushing memory I held off as long as possible: *Cameron*.

My breath stills and my eyes squeeze shut. I wrap my arms around my stomach. *Hold on, Cassandra.* I have to hold on just a little bit longer. I have to find

Ava so she can help me… Ava. Where is Ava?

I slide off the narrow mattress and fumble to the side table where a small bag sits. My foot hits a boot, and I lean down to run my hands over tall leather. This is good.

A few clicks, and I'm in the bathroom. A chunky sweater and filmy, short skirt are quickly on. Returning to the dresser, I roll on the knee socks and stick my feet in the boots. I'm ready to face what comes next when the door opens slowly.

I wish I had my glasses. I wish there was more light in this room. I don't know who's standing there, so I wait… for the voice that crumbles my insides.

"You're dressed. You're—"

My involuntary cry cuts him off, and I run to meet him at the door. His arms go around me, and I'm holding his waist, squeezing him and crying. My body won't stop shaking, and the emotions pulse in my chest with every heartbeat.

"Cameron!" I'm soaking his shirt with my tears, but I can't seem to care. All I can do is hold him. "Cameron…" It's a shattered whisper.

"Hey." His voice is soothing. "It's okay. You're okay now."

"But…" I hiccup a breath and step back, still holding his forearms. "You were shot."

"Almost." He lifts my hand to his forehead. I feel the bandage on the side as he continues. "I guess it was too dark? Still, it knocked me out. Logan found me." He reaches up and lightly touches my head. "We're twins again."

Tears are still in my eyes, and I start to laugh as gratitude heals the pain in my chest. I step forward again to hug him so tight.

"I'm so happy we're twins again."

"Not true. You always hated that." He laughs and squeezes me again before struggling out of my clinging hold. "I'm happy you're okay."

"Take me home?" My hand slides to the crook of his arm.

"Sure."

*  *  *

My brother says goodbye as I open the metal door to my apartment building. It's been so long since I was here. It's the first time I enter without fear.

Cameron briefly filled me in on the drive home — as he tolerated me holding his hand and touching him every few minutes. Blix is dead, Dev is dead, and Taz is in prison. He didn't say if I would be taken into custody — I don't know if that's what Reggie wanted — but I'm not hiding. They know where to find me when they're ready.

Stepping into the dark hallway, I look up the narrow flight of stairs, wondering if...

*Click, click, click...*

*The noise of doggy nails on hardwood.*

*Yip! Yip!*

Tears spring into my eyes again. "Henri?" I grab the rail, and he yips again, his nails dance on the floor above. "Henri! I'm home!"

I don't hesitate this time. I jog straight up the stairs and drop to sit on the top one. The little dog is in my lap licking the tears off my face, and my smile is so big. I can't stop laughing, and of course, he gets me right in the mouth.

"Oh!" I spit, trying to catch his happy muzzle as it dances all around my face. "So French!"

This time when the door down the hall opens, a sharp command in French is not forthcoming. Instead heavy footsteps make their way to where I'm sitting, petting the ecstatic little dog.

"Bonjour, Cassandra," Luc says. "I'm happy to see you home."

"Merci, Luc." I smile up at him.

He makes a grunting noise and with a shuffle, he turns and starts back to his apartment. A clucking sound, and Henri hops out of my lap to take off after him. I sit for a moment looking in their direction, trying to decide what to do now.

I don't have my phone. I don't have anything, but I always leave that spare key above my door. I'm about to stand and head inside when I hear a banging on the metal door below. My brow furrows, and I'm about to speak when I hear the buzzing release of the lock. It opens with a clatch, and I'm frozen on the spot.

Who...

"You left without telling me."

The breath leaves my body at the sound of Logan's voice. He's here, and I can't decide if I want to cry or laugh... or allow him to take me into custody.

"I'm sorry." Is what I manage to say. "Cameron was there... H-he's alive." I'm still overwhelmed by the reality of that, and my eyes heat.

Heavy boots take my stairs two at a time, and I exhale *What?* just before I'm scooped up in two massively strong arms.

"You're alive." Logan's deep voice is at my ear. He kisses my neck, my temple.

Leaning forward, I wrap my arms around his neck. My legs are around his waist, both his arms are around my lower back, and I bury my face in his collar. For several minutes, we only hold each other that way.

Both of us are breathing fast, and it feels as though we're melting into one another right here on the landing in front of my apartment.

At last he lifts his head. "I'm not letting you leave me again."

Nodding quickly, I don't even consider arguing. "Okay."

"These last few days were a fucking nightmare."

Lowering my face to his shoulder, I nod again. "What happens now?"

"Can you get in your apartment?"

With a sniff, I lower my legs. He releases me and waits while I reach along the top of my door until my fingers make contact with the small piece of metal. I unlock the door, and we step inside the tiny room.

"Let's pack up and move everything to my place."

But my stomach twists unexpectedly at his words. "Wait…"

He's with me again, and in the bright interior of my tiny apartment, I can make out his dark form looming over me. He cups my face in one hand and slides his thumb over my cheek.

"What's the matter, Sass?" His voice is melted sunshine in my chest, and I don't really know the answer to his question. All I've ever wanted is him standing here saying these things. I want him, us, together. Yet, at the same time…

"It's all happening so fast. I-I just woke up, and I don't even know… Where is Ava? Is she okay?"

He sits on my bed and large hands circle my waist. "Come here." With a gentle pull, I'm sitting on his lap in a straddle facing him, my hands resting on his shoulders. "Ava is fine. She got hit on the head pretty hard, but it wasn't concussive. She's back at the palace."

"I'm so glad... But..." Another vision is in my mind, and I can't tell if it's real or a fantasy.

Long fingers trace the hair off my cheek. "What is it?"

"Blix." Blinking fast, I remember Logan shouting in pain. I remember my insides filling with fear, anger, and adrenaline. I remember fighting through my own pain, calling on all the strength I had left in me to stop the madman. I remember the scraping of knife against bone.

"I wanted to hurt him. I wanted to—" I'm afraid to say what I hope I did. Will it make me as savage as Blix?

"What did you want, my love?"

So much warmth and safety is in his beautiful voice. I know I can tell him everything, even my darkest truths. I realize now I always could. "I wanted to kill him. But... not just kill him." I have to whisper it. "I wanted to make him suffer."

An edge of anger is in Logan's voice. "That bastard is no longer a threat to you or anyone else."

I slide my fingers along his collar thinking about those final seconds. "How did he die?" I'm quietly hoping...

"When we got there, he was sitting on the floor. He'd nearly bled out from a knife wound to the neck—under his jaw."

"But... that didn't kill him?"

"It probably would have. I had to cut the ropes holding you, and that bastard stabbed my leg."

"I remember that part." My fingers tighten on his shoulders. "You were in pain. I heard you, and I didn't know how bad it was."

A grin is in his voice now. "I couldn't believe it. You stabbed him in the fucking face, Kass. You're a fucking badass."

I'm going to hell, and I don't even care. Pride surges through my chest. "Did that kill him?"

"It probably would have. I wasn't patient enough to wait."

I lean forward, wrapping my arms around my guy. "You killed him?"

"I finished him off."

Turning my face, I kiss his neck as I slide my fingers along his beard. "So it really is over."

Strong arms surround me, and he leans down to find my mouth. I lift my head and cup my hands on each side of his square jaw, kissing him deeply. Our mouths move faster. His lips chase mine, mine chase his, and heat roars to life low in my pelvis.

I thread my fingers in his soft hair. My hips are moving, rocking against his waist, and his hands slide up my thighs and under the filmy skirt I'm wearing. When he reaches the center, my mouth breaks away.

"Oh, god…" I gasp.

Warm lips cover the skin on my neck, but it's his long fingers tracing a path along the seam of my panties that has me falling apart. They circle, moving closer until…

"Oh, yes!" I moan.

My thighs jump in ecstasy as his fingers glide over my clit, massaging and taunting. He lifts me and turns us so I fall on my back on the bed.

"I've missed this so much," he groans, sliding down my legs and flipping my skirt over my stomach. "I want to taste you."

He's on his knees, grasping the sides of my panties and pulling them down and off. Just as fast he spreads my thighs apart, wrapping his arms around them and dragging me across the bed to his mouth.

"Ahh!" I wail as his beard teases my sensitive skin. I'm burning up from the orgasm smoldering in my bloodstream.

His warm tongue makes a slow pass over my clit before moving down and tasting me deeply. My body shivers and tingling heat floods my pelvis.

"Logan! Logan..." I'm on the edge, and he gives me one more slow pass before leaning back to unfasten his jeans.

I hear them slide down, and I'm so wet and ready for his fullness. I lift my hands to reach for him. His hands meet mine, and our fingers entwine just as he leans forward, bracing on his elbows. One hand leaves mine, and he reaches between us, lining his cock up at the entrance to my core.

"Jesus, Sass. You're so beautiful." And with a firm thrust, he sinks deep inside, stretching and massaging me in the most erotic way.

I cry out from the delicious feel of him moving faster, hitting my clit as my insides twist and pull together into one irresistible ball. Until with another thrust, and another...

I explode with a loud cry, my back arching off the bed. The pleasure is so intense, I feel like I've left my body. Only his strong arms carry me through the flood of pleasure ravaging my insides.

My hands clutch his broad shoulders. He groans and grinds out my name like a prayer. He's so close. I lean up and plant my lips on the top of his chest, slipping out my tongue to taste the salt of his sweat. I stretch up to kiss the base of his neck, and when I bite his skin, he erupts.

"Fuck," he growls holding my body flush against him. He's in me, filling me, balls deep, and I feel every pulse of his cock as his orgasm jerks him repeatedly.

His head is against my shoulder and with every pulse, he exhales the most amazing low groan. It causes my pussy to clench around him again as if I can't get enough.

"Fuck me, you feel so good." He finds my mouth and kisses me deeply. Our mouths seal together, and salt is on both our tongues as they entwine.

My hands fumble to his cheeks, and I pull his face closer, kissing him harder. Another pulse deep inside me, and I whimper. It's so good. Our mouths break apart, and he lifts his chin.

"I think I made it to heaven that time," he laughs, and I can't resist touching the tip of my tongue to the hollow between his collarbones.

"You brought me with you." I smile, savoring the feel of his massive body in my arms, between my legs, deep inside me.

This is exactly right. This is how it's supposed to be. His face drops down, and he kisses my temple, my cheek, the side of my jaw. We roll to the side, and he slips out, pulling me against his chest. Strong arms surround me with love and warmth and safety.

"You're coming with me now, to my place." It's not a question, and I don't argue. Still, he touches my chin with his thumb. "I want to hear you say it."

That makes me grin. "I'm going home with you now."

Both his arms go back around me, and I'm rewarded with another lingering kiss. "I love hearing those words together."

"Home?" I ask.

"With you."

I nestle into his embrace. "You've always been my home since that first day on the beach. I saw you and something inside me changed."

His fingers trace down the line of my back making me shiver. "That summer was so perfect it was hard to believe." He kisses my head. "We were so young, and I'd found you. I never got over you, Sass. I kept looking for you everywhere."

"When I think of love and happiness, you're the only face I see."

He leans back to cup my chin, lifting my lips to his. "It will always be that way, from now until the end of our days."

Warm lips cover mine, and the world fades away. I'm safe in his loving arms, and I never plan to leave. We lost each other. I made mistakes. I was dirty, and I couldn't imagine ever being clean enough or good enough for my wonderful man.

Now through a miracle of fate, I've been given a second chance, and it's a gift I won't take for granted.

His lips move to my cheek, and he speaks directly in my ear. "I love you, Sass."

Joy expands so rapidly in my chest, my eyes heat. "I love you, Logan Hunt."

It's a promise from the depths of my soul. He's the home I've longed for, he's my euphoric desire, and he's my enduring future. I see our love as clear as a painting. Not a blurry Monet, but a Renoir—detailed and precise lines.

I fell in love and my eyes were closed, so I stayed there. Now my heart's eyes have been opened, and I see everything worth seeing. I don't need unique or extravagant words. What we've found is quite simple. It's forever.

Our happily ever after.

The end.

# Epilogue: After

*Logan*

Brilliant white light floods my enormous studio apartment. Since Kass moved in six months ago, we've done all we can to maximize the amount of natural light filtering into the space. I was resistant at first, until I realized how much it helps her see objects... in particular me. Once I got it, she had to stop me from picking up a can of reflective paint at the store.

The memory makes me laugh.

"What's so funny?" Her voice is lazy this morning.

It's ten, and we've just spent the last half hour making love. Now she's sitting up in bed, and I'm lying on my back in her arms. My head rests on a pillow beside her breast, and she still has a leg tossed over my stomach. I reach up to cup the back of her shoulder.

"I was thinking about reflective paint." Turning on my side, my mouth is right at her growing midsection. "We might decide to rethink all this light once the baby comes."

"Hmm... or he'll learn to sleep even when it's not completely dark?"

"So it's a boy now?" I reach up to move a lock of pale blonde hair off her face.

"He kicks so much. I've decided it must be a boy." Her chin drops, and she slides both palms over her cute baby bump. "A girl would be more relaxed in there."

"Based on what scientific evidence, Mrs. Hunt?" I confess, I love calling her that.

She giggles and leans straight into my face to kiss me. "Absolutely none, Mr. Hunt."

Her full breasts slide over my chest, and my cock twitches. I'm feeling my second wind rising, and I cup her breast, rolling her hardening nipple between my fingers. Reaching behind her neck, I pull her closer for a deeper kiss. She moans opening her mouth to let our tongues curl together, but with a groan, she pulls back.

"I have to go." Her leg untwines from around my waist, and she tries to get up.

"Hang on." I catch her by the waist and roll her onto her back underneath me. "Why do you have to go?"

"Logan!" she laughs, pushing against my shoulder. "Ava is having a tea for us today. You know this! I can't be late!"

My lips twist into a frown. "A tea?"

"She's being so sweet. You'd think we were related by how excited she is about the baby."

I bend down and plant a kiss just above her navel. "Kid, you are about to be so spoiled." That gets me another laugh, and I move to the side so she can get out of the bed.

"Where is this tea happening?" I lean against the pillows watching her skip over to the dresser and go through her system of selecting what to wear.

"Occitan. Have you listened to anything I've said?" She's my adorable, naked little pregnant lady. My wife. My badass, blind wife, who won't back down from cutting out the eyes of a monster.

When Ava told me what they'd done, their plan to kill Blix, I wavered between admiration and total, absolute fury.

They went after that fucking madman. They actually *allowed* themselves to be kidnapped by him on the slim chance the two of them could outsmart him. The thought of it provokes a fist of rage so hot in my chest, even now with the bastard dead and in the ground I have to distract myself. Still, it is amazing he's dead in part because my gorgeous wife stuck a push dagger in his throat and a Bowie knife in his eye.

Admiration mixed with anger mixed with anxiety is a curious emotion... I'm calling it *Adanxety* in honor of my wife's obsession with unique words.

I'm getting pretty familiar with how it feels.

Rowan's response was somewhere in the vicinity of nuclear fury. He doubled the watch on Ava and lectured her in front of Freddie and me on the level of freedom he allows her and what will happen if she abuses it again.

Naturally she was livid at his response. Her sapphire eyes blazed like a gas fire, and I worried for a few minutes she would leave for Tortola. Kass had only just moved in with me, and I wasn't confident she would uproot and go with me after her. Still, I knew Rowan would order us to follow his wife.

It was a tense hour and a half waiting for the king to calm down enough to find his wife and smooth her ruffled, independent feathers. Help came from an unexpected source when the grand duke gently reminded his nephew the Wilder sisters did not come from a royal background. He went even further to remind him exactly how Ava and Zelda did grow up — on the streets hustling for food and shelter.

That crisis had been averted, and to my knowledge Kass is none the wiser. She and Ava are inseparable, and Ava even secured Kass the job as chief diplomatic interpreter for the king in all his meetings of state. In return, Rowan appointed me as guard to his chief diplomatic interpreter, and I couldn't have been happier with the assignment.

Kass's need for autonomy frustrates me, but I respect it. She doesn't want to be dependent on anyone. After the years she spent as a slave to Blix and his orders, she needs to feel like she's in control of her life. That much I understand, and she's found a powerful ally in the queen regent.

The two are fiercely loyal since their victory over the forces of evil. I focus on the fact that we *did* find them in time, and neither was seriously injured... and not on what might have happened.

Ava has only been angry with my wife once as far as I know — when we ran straight from the doctor's office to city hall to get married after we confirmed we were pregnant. It had been an impulsive decision, but it had also been joyous and romantic. Neither of us have family — other than Kass's little brother, and Cameron had been all too willing to meet us for the brief civil ceremony.

We'd been overflowing with love for each other, and the only thing that could have made it better would be to pledge ourselves officially to each other for all time. So we'd done it. Then we left immediately for Campania. We spent three sex-filled days in that beautiful little hamlet by the sea. We'd always said we'd go there, and I wanted nothing more than to watch the sun rise and set over my new wife's naked body with the noise of the sea in the background.

When we finally returned, blissed out and glowing, Ava threw the most elaborate celebration for a non-royal family to date, and I'm pretty sure her ruffled feathers over missing the ceremony are now soothed.

Kass returns, filling the room with her scent of clean linen and jasmine. She's so pretty wearing a loose, floral dress with her long hair flowing down her back.

"Are you heading over now?" I can't keep the grin out of my voice as I watch her move around the room as easy as any sighted person would.

"Come when you're ready." She skips over to kiss my lips. "Rowan has much to discuss with you, I'm sure. He nearly came to verbal blows with the Spanish ambassador on Thursday."

"You're liking your job." I catch her face and kiss her once more before she leaves me.

"I love it." She smiles and runs her palm down my cheek. "Almost as much as I love you."

Hearing those words from her will never stop making my life, I'm sure of it. "And I love you, Sass."

She skips out the door, and I grab my phone. Only one thing would make her happier, and I shoot a text to her brother to be here in a half hour so he can go with me.

It's funny how life turns around in the most unexpected way. A year ago, I wanted to resign. I'd been at the lowest point of my adult life. Coming off the Zelda job, I'd realized I had no one, and I had no prospects of finding anyone.

I came back here and everything changed. Our road is exciting and challenging and meets every need and desire I've ever had for love and life.

I can't imagine it any other way.

* * *

*Up next is DIRTY THIEF, Rowan and Ava's glamorous, seductive, and unforgettable love story, coming Spring 2017!*

*Fill out this form and get an exclusive email alert when it's live:*
*http://www.subscribepage.com/DTSignup*

*Or get a text alert:*
*Text "TiaLouise" to 64600 Now!\**
*\*(U.S. only)*

\* \* \*

**Are you on Facebook? Join the Dirty Players Discussion Group and chat all about the story with fellow readers:**
*www.facebook.com/groups/DirtyPlayersTLM*

\* \* \*

*Never miss a new release!*

**Sign up for my New Release newsletter**, and get a **FREE Subscriber-only Bonus Scene** from *One to Love*! **(http://smarturl.it/TLMnews)\***

## *Your opinion counts!*

If you enjoyed *Dirty Dealers,* please leave a short, sweet review wherever you purchased your copy.

Reviews help your favorite authors more than you know.

*Thank you so much!*

* * *

# BOOKS BY TIA LOUISE

*Signed Copies* of all books can be found online at: http://smarturl.it/SignedPBs

### THE ONE TO HOLD SERIES

NOTE: All are stand-alone novels. Adult Contemporary/Erotic Romance: Due to strong language and sexual content, books are not intended for readers under the age of 18.

*One to Hold*

Derek Alexander is a retired Marine, ex-cop, and the top investigator in his field. Melissa Jones is a small-town girl trying to escape her troubled past.

When the two intersect in a bar in Arizona, their sexual chemistry is off the charts. But what is revealed during their "one week stand" only complicates matters.

Because she'll do everything in her power to get away from the past, but he'll do everything he can to hold her.

\* \* \*

*One to Protect*

When Sloan Reynolds beats criminal charges, Melissa Jones stops believing her wealthy, connected ex-husband will ever pay for what he did to her.

Derek Alexander can't accept that—a tiny silver scar won't let him forget, and as a leader in the security business, he is determined to get the man who hurt his fiancée.

Then the body of a former call girl turns up dead. She's the breakthrough Derek's been waiting for, the link to Sloan's sordid past he needs. But as usual, legal paths to justice have been covered up or erased.

Derek's ready to do whatever it takes to protect his family when his partner Patrick Knight devises a plan that changes everything.

It's a plan that involves breaking rules and taking a walk on the dark side. It goes against everything on which Alexander-Knight, LLC, is based.

And it's a plan Derek's more than ready to follow.

\* \* \*

### One to Keep

*There's a new guy in town...*

*"Patrick Knight, single, retired Guard-turned private investigator. I was a closer. A deal maker. I looked clients in the eye and told them I'd get their shit done. And I did..."*

Patrick doesn't do "nice."

At least, not anymore.

After his fiancée cheats, he follows up with a one-night stand and a disastrous office hook-up. His business partner (Derek Alexander) sends him to the desert to get his head straight--and clean up the mess.

While there, Patrick meets Elaine, and blistering sparks fly, but she's not looking for any guy. Or a long-distance relationship.

Patrick's ready to do anything to keep her, but just when it seems he's changed her mind, the skeletons from his past life start coming back.

\* \* \*

### One to Love

*Tattoos, bad boys, love…*
*Boxing, fame, fortune…*
**Loss.**

It's the one thing Kenny and Slayde have in common. Until the night Fate throws them together and everything changes.

It's a story about fighting. It's about falling in love. And it's about losing everything only to find it again in the least likely place.

\* \* \*

### One to Leave

*Stuart Knight is a wounded Marine turned Sexy Cowboy. Mariska Heron is the gypsy girl who stole his heart.*

Some demons can't be shaken off.
Some wounds won't heal.
Until a pair of hazel eyes knocks you on your ass, and you realize it's time to stop running.

\* \* \*

***One to Save***

*"I lost myself in the darkness of trying to protect you..."*

Some threats come at you as friendly fire.
Some threats take away everything.
Family won't let you go down without a fight.

The Secret isn't as secure as Derek's team originally thought it was, and a person on the inside of Alexander-Knight is set on exposing him, breaking him, and taking away all he holds dear.

Refusing to let anyone suffer for his crimes, Derek takes matters into his own hands. He's exposed, he's defenseless, but his friends are determined to save him.

\* \* \*

***One to Chase***

*Paris fashions,*
*Chicago nightlife,*

*Secrets and lies...*
*Welcome to the North Side.*

Marcus Merritt doesn't chase women. He doesn't have to. But when the spirited and sexy blonde who left him wanting more shows up in his

office looking for work, little things like the rules seem ready to be rewritten.

Amy Knight is smart, ambitious, and back home in Chicago to care for her mother. A courtesy meeting with one of the top lawyers in the city should be a boost to her career...

Until the polished green-eyed player turns out to be the same irresistible "random" she hooked up with at a friend's wedding in Wilmington. Bonus: He's the brother of her older brother's new wife. What the hell?!

Who's chasing whom? It all depends on the day. ***Or the night.***

\*\*\*

### *One to Take*

*Stuart Knight is a wounded Marine turned Sexy Cowboy. Mariska Heron is the gypsy girl who stole his heart. Now they're fighting for their Happily Ever After...*

> Life is never simple.
> Even perfect couples face storms.
> The question is whether our love is strong enough to survive.
> I believe it is.

> She told me to leave.
> If I leave, I take her with me.
> ~Stuart Knight

\*\*\*

## PARANORMAL ROMANCES

### *One Immortal*

*Melissa is a vampire; Derek is a vampire hunter.*

When beautiful, sad Melissa Jones flees to New Orleans with her telepathic best friend, she is looking for a cure—not an erotic encounter with a sexy former Marine.

Derek Alexander left the military intending to become a private investigator, but with two powerful shifters as partners and an immunity to vampire glamour, he instead rose to the top in paranormal justice.

At a bar on Bourbon Street, Derek and Melissa cross paths, and their sexual chemistry is off the charts. Acting on their feelings, they are pulled deeper into an affair, but Melissa is hiding, hoping to escape her cruel maker.

It doesn't take long before the shifters uncover her secret. Still, Derek is determined to confront the Old One and reclaim her mortality—even at the risk of losing his.

\* \* \*

*One Insatiable*

**(Loosely based on the Hades & Persephone myth.)**

*One wounded panther, one restless lynx: One insatiable hunger.*

Mercy Quinlan is a whip-smart lynx and the youngest in her shifter clan. She's tough and independent and dreams of escaping her alpha sister's control and living life on her own terms.

When a lone black panther shows up in her hometown, Mercy is intrigued. He's just passing through, which makes him perfect... Along with his broad shoulders, defined muscles, and sexy fighter moves.

Koa "Stitch" Raiden is picking up what's left of his broken life. Exiled from his black panther clan, he's running from Princeton to Seattle when he's drawn to Woodland Creek.

He's aware Mercy is watching him. What he doesn't know is the sexy little vixen who sneaks through his window each night is both the trouble he doesn't need and the hope he can't live without.

\*\*\*

## THE DIRTY PLAYERS DUET

***Cinderella*** **meets** ***Ocean's Eleven* in this CONTEMPORARY ROMANCE DUET featuring secrets, lies, royal high jinks, scams and double-crosses; breathless, swooning lust, cocky princes, dominant alpha future-kings, and crafty courtiers, who are not always what they seem.**

### *The Prince & The Player (#1)*

*Let the games begin...*

Runaway Zelda Wilder will do whatever it takes to secure a better life for her and her sister Ava. Crown Prince Rowan Westringham Tate will do whatever it takes to preserve his small country.

When Zee is blackmailed into helping a vengeful statesman take down Rowan, she never expects she'll be pulled into a web of lies and international intrigue-- much less that she'll find herself falling for Cal,

Rowan's "playboy" younger brother.

Ava's no help, as she finds quiet walks in the moonlight discussing poetry and leadership with the brooding future king irresistible. Even more irresistible is kissing his luscious lips.

They're in over their heads, and the more time passes, the more danger the sisters are in. Shots are fired, and it's soon clear even a prince might not be able to rescue these players.

\* \* \*

*A Player for A Princess (#2)*

*From the Mediterranean to the Caribbean, the game continues…*

Zelda Wilder is on the run, this time from the ruthless assassins who've decided she knows too much to live.

"Playboy Prince" MacCallum Lockwood Tate isn't about to let the beautiful player who stole his heart get away — if only he could decide whether he wants to save her or strangle her for her dangerous choices.

After tracking her down to a casino in St. Croix, Cal follows Zee back to Tortola where he intends to keep her safe. One problem: Zelda's criminal liaisons are two steps ahead of her.

Lives are threatened, and all of the players' skills are tested in this plot to capture a killer and save a princess.

\* \* \*

# Acknowledgments

This is always the hardest part of every book for me. SO many people help me with each new book in a myriad of ways—from my beta readers Ilona, Lisa, and Helene, to my eagle-eyed proofer Candy, you guys are rockstars!

My hardest critique partner, Mr. TL has gotten better at not making me cry with his critiques... LOL! To the authors who graciously made room in their crammed schedules to give me a read and a kudos—I appreciate YOU so much more than I can say... You have no idea.

My author-buds Aleatha, Ilsa, Elle, Katie—thank you from the bottom of my heart.

Special thanks to Hang Le for the beautiful cover design. You're a genius. And to every reader who makes teasers, please know those beautiful little works of art flood my insides with so much joy!

HUGE THANKS to Heather Roberts for her tireless advice and guidance. It's so great to have you on my team. I appreciate YOU.

To my BABES and to the DIRTY PLAYERS Facebook groups, *Thank You* for giving me a place to relax and be silly. THANKS to ALL the bloggers who have made an art and a science to book loving. I couldn't do this without you!

To everyone who picks up this book, reads it, loves it, and tells one person about it, you've made my day. I'm so grateful to you all. Without readers, there would be no writers.

Lots of love,
<3 *Tia*

# EXCLUSIVE SNEAK PEEK

*The Prince & The Player*
(Dirty Players, #1)
© TLM Productions LLC, 2016

*Zelda Wilder*

My legs are wet. Thunder rolls low in a steel-grey sky, and the hiss of warm rain grows louder. I lean further sideways into the culvert, closer against my little sister Ava's body, and grit my teeth against the hunger pain twisting my stomach. There's no way in hell I'm sleeping tonight.

Reaching up, I rub my palm against the back of my neck, under the thick curtain of my blonde hair. A shudder moves at my side, and I realize Ava's crying. We're packed tight in this concrete ditch, but I twist my body around to face her.

Clearing my throat, I force my brows to unclench. I force my voice to be soothing instead of angry. "Hey," I whisper softly. "What's the matter, Ava-bug?"

Silence greets me. She's small enough to be somewhat comfortable in our hideout. Her knees are bent, but unlike me, they're not shoved up into her nose. Still, she leans forward to press her eyes against the backs of her hands. Her glossy brown hair is short around her ears and falls onto her cheeks.

Our parents were classic movie buffs, naming her after Ava Gardner and me after Scott Fitzgerald's crazy wife Zelda. We pretty much lived up to our monikers, since my little sister wound up having emerald green cat eyes and wavy dark hair. She's a showstopper whereas I'm pretty average—flat blue eyes and dishwater blonde. So far no signs of schizophrenia (*har har*), but you can bet your ass I can keep up with the boys in everything, which brings us to this lowly state.

"Come on, now," I urge. "It can't be as bad as all that."

Her dark head moves back and forth. "I'm sorry." Her soft whisper finally answers my question. "This is all my fault."

"What?" Reaching for her skinny shoulder, I pull her up. She's the only person I've ever known who looks pretty even when she's crying. "Why would you say something like that?"

"I tried cutting my hair off. I tried not brushing my teeth—"

"Don't be doing shit like that!" I snap, turning to face front. The rain keeps splashing on my side getting me even wetter. "We can't afford a dentist."

"I don't know what to do, Zee."

Pressing my lips together, I clench my fists on top of my knees. "We ain't going back into no foster home. I'll take care of us."

"But how?" Her voice breaks as it goes high in a whisper.

"Hell, I don't know, but I got all night to figure it out." I press my front teeth together and think. We're not that far from being legal. I'm seventeen, but Ava's only fifteen. Looking at the sand on my shoes, I get an idea. "We got one thing going for us."

"What's that?" My little sister sniffs, and I hear the tiniest flicker of hope in her voice. She'll trust whatever I tell her, and I take that responsibility very seriously.

"We live in the greatest state to be homeless. Sunny Florida."

"Okay?" Her slim brows wrinkle, and the tears in her eyes make them look like the ocean.

"We don't have to worry about getting cold or anything. We don't have to worry about snow..." I'm thinking hard, assembling a plan in my mind. "During the day, we fly under the radar—keep your head down, don't attract attention. I'll see what I can find us to eat. At night we can sleep on the beach. Or here, or hell, maybe one of these rich assholes forgets to lock his boathouse. Have you seen how nice some of these boathouses are? They're like regular houses!"

Her eyes go round with surprise. "Why are they like that?"

"Hell, I don't know. Rich people are crazy. Some rich men even get their nails polished, and they aren't even gay!"

Air bursts through her lips, and she starts to laugh. I smile and pull her arm so she can lie down with her face on my bony, empty stomach. "Now get some sleep."

The rain is tapering off, and my little sister is laughing instead of crying. I don't have any idea if anything I just said is possible, but I'm going to find out. I'll be damned if I let another foster asshole touch her. It's what Mom would expect me to do. I'm the biggest. I have to take care of us, and I intend to do it.

\* \* \*

*Crown Prince Rowan Westringham Tate*

The navy fabric of my father's uniform coat stretches taut across his shoulders. It's the tangible warning sign his anger is rising, and the person addressing him would do well to *shut up.*

"Monagasco has been an independent nation for eight hundred years." His voice is a rolling growl pricking the tension in my chest.

The last time my father started on our nation's history, the offending party was thrown out of the meeting room by the neck. He's getting too old for such violent outbursts. I worry about his heart... and my future. My *freedom*, more specifically.

"I think what Hubert was trying to say—" The Grand Duke, my mother's brother Reginald Winchester, tries to intervene.

"I KNOW what Hubert is trying to say!" My father (a.k.a., The King) cuts him off. "He thinks we should cede our southwestern territory to Totrington! Even though their raiders and bandits have pillaged our farms along the border for *generations*!"

Leaning back in my heavy oak chair, I steeple my fingers before my lips and don't say what I want. As crown prince, I've attended these meetings for three years, since I turned nineteen. I've learned when to speak and when to discuss things in private with my father.

I could say I agree with Reggie, we should consider a trade agreement with our neighboring nation-state, but I'm more concerned about the King's health. I've never seen him so worked up before.

"Independence at all costs," he continues, his naturally pink cheeks even pinker. "We will not give those savages an open door to the control of Monagasco."

"No one's suggesting—"

"Shut UP, Hubert!" My father shouts, and I glance down to avoid meeting the earl's offended eyes.

Hubert's sniveling voice is like nails on a chalkboard, and I privately enjoy my father chastising him. I've always suspected him of conspiring with Wade Paxton, Totrington's newly elected Prime Minister, from the time when Wade was only a member of their parliament.

"I've had enough of this." My father walks to the window and looks out. "I'd like to speak to Rowan in private. You can all go."

"Of course." Reginald stands at once, smoothing his long hands down the front of his dark coat.

Tall and slender, with greying black hair and a trim mustache, my uncle embodies the Charmant line of our family. I inherited their height and Norman complexion. My father, by contrast, is a Tate through and through. Short, pink, and round.

As soon as the room is cleared, he stalks back to the table, still brooding like a thunderstorm. "Reggie's in league with them as well," he growls.

"Not necessarily." My voice is low and level, and I hope appeasing. "My uncle does have an idea, and of the two, it's the least offensive. Hubert would combine our countries and walk away—"

"Exactly!" Father snaps, turning to face me, blue eyes blazing. "My own cousin, born and reared in our beautiful land. He's been promised a place in the new government, I'll bet you. They'll throw the lot of us out—behead us if they can."

"I'm pretty sure beheading is no longer tolerated in western civilization."

"Harumph." He's still angry, but at least he's calmer. "It would break your mother's heart. The Charmants founded Monagasco. We can't let those Twatringtons in."

His use of the unofficial nickname for our southwest neighbor makes me grin. Rising from my chair, I brace his shoulder in a firm grasp.

"We won't let that happen." Our blue eyes meet. It's the only feature we share. He's a few inches shorter than me, but he makes up for it in stubbornness. "We're flush with reserves, and the economy can change at any time."

His thick hand covers mine. "I'm doing my best to leave you a strong country to rule. The country I inherited."

"We would do well to reduce our dependence on foreign oil reserves." He starts to argue, but I hold up a hand as I head for the door. He's finally calm, and I'm not interested in riling him up again. "In any event, you'll be around long enough to see the tides turn. Now get some rest." I'm at the enormous wooden door of the war room. "We can't solve all our problems in one day."

"Goodnight, son."

The tone in his voice causes me to look back. He's at the window, and a troubled expression mars his profile. A shimmer of concern passes through my stomach, but I dismiss it, quietly stepping into the dim hallway. It's enormous and shrouded with heavy velvet curtains and tapestries.

I grew up playing in these halls, hiding from my mother and chasing my younger brother. I'm tired and ready for bed when the sound of hushed voices stops me in my tracks.

"Pompous ass. He's going to kill himself with these outbursts. We need to be ready to move when that happens." The glee in Hubert's sniveling voice revives the anger in my chest. I step into the shadows to listen.

"By climbing into bed with Wade Paxton?"

I recognize my uncle's voice, and my jaw clenches. *Is Father right? Is Reginald conspiring with that worm against the crown?*

"Wade Paxton would unite the kingdoms and make us both leaders in the new government."

"Wade Paxton is a thug."

"Not very respectful verbiage for the Prime Minister of Totrington, also known as our future partner."

"He's no better than one of those mob bosses on American television. Savage." Reggie's voice is laced with snobbery. "He'd tax the people and change the very nature of Monagasco."

Hubert's tone is undeterred. "Some things might change, but as leaders, you and I can help maintain the best parts, the heart of the nation. Once Philip is out of the way, of course, which could be sooner than we think."

My fists tighten at my sides. I'm ready to step out of the shadows and shake Hubert's traitorous neck until his teeth rattle. The only thing stopping me is my desire to hear the extent of this treachery.

"You're right about one thing," Reggie says. "Philip's health is tenuous. We need to be prepared to act should a crisis arise."

"What about Rowan? If he's not on our side, we could end up in the same position—and with a much younger king to wait out."

"Possibly." My uncle pauses, and I feel the heat rising around my collar.

"Wade has a plan for managing such a contingency. Should Rowan prove... difficult."

"I'm sure he does," Reggie scoffs. "And Cal? Shall we wipe out the entire Tate line?"

Hubert's voice is low and wicked. "Perhaps being in league with a 'thug' as you put it has its advantages."

*How dare these bastards!* What they're saying is high treason! My body is poised to move when Reggie's words freeze me in place.

"I'm sure Wade's tactics won't prove necessary. When the time comes to do the right thing, we can count on Rowan."

*Count on Rowan?* Is it possible he thinks I would even consider a merger with Twatrington? Their voices recede down the corridor as my level of disgust and loyalty to my father rises. The king has had a difficult evening. I'll let him rest tonight, but I will present him with this conspiracy first thing tomorrow. Reggie is right. When the time comes, I will do the right thing.

Looking back, I had no idea the time would come in less than twenty-four hours...

\* \* \*

**The story continues in The Prince & The Player. Get your copy on all eBook retailers, in audiobook, and in print format.**

# About the Author

The "Queen of Hot Romance," Tia Louise is the Award-Winning, International Bestselling author of the One to Hold series.

From "Readers' Choice" nominations, to *USA Today* "Happily Ever After" nods, to winning the 2015 "Favorite Erotica Author" and the 2014 "Lady Boner Award" (LOL!), nothing makes her happier than communicating with fans and weaving new tales into the Alexander-Knight world of stories.

A former journalist, Louise lives in the center of the USA with her lovely family and one grumpy cat.

**Books by Tia Louise:**
*One to Hold* (Derek & Melissa), 2013
*One to Keep* (Patrick & Elaine), 2014
*One to Protect* (Derek & Melissa), 2014
*One to Love* (Kenny & Slayde), 2014
*One to Leave* (Stuart & Mariska), 2014
*One to Save* (Derek & Melissa), 2015
*One to Chase* (Amy & Marcus), 2015
*One to Take* (Stuart & Mariska), 2016

*The Prince & The Player*, 2016
*A Player for A Princess*, 2016

**Paranormal Romances** (all stand-alones):
*One Immortal* (Derek & Melissa, #SexyVampires), 2015
*One Insatiable* (Koa & Mercy, #SexyShifters), 2015

**Connect with Tia:**
Website: www.AuthorTiaLouise.com
Sign up for Tia's Book News: *http://smarturl.it/TLMnews*

Made in the USA
Charleston, SC
20 January 2017